CHERUB

NEW GUARD

Robert Muchamore

Hodder
Children's
Books

HODDER CHILDREN'S BOOKS

First published in Great Britain in 2016
by Hodder & Stoughton
This paperback edition published in 2017

1 3 5 7 9 10 8 6 4 2

Text copyright © Robert Muchamore, 2016

The moral rights of the author have been asserted.

A CIP catalogue record for this book is available from the British Library

ISBN 978 1 444 91414 6

Typeset in Goudy by Avon DataSet Ltd,
Bidford-on-Avon, Warwickshire

Printed and bound in Great Britain by Clays Ltd, St Ives plc

The paper and board used in this book are from well-managed forests
and other responsible sources.

Hodder Children's Books
An imprint of Hachette Children's Group
Part of Hodder & Stoughton
Carmelite House
50 Victoria Embankment
London EC4Y 0DZ

An Hachette UK Company
www.hachettechildrens.co.uk

CHERUB™

Robert Muchamore worked as a private investigator before starting to write a story for his nephew, who couldn't find anything to read. Since then, over twelve million copies of his books have been sold worldwide, and he has won numerous awards for his writing, including the Red House Children's Book Award.

Robert lives in London, supports Arsenal football club and loves modern art and watching people fall down holes.

For more information on Robert and his work, visit **www.muchamore.com**, where you can sign up to receive updates on exclusive competitions, giveaways and news.

BY ROBERT MUCHAMORE

The CHERUB series:

1. The Recruit
2. Class A
3. Maximum Security
4. The Killing
5. Divine Madness
6. Man vs Beast
7. The Fall
8. Mad Dogs
9. The Sleepwalker
10. The General
11. Brigands M.C.
12. Shadow Wave
13. People's Republic
14. Guardian Angel
15. Black Friday
16. Lone Wolf
17. New Guard

The Rock War series:

Rock War
Boot Camp
Gone Wild

and coming soon

Crash Landing

The Henderson's Boys series:

Start reading with *The Escape*

WHAT IS CHERUB?

CHERUB is a branch of British Intelligence. Its agents are aged between ten and seventeen years. Cherubs are mainly orphans who have been taken out of care homes and trained to work undercover. They live on CHERUB campus, a secret facility hidden in the English countryside.

WHAT USE ARE KIDS?

Quite a lot. Nobody realises kids do undercover missions, which means they can get away with all kinds of stuff that adults can't.

WHO ARE THEY?

About three hundred children live on CHERUB campus. Among them are brothers RYAN SHARMA (17), twins LEON and DANIEL (14) and THEO (11).

JAMES ADAMS is a former CHERUB agent. After three years studying for his degree in the United States, James now works as a mission controller on CHERUB campus. He has been engaged to long-term girlfriend KERRY CHANG for two years.

CHERUB STAFF

With its large grounds, specialist training facilities and combined role as a boarding school and intelligence operation, CHERUB actually has more staff than pupils. They range from cooks and gardeners to teachers, training instructors, nurses, psychiatrists and mission specialists. CHERUB is run by its chairman, EWART ASKER.

CHERUB T-SHIRTS

Cherubs are ranked according to the colour of the T-shirts they wear on campus. ORANGE is for visitors. RED is for kids who live on CHERUB campus but are too young to qualify as agents (the minimum age is ten). BLUE is for kids undergoing CHERUB's tough one-hundred-day basic training regime. A GREY T-shirt means you're qualified for missions. NAVY is a reward for outstanding performance on a single mission. Ryan Sharma wears the BLACK T-shirt, the ultimate recognition for outstanding achievement over a number of missions. When you retire, you get the WHITE T-shirt, which is also worn by some staff.

1. SHORTS

10 minutes late. Traffic nightmare!!!!!
> *No worries. Mum won't be back for hours.*

Getting XXX cited. You wearing the cut-offs, like in that pic?
> *As agreed, you old perv* ☺☺☺

Leon heard the BMW roll on to a driveway strewn with brown leaves. The fourteen-year-old bounded two steps at a time, coming down to the front door as the car flashed to show it was locked. Its driver approached, his bulky outline shimmering through frosted glass.

Leon wore frayed denim shorts a size too small, grubby trainer socks and a black muscle vest. His hair was bleached and tight-cropped, showing a silver cross in his right earlobe.

'Hey,' Leon said, grabbing the latch and staring down, embarrassed.

The BMW on the drive was a year old. Nigel was forty-two, wearing bottle-green slacks, Ralph Lauren short-sleeve tight around the gut and four grand's worth of Carrera watch. The expensive look was spoiled by twisted teeth and choking aftershave.

'Finally here,' Nigel said, as he crossed the threshold and made a little clap. 'You look really nice.'

Leon smiled coyly, then looked alarmed. 'Take your shoes off. My ma is a carpet Nazi.'

'Of course,' Nigel said, peeling slip-on brogues as he glanced around the little hallway, at family pics and a coatstand. 'Your parents?'

'Don't worry, old man,' Leon said, smiling and resting one hand on the wooden knob at the bottom of the stair rail. 'My sister is at uni. Mum's at the Trafford Centre, and she's left me dinner to heat up.'

'Cool beans.'

'Drink?' Leon asked. 'Tea, Coke, water?'

'I'm OK.'

Leon shrugged. 'You got something for me?'

'Absolutely.' Nigel pulled out a roll of twenties. 'Three hundred, as agreed.'

Leon pinged off an elastic band, then quickly counted the notes before shoving them into his front pocket.

'I'll have enough to go to V-Fest with my besties. And get my Xbox fixed.'

'I can't believe I'm here after all the messages we've sent each other.'

'Me too. Hang on a sec while I grab myself a Coke.' Leon backed through a door into the kitchen, seeing his twin Daniel, plus a larger man in a smart suit. As soon as Leon gave the thumbs-up, the pair hurried out into the hallway, pursued by a stocky woman with a pro camcorder balanced on her shoulder.

'Nigel Kinney,' the suited man announced. 'I'm Jason Nolan from the Paedophile Hunting Network. Would you like to tell me why you came here this afternoon?'

Twins Leon and Daniel watched through the doorway as the camera operator zoomed on Nigel, who held hands in front of his face.

'Mr Kinney,' Jason Nolan demanded. 'PHN has been tracking your behaviour. What have you got to say for yourself?'

Nigel spluttered. 'I didn't lay a finger on him. I didn't plan on doing anything illegal.'

'But we have hundreds of messages, Mr Kinney,' the presenter pushed. 'You sent and requested sexually explicit images. Our hidden camera just filmed you paying Leon three hundred pounds.'

'I don't understand,' Nigel said, backing up behind the coatstand but pursued by the camera operator. 'You're not the police?'

'No we are not the police,' Jason explained. 'We are a totally independent organisation that tracks the vile behaviour of people like yourself. We will send all of our evidence to the police and you may face prosecution. We will also put a video about your activity on our Paedophile Hunting YouTube channel.'

'I didn't touch him,' Nigel shouted. 'I just came here to hang out and play Xbox with the boy.'

Leon shook his head at his twin Daniel, as Nigel and the camera operator continued their dance around the swaying coatstand.

'If you're not police you can't arrest me,' Nigel blurted.

'We're not stopping you leaving,' Jason said, aiming a hand towards the exit. 'But we will make sure that your wife sees all the evidence, for the sake of your twelve-year-old son. And we'll also be notifying your employer.'

'I'm leaving,' Nigel shouted, hands over face as he barged the camera operator and made for the door.

'What do you think your eighty-two-year-old mother will think about this when she finds out?' Jason demanded. 'Are you ashamed of yourself?'

'I never laid a hand on him,' Nigel said tearfully, as he fumbled with the door catch.

'But you were convicted of two sex offences in 1998, while doing a summer job at a holiday camp,' the presenter noted. 'Have you got anything to say to those victims? And how many other boys are there that we don't know about, Mr Kinney?'

Nigel spun around in the hallway, then pounded the wall. 'You've stolen my shoes. Where are my shoes?'

'Nice knowing you, pervert,' Leon taunted. 'How do you like my tight little shorts now?'

'This is entrapment,' Nigel shouted, pointing at Leon. 'He set me up . . . What have you done with my damned shoes?'

'I'm sure they're around somewhere, Nigel,' Leon teased.

Nigel started wagging his finger in presenter Jason's face. 'I have a very, *very* good lawyer. If you put this online I will sue you for every penny you have.'

Jason smiled to the camera. 'Paedophile Hunting takes legal advice on everything we do, Mr Kinney. Perhaps you'd like to take my business card so that your lawyer can contact me?'

'Pricks,' Nigel shouted, as he gave up on finding his shoes, grabbed car keys from his pocket and opened the front door. 'May you rot in hell.'

Leon and his twin gave Nigel two-fingered salutes as he stumbled on to the leafy driveway in his socks. They stood behind the camera operator as she filmed Nigel getting into his car, revving the engine and squealing his rear tyres as he backed off the drive.

Everyone paused for breath, then smiled.

'Nicely done,' the camera operator said, as she switched off and took the bulky cam off her shoulder.

Jason grinned and led the quartet in a round of high fives. 'You boys were great.'

'How long till the video goes live on your YouTube?' Daniel asked.

'I'll upload the footage to my edit guy in London. He should have something online by this evening, and we'll send the evidence to the cops by tomorrow morning.'

'And you've *got* to blur our faces,' Leon said firmly. 'We could get in a lot of trouble with our 'rents for getting involved in this.'

'For sure,' Jason agreed. 'There is one thing though.'

'What?' Leon asked.

'Your contact, the one who got us intelligence on Nigel Kinney's previous convictions and stuff. Is there any way I could talk to them personally?'

The twins shrugged. Daniel answered, 'We'll help you again if we can.'

'But our contact is personal,' Leon added, before checking the time on his phone. 'Can you run us to the station? Our dad will go ape if we don't make it home before six.'

'Sure,' Jason agreed, before glancing at his camera operator. 'You mind starting the clean-up here while I drop the boys off?'

As the camera operator nodded, Jason grabbed his car keys, but Leon had disappeared into the living-room.

'We need to shift, Leon,' Daniel said anxiously. 'There's only one train an hour and it's due in fifteen.'

'I know,' Leon agreed, as he grabbed a set of black trackie bottoms draped over a leather couch. 'But I don't care how late we are, I'm not going out in public in these dumbass shorts.'

2. BALLS

'It's weird,' James Adams admitted, as he sat at a circular table in Channing's restaurant, twelve miles from CHERUB campus, eating a starter of deep-fried risotto balls. The twenty-four-year-old former CHERUB agent sat close to his fiancée Kerry Chang, while long-term friend Bruce Norris sat opposite with bean salad and a nasty black eye.

'What's weird?' Bruce asked.

'When I shut my eyes, it's like yesterday that my mum died,' James explained. 'Waking up on campus, meeting you guys for the first time. Being a cherub . . .'

Bruce paused to count on his fingers. 'Thirteen years, pal.'

'And in my head, when I'm working on campus and one of the kids is up to something I feel like I'm one of them. But then I have to do a double-take, and be Mr

Mission Controller and get them to listen and behave.'

'Can I taste?' Kerry asked, not waiting for an answer before stabbing half a risotto ball with her fork.

'You always do that,' James moaned.

'What?' Kerry growled.

'You say you don't want a starter and then you eat half of mine.'

Kerry turned sideways, gave James a quick kiss before poking his slightly bulging stomach. 'You don't need the calories, fat boy.' Then she pointed across the table. 'Look at Bruce, all tanned and muscly from Thailand.'

'I can't help it,' James said. 'I'm stuck behind a desk most of the day.'

'He failed his staff fitness assessment on campus,' Kerry said. 'And frankly, I'm fed up looking at his paunch.'

'It's just my build,' James protested. 'Body fascist.'

'So anyway,' Bruce said, pausing as a waitress swept by close enough to overhear, then speaking to Kerry. 'What are you doing now? Are you on campus?'

Kerry shook her head. 'I visit weekends. If James is around and I'm not working.'

'She sold her soul to the devil,' James added.

Bruce looked confused, before Kerry explained. 'Unlike *certain* boyfriends of mine, who inherited hundreds of thousands of pounds from their mother and ride around on fancy motorbikes, I have to *earn* my keep.'

'Hear hear,' Bruce said, scowling at James

because there had been nothing to inherit from his parents either.

'Kerry works in the City of London,' James explained. 'Evil French bank, securitised leasing.'

'They're not evil,' Kerry protested.

'What's securitised leasing?' Bruce asked.

Kerry shrugged. 'You don't wanna know.'

'So is it fun?' Bruce asked.

Kerry snorted. 'Nope.' Then looked disappointed. 'Salary's great, but you work stupidly long hours, preparing trading reports and . . . I don't even want to talk about it.'

'So quit,' Bruce said. 'Dump the flabby boyfriend and come live with me, teaching martial arts in the sunshine.'

James gave Bruce the finger across the table, before dipping a piece of bread in olive oil.

'A few years,' Kerry said. 'A couple of good bonuses and I can afford to quit and do something more satisfying.'

'Banker bonuses,' Bruce laughed.

'I told you she sold her soul,' James added.

Kerry folded her arms, but was only pretending to be upset. 'I miss being a cherub. And when I'm at work, listening to all these Oxbridge-educated toffs going on about their gap year antics, I want to knee them in the gonads and tell them that I helped bring down a major drugs ring when I was twelve years old.'

'So who else is coming to the party tomorrow?' Bruce asked.

'Loads of people,' James said. 'Kyle, Gabrielle,

Callum, Connor, Michael. And people I've not seen for yonks, like Arif and Dana.'

'Dana,' Bruce snorted. 'What about your sister?'

'Lauren's coming with Rat.'

'Nice,' Bruce said. 'Probably in Rat's private helicopter.'

James and Kerry both laughed. 'I don't think he's in the private helicopter league,' Kerry said. 'But I heard Rat inherited well over twenty million from his crazy cult leader father.'

'AAARGH!' Bruce said, enthusiastically pounding the table as a waitress approached with three main courses. 'It's gonna be so cool seeing all the old faces again.'

*

Most older CHERUB agents took a trip off campus when they got a free Saturday afternoon, but Leon and Daniel's train got held up, meaning it was past seven when they detrained at the station nearest to CHERUB campus.

'We're *so* screwed,' Daniel said, as he stepped out of the unmanned ticket hall and glanced around. Sometimes there was a bus from campus waiting to pick up kids. 'Shall we use the taxi account?'

Leon shook his head. 'If we charge a taxi, campus will know we're coming. If we rock up at the gate unannounced, we might just slip through unnoticed.'

'Forty minutes at a brisk jog,' Daniel said thoughtfully. 'There's a ton of guests arriving for the blow-up party, so security *might* have their eye off the ball.'

Like all CHERUB agents, the twins had to stay in top shape, so the 8km run was a breeze. They were on the last stretch towards campus when Daniel had a sudden thought.

'Don't forget my half of the money.'

'What money?'

'The three hundred that Nigel gave you,' Daniel said.

Leon scoffed. 'No way! I took all the risks. I had to put on those stupid shorts and have the pervert leering at me.'

'Risks,' Daniel said. 'What *risks!* He's got no skills. If Nigel tried something you could have broken his arm in ten seconds flat.'

'I suffered mental trauma,' Leon said.

'Half of that three hundred is mine, Leon.'

'I'll give you fifty quid, just to shut you up.'

'Stop being a dick!' Daniel said, outraged. 'Fifty-fifty.'

'Possession is nine-tenths of the law.'

Daniel gave Leon a shove. It was enough to knock him off stride, but he managed to stay upright.

'I want my half,' Daniel demanded.

'I'll race you for it,' Leon said. 'First one to the campus gate. Go!'

The twins weren't identical, but nor was there much between them in size or speed. Daniel knew that if he took the bait, he wouldn't catch his twin, who was already ten metres ahead. All this became academic when Leon took a slight bend in the road and got flashed full beam from an army-green Land-Rover, parked alongside the road.

'Evening boys,' a burly campus security guard announced grandly, as the pair stopped running and sensed doom. 'I'm Briggs and you two are way past your curfew time.'

Since campus appeared on maps as a military facility, the guards on its perimeter drove army-style vehicles and wore military police uniforms.

'We went swimming in town,' Daniel said hopefully. 'There were some girls from that boarding school, and we lost track of time.'

'Really,' Briggs said, unconvinced. 'You could have texted to say you were late. But for some reason your phones were off, so we couldn't track them. Almost as if you didn't want us to know where you were.'

'I . . .' Leon stuttered.

'We . . .' Daniel added.

'You two are in a lot of trouble,' Briggs said, as his hand beckoned the pair towards the back seat of the Land-Rover. 'The sooner you start telling the truth about what you've been up to, the better the chance that you don't get kicked out of CHERUB.'

3. TRAUMA

After stepping aside from the stressful post of CHERUB chairman, Zara Asker now had a part-time role dealing with serious disciplinary measures. She yawned as she walked into the security post just inside campus' main gate and got caught off guard by two faces she'd not seen in years.

'Older no wiser,' Kyle Blueman said, as the former CHERUB agent gave Zara a hug. Gabrielle O'Brien was right behind, but Zara did a double-take.

The practicalities of campus life and training make it hard for girls to dress up for anything but special occasions. Gabrielle appeared to be making up for lost time, with elaborate extensions to her plaited hair, heavy make-up and mad heels.

'You look like a model,' Zara said. 'Wow!'

'It's weird you're not chairman any more,' Kyle noted.

'My husband is welcome to it,' Zara said. 'It's a twenty-four-seven job. And I'd love to stay and chat, but I have a pair of idiots to crucify.'

Zara dropped the friendly tone as she stepped past the X-ray machines used to examine baggage and down a short hallway to the waiting area where Leon and Daniel had spent the last two hours, nervously awaiting their fate.

'Office, now,' Zara snapped, clicking her fingers.

The twins had been allowed to shower and dress in their CHERUB uniforms, complete with navy shirts. Leon felt a shudder as Zara joined Briggs' brooding presence across a desk top laid out with evidence. Computer printouts of phone messages, three hundred pounds, train tickets to places the boys weren't supposed to have been . . .

'Sit down.'

The twins eyed one another uneasily as they sat on hard plastic chairs. The gloomily lit room had bare concrete walls, a pair of CCTV cameras and a metal door so that it could be used as a cell if necessary.

'We know what you did,' Zara began. 'Every lie you tell will just get you deeper into trouble. What I don't understand is *why* you did this. What significance does Nigel Kinney have for you?'

Daniel looked a bit surly. 'He's a paedophile. He's getting what he deserves.'

'We knew there was a good chance we'd get in trouble,' Leon added. 'We'll take our punishment.'

Briggs thumped on the desk top. 'We didn't

ask you for a moral justification. You were asked a specific question.'

Zara looked more startled by Briggs' reaction than the two boys, and gave him a thin-lipped *I can handle this* look.

'Kinney?' Zara said firmly.

Leon looked at Daniel, and got a nod before beginning to explain. 'We did a mission in Sheffield last year. There was a kid there, Brent Johnson. Nice guy, year younger than us. But he was messed up. Cutting himself, nightmares. He'd been abused by Nigel Kinney and some other guy since he was about ten. Cops didn't press charges because Brent was too messed up to go through a trial.'

'Kinney had previous convictions, but you're not allowed to mention that to a jury,' Daniel added.

Zara shook her head slowly. 'So you contacted the Paedophile Hunting Network?'

'Sure,' Leon agreed. 'At first we just got hold of a copy of Kinney's criminal record and sent it to the paedo hunters, hoping they'd make him a target. But they get a lot of tip-offs and they're a tiny organisation.'

'So you agreed to help?' Briggs asked.

Leon nodded. 'We hacked Kinney's office computer and found a site he was using to speak to young boys. So I joined up and started sending him fake messages. Said I was short of cash and would like to meet up.'

'Then we got the paedo hunters to set up the final sting,' Daniel added.

'I'll take whatever punishment,' Leon said. 'But I'm not ashamed of what we did.'

'You can't be vigilantes,' Briggs growled. 'CHERUB has bigger fish to fry and you risked organisational security by making unauthorised access to police records.'

Zara gave Briggs another *calm down* look. 'Guys,' she began. 'I have four children and the idea that anyone who wants to harm them is out there makes me sick. Online grooming is a serious and growing problem and everyone should be more aware of it. But you are CHERUB agents. Our targets are major terror groups, drug cartels, people smugglers, weapons dealers. We're not in the business of getting revenge for one wronged child. You've broken dozens of rules.'

'When news about this gets out on campus, you'll probably be regarded as some kind of heroes by your fellow agents,' Briggs added. 'If we don't hit you hard, who knows where it'll lead?'

Leon and Daniel allowed slight smirks at the thought that they'd be considered heroes.

'Don't you *dare* smile,' Zara said, wagging a finger. 'Although I'm in charge of matters of severe breaches of discipline, I have to follow guidelines laid down by the ethics committee. Under those guidelines, you have breached so many rules that the case for permanent exclusion from CHERUB is absolute.'

Zara paused to let this sink in. The twins avoided eye contact with each other and Leon's breath juddered, like he was going to cry.

'However,' Zara said. 'I do have slight wiggle room

in cases where agents act out based on traumatic events they've seen while on missions. And I suppose you *could* argue that you were upset after encountering Brent Johnson and that is the reason why you acted the way you did.

'So, I'm going to give you two choices. The first is that you're discharged honourably from CHERUB. You can live with a member of staff near to campus, so you'll still get to see your brothers Theo and Ryan.'

Leon's jaw dropped. 'I thought you said there was wiggle room . . .'

'Let me finish,' Zara said firmly. 'Your second choice will be to remain on CHERUB campus, but you'll face severe sanctions. Namely, two months of heavy drill and ditch digging, followed by a further two months during which you'll be suspended from missions.'

The twins gasped. 'Two months of heavy drill!' Leon blurted.

'I never heard of anyone getting more than two weeks,' Daniel added.

'You'll also be expected to tell none of your friends what you're being punished for,' Briggs added. 'Not even your brothers.'

'No cherub is ever forced to undergo punishment,' Zara said. 'You can quit now, you can quit at any time.'

Leon looked across at Daniel. 'I got twenty-four hours' heavy drill that time I drank all the cider and puked in French class. It was full on. I'm not sure I could hack two months.'

Daniel had never been made to do heavy drill. 'Worse

than basic training?'

'Way worse,' Leon said.

Zara stood up and signalled Briggs to do the same. Then glanced at her watch.

'Quit CHERUB, or two months' punishment. I'll give you ten minutes to make up your mind.'

Zara and Briggs headed out. The twins jolted as Briggs locked them in with a metallic clank. As the boys looked at one another, Daniel eyed a picture of Nigel Kinney on the desk.

'We always knew there was a good chance we'd get caught,' Daniel said sadly. 'Maybe it wouldn't be so bad, just being an ordinary kid.'

Leon nodded. 'There are so many hot girls at that Catholic school down the road.'

Daniel looked up at one of the cameras. 'They can probably hear what we're saying.'

'But on the other hand,' Leon said, as he flicked his cheek anxiously. 'We've got the whole rest of our lives to be ordinary.'

4. MAGGOTS

CHERUB campus was Sunday-morning quiet as a blonde twenty-two-year-old stepped up to a set of doors, dressed in tight-fitting cords and tatty Converse. She leaned forward, staring into a black square with a green light flashing above it. After a moment, a screen beneath the panel lit up with *Lauren Adams, access granted.*

The snaking mission control building on CHERUB campus had recently undergone refurbishment, with new floorboards and modern art. The heart of the building was a small control room aglow with computer screens. From here, the sixty or so CHERUB agents and their adult controllers who are on a mission at any given time can call in an emergency, request backup, equipment or a link to specialists whose skills range from hacking an encrypted file to making sure that a traffic light turns red when it needs to.

Branching off were three smaller control rooms, which were manned during the critical phases of CHERUB's individual missions.

After passing through, Lauren entered a broad corridor, with securely locked offices on one side and full-height glass overlooking forest on the other. Halfway along, a boy and a girl looked nervous in their grey CHERUB shirts, yet to hit their teens and about to get briefed on their first mission.

The last office had a sign Lauren found slightly ludicrous: *James Adams – Mission Controller.*

Before Lauren could knock, a stocky seventeen-year-old in a black CHERUB shirt opened the door and almost crashed into her with an armful of papers. After an exchange of *sorries*, Lauren stepped into a plush corner office, with bookshelves, trendy walnut desk and a pair of leather sofas either side of a coffee table.

The view, down a gentle slope over golden trees, was spectacular. Unfortunately, James Adams let down the ambience, dressed in gym clothes, one holed sock propped on his desk and surrounded by coffee mugs, box files and mounds of paper. He was on the phone, so he gave Lauren a thumbs-up and pointed her wordlessly towards a couch.

'John . . .' James told the phone. 'She's a sixteen-year-old girl and her whole wardrobe got smoked in the fire at the end of the mission. I just told her to get what she needed . . . I realise I should have set a budget, John. But how was I supposed to know she was going to go to London and spend eight hundred pounds on shoes?'

Lauren smirked as she slid a backpack down her arms, settling on the only part of the couch that wasn't covered in files. As James continued talking, the black-shirt girl came back in with a roll of thick orange bags, which Lauren knew were for stuff that had to be incinerated on campus.

'I'm Fu Ning,' the girl told Lauren quietly, as James continued on the phone. 'You must be his sister, Lauren.'

Lauren nodded. 'My brother must be a pain to work for.'

Ning smiled. 'He's cool, just disorganised.'

James was continuing his conversation with his boss. 'Birmingham?' James said. 'I know about the recruitment. I told you Thursday in the team meeting, I've got Leon and Daniel Sharma lined up for that job . . . What? . . . Are you serious? How can they not be available for missions? . . . I need those two guys. I'll give Zara a call and try to twist her arm. If it's not too serious she might let me have them back . . . Right, I'll be here until noon I guess. Speak in a bit.'

James sounded frazzled as he put down his phone.

'Working hard?' Lauren asked, as James stood and gave her a hug.

'Sunday morning,' James said, as the pair embraced. 'I should be in bed with Kerry. The hours she works, and the hours I work, we barely see each other.'

'What was that about shoes?'

'God,' James said, smacking his forehead as Ning broke out in a huge smile. 'I was on a mission, girl gets all her clothes burned. She's really upset, so I'm like *don't worry, take a nice shopping trip to London and get whatever you need*. I fixed up a debit card and she spent four and a half grand. Totally destroyed the mission budget. John Jones is furious.'

'You told a sixteen-year-old girl to go to London and buy whatever she wanted?' Lauren scoffed.

'She's a great kid,' James protested, as Ning and Lauren struggled to contain their laughter. 'I've never seen her wear anything other than joggers and a hoodie. I didn't expect her to do that.'

Lauren smirked. 'It's almost as if *someone* trained her to manipulate adults and get what she wanted.'

'Fair point,' James said, shaking his head. 'So what's up in your world? Still racing cars?'

'Team's all set up for the new season,' Lauren said. 'Rat put up some seed funding, but now we're fully funded through sponsorship, unless I crash too many cars.'

'When's your season start?'

'Still got four months.'

'Scared?'

Lauren nodded. 'It's a jump. I had a hundred and twenty horsepower in the single-seater formula. This is a saloon car, topping out at five hundred.'

'Try not to get killed,' James suggested.

Lauren grinned. 'You know me, James. I'm not the kind of person who wants to be stuck at a desk behind a mountain of paperwork.'

'Up yours!' James said, giving his sister a playful dig in the ribs.

Lauren grabbed James' arm and tripped him on to the couch, but he had to run for the phone before things could escalate.

'James Adams speaking . . . You need *what*? Well can't you get some of the carers down at The Village to round up a bunch of kids? . . . Why is this even a mission control problem? . . . OK, fine, I'll do it.'

James slammed the phone down and looked so stressed that Lauren took pity and pulled a sarcastic comment.

'Five hundred and fifty boxes of mission control files in the basement of the main building,' James explained. 'They were supposed to be moved a week ago, but it got held up by the asbestos removal team and apparently John Jones forgot. So, are you girls up for some heavy lifting?'

*

Barefoot, dressed only in shorts and T-shirts, Leon led his twin by a couple of paces, weighted down by a huge pack and with a stocky Aussie instructor named Capstick in his ear.

'Faster, Sharma,' Capstick roared. 'If you're not at the top of this hill in one minute, I will take you down to the bottom. I will put another ten-kilo weight in your sack and I will make you run this whole circuit again from scratch.'

Daniel's instructor was no less intimidating. 'Too slow, cupcake,' Instructor Smoke yelled, kicking him in the back of the legs and sending him sprawling before skimming her boot through a puddle and spraying his face with mud. 'On your feet, stat!'

Leon glanced back.

'Don't look at him,' Capstick roared. 'Move your butt.'

Daniel tried to pull himself up, but he'd been drilled since sunup, with planks, push-ups and a half-hour standing with the heavy pack held high above his head. There was no strength in his arms.

'I can't,' Daniel moaned, as he noticed blood between his toes.

'What's the matter?' Instructor Smoke demanded. 'Nothing wrong with a bit of blood. What do you want, a kiss better? Get on your damned feet.'

Daniel tried, but his arms gave out again.

'UPPPP!' Smoke ordered, as she lost patience and yanked Daniel to his feet by the strap of his backpack. 'Now shift before I kick you down again.'

Leon had reached the top of the hill and groaned with relief as he dumped the pack on the ground before doubling up, gasping.

'On your knees, both of you,' Capstick shouted, when Daniel finally stumbled to the top of the hill. 'Hands on heads.'

The ground was muddy, so the position wasn't too hard on the knees. Both boys gasped, while Daniel was now feeling the pain in his foot. The two instructors moved right into the boys' faces and started a verbal barrage.

'You are pathetic.'

'Maggots!'

'You bring shame to the CHERUB T-shirt, maggots.'

'Wrecked on day one. Do you really think you can take sixty days of this?'

'Why put yourself through the misery? You can't beat us, maggots.'

'Quit now. Go live the easy life. Geography homework and a girl with nice long legs.'

'Are you crying, Daniel? Is that a tear in your eye?'

'No sir,' Daniel lied.

'You wanna quit, maggots?' Smoke roared.

'No ma'am,' the twins shouted.

The two instructors stepped back, smiling at one another.

'You boys stay right there on your knees,' Capstick demanded. 'Keep hands behind your heads. Don't speak, don't move.'

'We'll be back in two hours,' Smoke added. 'If you're very lucky, we might bring you some food.'

5. BOXES

Lauren Adams got a twinge of nostalgia as she crossed leaf-strewn grass towards CHERUB campus' seven-storey main building. The dishes and aerials that had adorned the roof were gone, the outer cladding removed, leaving a concrete skeleton and a dolls-house-like view into bedrooms and offices stripped of everything that wasn't screwed to a wall.

The ground-floor canteen made her particularly sad, remembering the sense of excitement when you came out of lessons and looked forward to seeing the gang. Everyone sitting around the tables, teasing and gossiping. Food fights. Early breakfasts with Rat when she first got the sense that she was falling for him . . .

'OK,' James said, as he stopped walking and turned around. Lauren was taken by the calm authority in her brother's tone. A teacher's voice. 'Listen up.'

Besides James, Lauren and Ning, a dozen teenaged CHERUB agents were in tow. They were a mix of reluctant volunteers and kids on punishment.

'I've got bad news and worse news,' James began. 'The bad news is that due to a balls-up, five hundred and fifty boxes of historic mission control documents were not shifted by the army logistics team, due to a delay in the asbestos removal work. The worse news is that the lift has been deactivated, so we've got to take all of them up four flights of stairs. Once they're up at ground level, the boxes have to be taken across campus on a truck and unloaded in the archival space beneath the mission control building. So let's hope we're all feeling energetic!'

'How long's it gonna take?' a girl of about fifteen asked.

James shrugged. 'Three hours, maybe. John Jones is rounding up a second batch of volunteers to help unload at the other end. And if you're not here on deferred punishment, we'll add fifty pounds to your spending accounts as a thank you.'

The volunteers seemed happier after hearing this and there was even a muted cheer.

'The interior is a demolition zone, so you must wear hard hats and hi-visibility vests. Do not stray away from the designated route.'

A temporary barrier circled the main building, its sole access point guarded by a sergeant from the Royal Engineers Corps. Like everyone else on the demolition team, she'd been living on campus for the past six weeks,

27

but was allowed no outside communication and had not been told where campus actually was. Her uniform would usually be topped with a green beret, but special orange ones had been issued, reminding young agents that she was not to be spoken to under any circumstances.

The sergeant counted everyone through the gate, issuing everyone with a numbered dog tag and strict orders that the necklace must be returned so that they could be counted out of the secure area. She then opened a portable cabin, and distributed yellow vests, dust masks and hard hats, while telling James where to find trolleys and other moving equipment. At the same time, a beeping truck was being reversed up to the gate and four more volunteers jumped out of the back, spurred by the prospect of making fifty quid.

Once they were all equipped, a second orange-hatted army engineer led the way inside, between yellow and black *danger high explosive* signs. The main doors had been removed to give work crews easy access. The usually polished floor was horribly scarred and James looked forlornly down the hallway leading to the old chairman's office, missing the wooden bench where he'd so often sat, drumming his foot as he awaited punishment.

But the most dramatic change was in the concrete columns that braced the main hallway that ran all the way to the dining-room at the back of the building. These had been drilled with dozens of three-centimetre-wide holes, into which had been dropped sticks of high explosive. Between sticks ran looms of brightly coloured wiring.

'Could this go off by accident?' a girl asked warily, as the army engineer led the way towards the stairs into the basement. James gave a nod, indicating that the soldier was allowed to answer.

'The explosive and detonators are very stable and I'm not aware of any demolition where there has been a premature explosion. What *can* happen is that the demolition happens incorrectly and only some of the charges go off. So please don't touch any wiring, and if any of you should accidentally drop something or trip and touch one of the looms, please let us know so that we can test the circuit.'

James and the engineer led the group down a back staircase to the first basement. Most furniture had been removed, but the decision had been taken to entomb some equipment in the explosion, including an ancient mainframe computer and thousands of document boxes that were no longer needed, but not so sensitive that they had to be incinerated.

After a stretch of floor, James found himself clattering down metal stairs, wrapped around a large cargo lift which he had never previously seen. At the bottom, the stairs continued down to a third basement, much to the astonishment of kids who'd lived in this building for some years but had no idea about these subterranean levels.

The engineer unlocked the door into a final stretch of corridor. There were no explosives, but like most buildings built before the 1980s, the mineral asbestos was used as fireproofing. Now known to cause cancer, every sheet of asbestos had to be removed so that its toxic dust didn't form part of the cloud when the building detonated. This hallway had been the last to be cleared, and the plaster and ceiling had been stripped back to bare concrete, with some dangerous-looking 1970s electrical wiring on show.

James felt intimidated when he stepped into a room which he realised sat directly beneath the campus dining-hall. There were two dozen rows of metal shelving, each stretching more than thirty metres. Everything had been cleared out, apart from the five hundred and fifty dusty box files, each one recently stickered with *Mission Control – do not destroy.*

Made from heavy card, each box was more than a metre deep, and James quickly realised that it would take two people to lift each one upstairs.

'OK,' James said, as his sister and several kids groaned at the magnitude of the task ahead. 'It looks like we've got our work cut out.'

*

Four hours later, James had backache and pit stains the size of dinner plates. The fourth and final truckload of boxes had been shifted and the last batch of exhausted kids were clattering upstairs with the metal trolleys.

'They worked hard,' Lauren said, giving James a smile. 'You're actually really good with the kids.'

'You think?' James said brightly. 'I always feel like a phoney.'

Lauren inspected dirty hands and a cracked thumbnail as she set off upstairs a few steps behind her brother. 'I'll never be a lady with these hands,' she said.

'Weird to think it'll all be under rubble in a few hours,' James said, when he reached the ground floor.

He should have headed on down the corridor, but there was no sign of the engineers and just a strand of *do not enter* tape keeping him from going on upwards.

'One last look?' Lauren asked, making James crack a huge smile because he was a quarter second behind in saying the same three words.

James straddled and Lauren ducked under. After furtive glances behind, the siblings moved quickly but quietly, tired from humping boxes but able to handle pain after years of CHERUB training.

'Saturday night hall parties!' James remembered, as he rounded the sixth-floor landing.

Lauren smiled and added, 'Pop tarts and instant mac and cheese in the mini-kitchen.'

With no glazing, human smells and central heating had been replaced by crisp outdoor air that made James feel like he was in a dream.

'Creepy as,' Lauren said, as the cold air caught skin damp from hard work.

As Lauren headed into the kitchen and opened cupboards, wondering what had happened to all the battered cutlery and amused to recognise a stain on the wall where her bestie Bethany had tripped up holding a glass of cranapple, James headed for his old room.

The bed and sofa were gone, but the fitted storage and bathroom fixtures were intact. It had been some other kid's room until a few months earlier. Some of her posters still adorned the walls. Inevitably, rain had encroached after the cladding got removed and the carpet near the missing external wall had a greenish tint from mould and dried-out bird droppings.

James stood as close as he dared to the missing external wall and looked out over campus. Preparations were taking place for the demolition party. Beyond that lay the main building's recently opened replacement.

Instead of rooms off of anonymous high-rise hallways, CHERUB agents now lived in one of five streets. Individual homes, monitored by carers, with public kitchen and living spaces downstairs and four to six private suites on each top floor. Cycle paths ran between, along with play areas and a circular area of grassland, with a relocated CHERUB fountain and benches which had been packed out every night through the summer.

At the farthest end, a long, arrow-shaped three-storey building contained the new dining-room, staff accommodation and leisure facilities including a cinema and theatre, a main assembly hall and an indoor play area for little red-shirt kids. The final building was a six-storey glass box known as *Town Hall*, which was where all the most senior staff, including Chairman Ewart Asker, worked.

Campus Village was larger and better in every sense than the dilapidated main building and junior blocks it had replaced. But James was still saddened by the loss of a place where he'd lived for the happiest seven years of his life and felt a tear well up. When he noticed a change in the light behind him he expected to see Lauren in the doorway, but it was the orange-capped army demolition expert.

'Sir,' she said, peevishly. 'This area is out of bounds. I must ask you to leave.'

Lauren loomed behind the sergeant, poking her tongue cheekily at James.

'Right,' James said, feeling guilty that he'd made the sergeant chase him up six floors. Then sad as he stepped out of his old room for the very last time.

6. HOSE

'There's nothing here for you maggots,' instructor Capstick roared. 'You gonna hold out for sixty days? You think this is bad? How's it gonna be when your joints stiffen up? When you're hungry? When you've been cold and wet for two whole weeks and there's still forty-five days to go? It is my personal mission to destroy you. So?'

'Not quitting, instructor,' Leon gasped, as he stood on one leg, with sweat streaking down a muddy face.

'No way,' Daniel added.

It was dark. The twins had been taken into the campus dojo and made to do ninety minutes' sparring against tough eighteen-year-olds. Then they got canned meat, biscuits and orange juice for dinner, followed by another march with the heavy packs, this time taking them through waist-deep drainage channels at the back of campus.

'Accommodation,' Capstick shouted, as he grabbed a battered army tent off the muddy ground and hurled it at just the right angle to knock both boys off balance. 'Build it, sleep in it. Instructor Smoke will be up super early for your first morning drill session.'

Daniel picked up the tent and squelched a few paces.

'Where do you think you're going?' Capstick roared.

Daniel pointed towards some trees where the ground was drier. 'I'll pitch it over there.'

'Here's good,' the instructor teased, sloshing his boot through mud to make his point. 'Crack on!'

The tent was a pop-up type. The twins had used them in basic training and had no bother unfurling and driving anchor pins into the mud. Capstick had vanished by the time they got to the tricky business of getting inside without filling the tent with liquid mud. There were also sleeping bags, which smelled like previous occupants had spent a lot of time in them.

The tent floor was keeping out the water, but it was squelchy and freezing as the twins huddled up, catching sounds wafting across campus.

'Sounds like the demolition party's in full swing,' Leon said, keeping it to a whisper in case there was a training instructor lurking outside with some extra torment. 'I'd kill for a cold Sprite and a plate of party food right now.'

'This is tougher than basic training,' Daniel whispered.

'I reckon it'll get easier,' Leon said.

'We'll get used to it?'

Leon shook his head. 'Capstick and Smoke are being extra tough to try and scare us. But think about it, we're trained agents. We've both got our navy shirts. They want us to get punished, but do you really think they want to lose us?'

'I still don't regret what we did,' Daniel said, squelching as he tried to get comfortable.

'Not for one millisecond,' Leon agreed.

'And you're probably right. They can't keep working us this—' Daniel stopped talking as his brother yelped. 'You OK?'

'There's a rock under the ground sheet and it just dug the spot where I took a hit in the dojo.'

'I don't care how uncomfortable this is,' Daniel said. 'I am gonna sleep so hard!'

Before Leon could respond, they heard boots splashing in the mud.

'He's back!' Leon said, sitting bolt upright.

Daniel rolled over and reached out to open the tent flap and take a look, but someone unzipped from outside first. There was a flash of torchlight through the flap, followed by the nozzle of a high pressure fire hose.

'We forgot shower time!' Capstick shouted, as torchlight caught the instructor's piercing blue eyes.

The hose ripped so hard that Daniel and Leon buried their heads as the freezing water hit the back of the tent with enough force to rip out its anchors and buckle one of the support rods.

As the tent shot backwards with the twins still inside,

Capstick kept blasting until the roof had collapsed and the water trapped inside was more than thirty centimetres deep. Leon tried scrambling towards the exit but the hose blast flipped him on to his back.

When the tent was several metres from its starting position, Capstick pulled out the hose and instead started blasting the powerful jet at the muddy ground. With so much water in the tent, the twins scrambled out in a brown slick, riding a surge from the back of the tent. The hose blasting at the ground left them stumbling blindly towards a wall of mud spray that was rapidly burying their tent, sleeping bags and any prospect of a dry night's sleep.

'Sleep tight!' Capstick beamed, as he finally cut the hose and began strutting backwards to disconnect it from a ground hydrant thirty metres away. 'Don't let the bed bugs bite.'

*

A party was going on by the athletics track across campus. Current staff and agents had been joined by six hundred guests from the organisation's past. James was a tad drunk as he strolled out of a toilet block, shaking his hands because the paper towels had run out. While a crowd chattered and drank in the centre of the track, he was surprised to see seventeen-year-old Ryan Sharma, sat on the banked area nearby, holding a half-drunk Peroni and staring anxiously at the moon.

James had worked with Ryan on two missions, and knew him too well to walk by. But Ryan's first reaction was to hide his beer.

'We're allowed two marked beers,' Ryan said, making James smirk.

'I'm mission control, not a carer,' James said. 'Get as drunk as you like, as long as you don't throw up on me.'

Ryan smiled and took a slug. James was the kind of cool adult he hoped he'd be a few years down the line. 'I've actually got a spare,' Ryan said.

James took the Peroni and squatted in the slightly damp grass beside Ryan. They both wore their party jackets. Ryan with a tie, James without.

'Let me guess,' James said. 'Girl broke your heart?'

Ryan sighed. 'Worried about my brothers, actually. They're on sixty days' heavy drill and it's all this big mystery. I have no clue what they did.'

James slugged beer and nodded. 'It's all been kept very quiet. Are you certain it's *sixty* days?'

'Zara told me herself.'

'I never heard of more than twenty-eight before now,' James said. 'I didn't think you got on too well with the twins?'

Ryan shrugged. 'Not really, but they're my brothers and I still love them. And my little brother Theo's upset because he's away on a mission and there's a rumour going around that the twins molested a girl or something.'

'Not a chance,' James said, very firmly. 'I have no idea what Leon and Daniel did. But I know one hundred per cent that if an agent did something like that there would be no punishment. You'd be kicked straight out.'

'That's what I told Theo,' Ryan said. 'But he's eleven

and all his mates are gossiping. And I've never known a situation where there's been a big hush-up. Or such a big punishment.'

'Pain in my arse too,' James said. 'I had your brothers lined up for a mission in the Midlands. I'm actually going to speak to Zara Asker tomorrow to see if I can still sort it. Deferred punishment or something. And I can't break confidentiality, but I'll certainly let Zara know that you and Theo are worried.'

'I think family deserves to know,' Ryan said.

James had noticed that people were starting to move away from the athletics track, towards a cordon with a small stage erected three hundred metres in front of the main building. 'Better shift if we want a decent view,' he said.

'Appreciate your help,' Ryan said.

Almost immediately, Ryan sighted his mates Alfie and Ning and jogged off. James got within fifty metres of the white cordon before catching up a big group of his ex-CHERUB pals, including Kerry, Lauren, Kyle, Bruce, Gabrielle, Dana, Rat, Bethany, Callum and Connor.

'If I may have your attention,' CHERUB's recently installed chairman Ewart Asker said, from up on stage. He was over forty but looked younger, in a tailored suit and with several stud earrings. 'We've blown a lot of stuff up on CHERUB campus over the years, but tonight we're really pushing the boat out!'

There was a big cheer, and lots of little kids smirked because the chairman seemed drunk.

'First off, a warning. In a few moments an electromagnetic pulse generator will be activated. This will not only knock out any hidden cameras and unauthorised drones from surrounding airspace, it will fry *any* small electrical item that has been left on within half a kilometre of the explosion. So please, make sure those digital cameras, Android phones and Apple watches are switched off!

'Second, I would like to thank the army engineers who've put so much hard work into the demolition preparations. Sadly, since CHERUB doesn't exist, only a skeleton crew of two remain on site to watch the results of their handiwork.

'There has been much debate on who gets to press the button to destroy the main building,' Ewart continued, as he pointed a finger at a control console. 'In the end, our engineers have constructed a console with three buttons that must all be pressed to activate the demolition charges. The first button will be pushed by a man who needs no introduction to most of you.'

A round of applause broke out as a stooped old geezer began walking up the steps on to the small stage, aided by Zara Asker.

'Mason LeConte was a hero of the French resistance during World War Two, fighting alongside our founder Charles Henderson.[1] He later became one of the first batch of CHERUB agents. He recently celebrated his ninety-second birthday, but he still puts in two shifts a

_____

[1] See the *Henderson's Boys* series for more information on how CHERUB began.

week at the vehicle shop here on campus.'

As Mason shook Ewart's hand and settled into a chair in front of the console, an *AHHH* sound began rippling through the crowd. A cute boy and girl in red CHERUB shirts were coming up the stairs on to the stage.

'They've been allowed to stay up late,' Ewart joked, as the two five-year-olds came on stage looking spooked. 'Joining the oldest surviving CHERUB agent, two agents of the future. Freddie and Sophia.'

As the two kids shyly stood at the detonator panel at either side of Mason, Ewart picked up an old-skool wired army telephone and spoke to the engineers.

'I have the all-clear,' Ewart announced dramatically, as cheers and whoops came out of a crowd close to a thousand strong. 'Let's have a nice loud countdown from ten, nine . . .'

'Eight,' James chanted, as he slid an arm around Kerry's back.

'Seven, six,' as Rat did the same to Lauren.

Ryan held hands with Ning and gave her a smile on five.

'Four, three,' Kyle shouted, as he remembered the day he arrived in the main building at nine years old. Scared out of his wits.

'Two,' everyone yelled, as floodlights illuminated the glassless hulk of the main building.

'One.'

Mason, Freddie and Sophia pressed their buttons on the detonator panel. The first of five sharp cracks erupted, starting at the bottom and working their way up seven floors. For a half-second it seemed as if something had gone wrong, but a low rumble began to build and everyone screamed and cheered as the front façade collapsed, followed by the floors behind, with the side walls coming in last.

'Holy crap!' James shouted, as the roar became deafening and a billowing cloud of dust erupted in all directions.

As the ground rumbled, banks of powerful hoses began misting the perimeter where the main building had stood, to help keep the dust under control. But even with water and nets in place, the crowd tasted grit in the air as the last defiant strut buckled. Then stunned silence became a cheer of relief, accompanied by a wailing *all clear* siren.

7. LYNX

Four days later
James eyed himself in the mirror. He pulled up the tatty white CHERUB T-shirt he was wearing and clenched his stomach muscles, struggling to make any kind of six-pack. He needed to eat less and exercise more, and decided to start by just having coffee for breakfast.

Since he was a fairly junior staff member, James' first-floor apartment wasn't huge and didn't have the luxury of a view over campus. But on the other hand, it was modern and rent free, comprising a bedroom, shower room, walk-in wardrobe and a combined kitchen and lounge. He'd added a few personal touches, including a large photo of his late mother, and black and white photos of retired Arsenal players.

After popping a pod into his Nespresso machine, James pulled a shirt up his arms, then sat at his glass dining-table and flipped up the lid of his laptop. There were fifteen e-mails since he'd finished work the previous night, but before he got to any of them he noticed his mobile was vibrating and saw *John Jones* on caller display.

'John,' James said, faking enthusiasm. It felt like he spent half his waking hours with his boss' voice in his ear.

'You're not in your office,' John noted.

James scowled. 'I didn't finish work until gone ten last night.'

John laughed. 'I'm not having a go, pal. I appreciate how hard you've been working these past couple of months with so many other controllers away on missions. You'll be going up a couple of notches when the pay review comes around in Feb.'

'Really?' James said, smiling at the prospect of extra cash.

'Gotta keep pace with that banker-bonus girlfriend of yours,' John joked. 'Anyhow, I've been nagging various people and Birmingham is good to go.'

'Seriously?' James grinned, relishing an escape from campus bureaucracy to head off on a mission.

'I'm just about to send through an e-mail with all of the details of the agreement.'

As soon as John hung up, James pocketed phone and keys and charged for the exit. He was halfway out the door when he had a realisation. After opening a shoe cupboard just inside the door, he pulled off the shoes he usually wore in his office and grabbed a trashed pair of combat boots, clad in dry mud.

Rather than leave mud flakes down the hallway and stairs, he kept the boots hooked over his fingers until he was out through the revolving door of the staff building. It was a school day, so the paved walkway through Campus Village's low-rise accommodation was deserted, apart from a cleaner picking up litter and leaves with an electric handcart.

The dining-hall was mostly empty. A circle of gossiping red-shirt carers, taking breakfast now that lessons had started, and kids who didn't have school because they were either preparing for or recovering from missions.

James grabbed bottles of orange, sandwiches and two packaged slices of carrot cake, and got a dirty look from one of the catering staff because he hadn't quite walked all the dry mud off his boots.

James found an electric cart and rode it across campus. He had to take a circuitous route, because a large area was cordoned off where army bulldozer crews were working to clear the rubble of the main building.

The cart was only designed for tarmac or damp grass, so James had to abandon his ride when he got to a wooded area near the back of campus. It had been a wet autumn and he was glad he'd picked the boots as he walked the last five hundred metres, down a path regularly churned by kids on training runs.

After using his fingerprint to enter the gates of the training compound, James found Leon and Daniel Sharma, stood to attention in a muddy clearing, dressed in combat boots and filthy CHERUB uniform. The drill instructor had planted a remote camera in the mud, so that he'd know if they moved.

'You look bloody terrible,' James said, as he noticed the boys' red eyes and mud-caked hair.

They didn't answer and instead looked anxiously at the camera sticking out of the mud.

'Did Capstick say why you've been made to wait here?' James asked.

'Nope,' Leon said.

James rustled a plastic bag and pulled out a sandwich. 'Hungry?'

The twins' eyes lit up, but instructors had been tricking and bullying the pair for a week, so they didn't take anything at face value. James flung the bag at Daniel, who ripped out a chicken and bacon sandwich. Leon seemed slightly miffed that the other sandwich was cheese and pickle, but still inhaled it in a few bites, despite muddy fingers.

'Thank you,' Leon said, as he guzzled his orange juice. 'So good.'

'Safe to say you're keen to get out of here?' James noted.

'Yes, sir,' the twins agreed.

'Call me James. Fortunately for you guys, I was about to offer you a mission when you decided to go vigilante on Britain's paedo population. It's taken a hell of a lot of arm twisting, but we've reached agreement with Zara Asker. If you accept the mission I offer . . .'

'We accept,' Daniel blurted.

James smiled. 'I haven't told you what it is yet.'

'Anything's better than this,' Leon added. 'Drugs, terrorists, bring 'em on!'

'The bad news is that you're not off the hook,' James explained. 'Your punishments will be suspended, and your sixty days' heavy drill will be reduced by one day for every two that you serve on the mission.'

'How long is the mission?'

'Two weeks,' James said. 'Three if you're lucky.'

'Any chance it could spiral?' Leon asked.

'A hundred and four days would suit us best,' Daniel added. 'Wipe out the rest of our heavy drill.'

James smirked as the twins made simultaneous starts on their carrot cake. 'I'll need the pair of you in my office at noon. So get back to your rooms and scrub up.'

*

'Sorry,' James said, running into his office holding a red plastic pouch. 'It's chaos around here. You're not the only ones who can't wait to get off campus.'

Leon and Daniel stood in front of James' desk. The pair now wore neatly pressed CHERUB uniform, comprising lightweight black boots, combat trousers and navy CHERUB logo T-shirts. Their hair was damp from a shampooing and there was a powerful aroma of Axe body spray.

'Sit,' James said, pointing to a couple of chairs that needed to be dragged across. 'What is it about teenage boys and body spray? You just need a *tiny* amount. You've made my office smell like a Thai brothel.'

'Sorry,' Daniel said.

But Leon grinned. 'Do you have much experience with Thai brothels?'

James raised one eyebrow, as he pulled two ruggedised Android tablets out of the red pouch and handed them across. 'If you want to go back to heavy drill, be my guest.'

As the boys leaned over to grab identical tablets, James noticed that the quick scrub up hadn't extended as far as the twins getting all the mud out from under their nails, and Leon's right ear seemed to have a leaf stuck in it.

'I'm assuming you've both seen one of these before,' James said. 'Each unit has a mission briefing and a bunch of background files. You can access the tablets using your agent number and thumbprint. Once you accept the mission, the data will be transferred into your personal data cloud and be accessible using the secure area of your smartphones.'

'What happened to paper briefings?' Leon asked.

'Too much risk of being carried off site,' James explained. 'All agent phones and laptops are set up to be remotely wiped if they're lost or stolen. I have to go man the control room while the duty controller takes his twenty-minute break. So, you guys stay here, read this through and I'll answer any questions when you get back.'

James charged out, then back again briefly to grab his phone off the desk as the twins started to read.

8. SKIP

CLASSIFIED
MISSION BRIEFING:
FOR LEON SHARMA AND DANIEL SHARMA
DO NOT PRINT, COPY, OR MAKE NOTES

MISSION GOALS

This mission has been given a dual classification, as an opportunity to recruit a CHERUB agent and to potentially gain insight into possible extremist activity in the Sandy Green area of Birmingham.

SANDY GREEN

Located 2km from the centre of Birmingham, Sandy Green is one of the most deprived areas of the UK. Over half of all children live in poverty and youth unemployment runs at more than 50 per cent. 70 per cent of the population is non-white, with Muslims forming the largest ethnic group.

While the vast majority of Muslims in Sandy Green have no sympathy for or connection to radical Islamic groups, the combination of poverty and unemployment means that the intelligence service regards Sandy Green as an area where there is a high probability of disaffected youths becoming involved with radical Islamic groups like Al Qaeda and Islamic State.

MISSION TARGET – OLIVER LAKSHMI

Oliver Lakshmi was born in 2004 and recently turned twelve. He is the son of an unknown restaurant worker, who is believed to have returned to India, and a mother who died following a drug-related stabbing in 2007. Since this time, Oliver has lived in a number of care homes and foster placements.

Oliver has been assessed with an IQ of 150, which places him in the cleverest one per cent of the population. Despite his intelligence, Oliver has been bored and disruptive at school, frequently bunking off. He has been involved in a number of serious incidents, including assaulting another boy at a care home and seriously injuring a teacher with clay modelling tools during an art lesson.

He has been in a number of fights and after being expelled from two secondary schools in Year Seven, he recently started Year Eight and now attends a Fresh Start programme designed to help disruptive pupils before eventually reintegrating them into normal classes.

Oliver has difficulty making friends with people his own age, and often describes them as dumb. He seeks out older kids for companionship, who he tries to impress with elaborate lies and various forms of bad behaviour, including theft from shops and breaking into cars.

THE ARSON

In April 2016, Oliver and two older boys burgled a flat in the Longsight area of Birmingham. During the burglary, a man returned home from work and confronted the boys. All three boys got away, but not before one of the older boys was grabbed and severely beaten by the householder.

Two nights later, Oliver and the boy who'd been beaten sought revenge. The pair poured petrol through the flat's letterbox and set it alight. The householder was out working a night shift, but his wife was badly burned while rescuing two small children, and the family dog died. The flat was gutted, and there was serious fire and water damage to four other homes before the blaze was controlled. Property damage was estimated at £350,000.

Scared of a lengthy spell locked up in a young offender institution with much older boys, Oliver told local police that he would give them information about a radical Islamic group operating in the Sandy Green area in return for being let off the arson charges.

The investigating officers had previously arrested Oliver for a number of minor crimes and picked him up when truanting from school. Knowing that Oliver was smart and had a tendency to invent elaborate lies, the officers logged his offer and followed procedure by forwarding it to MI5. However, nobody took the eleven-year-old's claim seriously.

Oliver's fourteen-year-old accomplice received a four-year sentence for the arson attack. Since Oliver was barely old enough to face criminal charges, he was sent for a detailed psychiatric evaluation, after which he was ordered to stay at a secure confinement facility. This would enable him to stay in his local area and carry on going to school, but ensure that he was closely monitored and subject to a strict curfew outside of school hours.

After four months of relatively good behaviour, Oliver has recently had his curfew and most other secure confinement conditions suspended.

THE ARREST

In July 2016, police arrested fifteen- and seventeen-year-old brothers in the Sandy Green area, acting on intelligence from MI5. The boys were linked to a series of armed petrol station robberies, the money from which was donated to a radical Islamic group.

When the teenagers' bedrooms were searched, evidence was found that the boys had begun saving up to run away to North Africa and receive military training from a radical Islamic terror group. The boys are currently being held in custody, awaiting trial for the robberies.

When they were brought in for arrest, one officer on duty remembered that the younger boy had been caught truanting with Oliver Lakshmi the previous summer. This suggests the possibility that Oliver really might have some kind of information on radical Islamic groups.

MISSION PLAN

Daniel and Leon Sharma will move into the privately run Nurtrust Care Residence (NCR) in the Sandy Green area, with James Adams as mission controller. The twins' role is to befriend Oliver Lakshmi and ascertain whether he has knowledge of Islamic terror groups, while simultaneously monitoring his behaviour to see if he will make a decent CHERUB recruit.

If information on radical Islamic groups is unearthed, an assessment will be made on whether to try and infiltrate the group, or to pass information on to the intelligence service and withdraw.

NOTE: ON THE 4TH DAY OF AUGUST 2016 THIS MISSION PLAN WAS PASSED UNANIMOUSLY BY THE CHERUB ETHICS COMMITTEE, ON CONDITION THAT ALL AGENTS UNDERSTAND THE FOLLOWING:

This mission has been classified MEDIUM RISK. All agents are reminded of their right to refuse to undertake this mission and to withdraw from it at any time.

9. ARRIVAL

James wanted to bring his motorbike, so he bent the *under-age agents should only drive if they have to* rule and let Leon and Daniel take a Focus ST with blacked-out windows from campus to Sandy Green.

James had rented a small flat above a Morrisons Local and had already been downstairs, sworn at the self-checkouts and made a brew by the time the twins tramped upstairs carrying some of his luggage.

'You can't park for shit,' Leon teased.

James looked down from a bare-bulb landing, with the apartment door open. 'What happened?' he asked.

'We parked the Focus in the lot out back, like you told us,' Leon explained, as he crossed the threshold into the grimly furnished studio. Campus staff had already delivered most of James' clothes and a pair of aluminium flight cases containing communication and surveillance equipment. 'This nutter tried to reverse park and it was a total fiasco.'

Daniel tutted. 'It wasn't *that* bad.'

'Did anyone see you?' James asked warily.

'Just some guy in a white van hooting,' Leon said, grinning.

'Cuppa?' James asked. 'Nurtrust is only a couple of hundred metres from here, so you'll need to be discreet when you visit me.'

After tea and chocolate digestives, James helped the twins take the remaining luggage out of the Ford and sent them off to Nurtrust. Leon pressed a buzzer on a barred door, set between a betting shop and a local council office. The voice through the intercom was indecipherable, but he pushed when it buzzed and the pair found themselves in a graffitied hallway that smelled of cleaning product.

There was an office at the top of a staircase and a Sikh man in jacket and jeans greeted the pair at the top.

'Leon and Daniel?' he said, offering a hand to shake. 'I'm Gurbir. Welcome to Nurtrust Sandy Green.'

They filled out forms and discussed rules. The whole time a girl in the next office sobbed helplessly. She was twelve and very skinny. She sat on an armchair with knees tucked under her chin and what looked like her worldly possessions split between a school backpack and a pair of canvas bags.

Daniel tried giving the girl a reassuring smile as Gurbir led them on a tour of what had once been the upper floor of a furniture showroom. A small kitchen gave off a smell of veg cooked to oblivion. There was a room with pool tables and vending machines, another with TV and battered recliner chairs.

'You're in rooms twelve and fifteen,' Gurbir explained.

They passed a locked corridor.

'Is that solitary, for if we misbehave?'

'We have nine secure rooms,' Gurbir explained. 'Only five are currently occupied and you're not allowed beyond that door, should you ever find it open.'

'What did the kids in there do?' Daniel asked, as he put his face up to a shatterproof pane in the locked door.

'There's nobody in there now,' Gurbir explained. 'Most of them are at school.'

'So they can come and go?' Leon asked.

Gurbir laughed. 'The courts set different rules and curfews for our secure residents, but this *isn't* a prison.'

They'd reached room twelve by this time. 'Daniel, you're directly across the hall. Toilets and showers are at the end. Showers are kept locked, so you have to get a key from the office and return it when you're finished.'

'Right,' Daniel said.

He threw his stuff into a room with a small window, a fold-down desk and a metal locker. It looked modern, but there was an oniony tang from the previous occupant and the window only opened inwards by about four centimetres.

Leon stuck his head around the door. 'Not exactly

spacious,' he said, then wrinkled his nose. 'It stinks like BO in here.'

'I noticed,' Daniel said sourly.

Out in the hallway, the sobbing girl was being led into room nine. A female social worker spoke in a soothing voice.

'Abigail, you'll only be here for a night or two, until you get a foster placement in a proper house. OK?'

She sobbed, and gave a weak nod.

'I'm just down the hall until seven, and I'll introduce you to the night staff before I clock off.'

As the twins unpacked, a few other noises started to break out. The twins could see into each other's rooms if they left their doors open and they saw kids coming past in school uniform. Most were fourteen to seventeen, but there were a couple of pre-teens.

Daniel was hunting for a socket to charge his phone when he saw Oliver shoot past. Their target used the toilet, dropped into room thirteen next to Leon and came out a minute later having swapped school gear for trackies and an Aston Villa shirt.

'Hey, neighbour,' Leon said.

'Hey,' Oliver replied, but didn't break stride.

The twins had seen photos, but were still surprised by Oliver's presence. He was average height for twelve, with a light brown complexion. But his build gave him the air of a little thug. Big neck, broad shoulders, thick arms, and legs stretching his Nike tracksuit bottoms to bursting.

'I'm Leon,' Leon said, as he trailed Oliver. 'Do you

know where I can get soap and a towel?'

'Call me Oli,' the twelve-year-old said, staring Leon up and down, seeing a well-muscled kid with a medium build and blond streaks in his hair. 'Ask in the office,' he said impatiently.

'Right,' Leon said.

At the end of the hallway, Oliver cut into the TV room. The only kid in there was on floor-cushions using an ancient Xbox 360, still in his school uniform. He looked older than Oliver, but was beanpole thin.

'Wes the weasel,' Oliver said fiercely. 'You got my money?'

'I don't owe you money.'

'You reckon?' Oliver said, pounding a fist into his palm as he closed in. 'Gimme a fiver.'

Skinny Wes dropped the Xbox controller and raised his arms over his face. 'I haven't got any money.'

Oliver shoved Wes off the cushions. Leon watched in mild horror as Oliver lunged, delivering three hard punches to the ribs and a kick in the thigh.

'I'm on the Xbox,' Oliver growled. 'Get out before I give you real beats.'

Wes scrambled up and limped out the door past Leon. Oliver smiled until he saw that he was being watched.

'You got a problem?' Oliver asked.

Leon smiled like he was OK with what he'd seen. 'What did he do to piss you off?'

'Skinny weasel,' Oliver explained, as he grabbed the controller off the floor. 'I always give him beats. I don't even wanna play. All the discs are scratched up so the games never work.'

'I've got a PS4,' Leon said. 'Haven't unpacked it yet, but it'll only take half a minute to set it up.'

'I had a PS4 and an Xbox One,' Oliver said, putting a hand on his hip. 'But I sold 'em. Needed the money for clothes and stuff.'

'Really?' Leon said, catching a whiff of bullshit stronger than the BO in Daniel's room. 'Got a bunch of games. You wanna play?'

'Played most of 'em already, probably,' Oliver said, shrugging. 'But yeah, whatever. Got nothing else to do.'

Daniel was coming out of his room with some air freshener he'd blagged from the front office.

'Gonna put the PS4 on,' Leon told him.

'That your brother?' Oliver asked, as Daniel walked past. 'Twins?'

'Non-identical,' Leon said. 'I got the good looks.'

Daniel did a noisy false laugh. 'Who are you kidding, bro? With your face like an ape's backside.'

10. TALES

Leon set up the PS4. He played *Call of Duty* with Oli and Daniel before switching to *FIFA16*. An older teen called Wilfred joined in for a bit, and a girl called Rhea came in and started flirting with Leon. She looked about fifteen, with make-up trowelled on.

'Smoking hot,' Leon said, as his eyes followed her out of the room. 'You think she was into me?'

Daniel was pissed off, because he reckoned he'd have got Rhea's attention if he'd only chosen to sit by the door, rather than down on the floor in front of the PlayStation.

'What room's she in?' Leon asked.

'S-four,' Oli said, then gasped as his shot on goal sailed over the bar. 'Aww, come on, bitch!'

'S?' Leon asked.

Oli glanced at Leon like he was dumb. 'S for psycho,' he said.

'What did she do?'

'I heard Rhea and her brothers went around mugging people,' Oli explained. 'She'd lure some guy, then her brothers would mug them and beat the crap out of them. Brothers are in young offenders for cracking some guy's skull.'

'Really?' Daniel asked, smiling. 'Looks like you've hitched your wagon to another winner there, brother.'

Leon shrugged and smiled. 'She's got a great ass, so I can live with a few tiny imperfections.'

Daniel tutted.

'Nooo,' Oli shouted, as he overhit a corner. 'This game is a pile of junk. It just does random bloody . . .'

Oli thumped the controller into a cushion then looked at Leon. 'You wanna take this over? I'm 3-1 down.'

'Give us,' Leon said.

Oli was a clammy beast, and Leon found it gross taking a controller smeared in sweat.

'Tackle!' Leon said, as he took the ball off Daniel and passed out wide before starting a run on goal. 'Come on, come on . . . Shit!'

'So I never finished my story,' Oli said.

Leon and Daniel both groaned internally. But Oli was their target so they had to listen.

'So I go into this McDonald's,' Oli said. 'And they're giving away free breakfast vouchers. But they're really busy and I can see the whole pile of vouchers. So I jumped across the counter and grabbed the book. And I had like, two hundred vouchers. And I was eating free Big Macs for like, two months.'

'I thought they were *breakfast* vouchers,' Leon pointed out.

'Yeah . . .' Oli said. 'I mean, they were mixed. Four different ones. Some were for Big Macs and apple pies and stuff.'

'Right,' Daniel said. 'Cool beans.'

Leon reckoned Oli was one of those guys who'll top any story you tell, and decided to put his theory to the test.

'Our older brother and his mate robbed a Burger King one time,' Leon lied. 'He got over eight hundred quid. Cops chased him and everything, but he got away with it.'

Oli nodded enthusiastically. 'I've been chased by cops *so* many times when I'm bunking school. One time me and this friend of mine took an iPad out of Selfridges at the Bullring. Sold it for four hundred.'

'Nice,' Daniel said. 'You should show us how you did it.'

Leon nodded. 'We could go robbing shops.'

Oli's bluff had been called and his smile vanished. 'I have to be so careful now though,' he blurted. 'Cos . . . Like, the store detectives all know me and shit. They've even got a special file on me.'

'Special file,' Daniel said, trying not to smirk as he caught his brother's glance. 'Wowee!'

'But I'd like to hang with you guys, for sure.'

'You seem cool,' Leon said, which made a huge smile erupt across Oli's face.

Leon was dominating at *FIFA*, but only got the score back to 3–2 before time ran out.

Daniel looked at Oli. 'You wanna play Leon?'

But Oli was looking out the door down the hallway. Abigail – the girl who'd been sobbing when the twins arrived – had been to the office to get a shower key. Now she'd emerged from her room with a towel and a bundle of clothes under her arm.

'I overheard Gurbir say that Abigail's mum was in a big car smash,' Daniel said. 'Touch and go whether she'll live.'

Leon nodded sympathetically, but Oli didn't seem to care. 'Boo-hoo,' Oli said. 'My mum died when I was three. What good's sobbing her head off gonna do?'

Oli's words made Leon and Daniel think about their mother dying of cancer. At the other end of the hallway, Abigail's slender frame unlocked a door and hopped into a small room with a shower cubicle at the back.

'You wanna mess with Little Miss Tearful?' Oli asked.

Leon wasn't keen. 'We could put a different game on.'

But Oli was on his feet. After stepping into the hallway and taking a few furtive glances, he hurried to Abigail's room, rattled her door and found that she'd had the sense to lock it. Undeterred, Oli beckoned Leon and Daniel.

'You wanna see something funny?' Oli asked.

The twins dashed along the hallway towards room nine. They instinctively wanted to tell Oli to leave

Abigail alone, but their mission was to find out whether Oli would make a decent CHERUB recruit and they'd get a better sense of his personality if they went along with his plan.

'I'll give her something to cry about,' Oli grinned, as he reached inside his tracksuit pocket and pulled a twenty-pence piece.

The boys heard water running as they closed up to the door of the shower room. A key with a big yellow *In Use* tag was in the outside of the door, which was locked with a bolt on the inside. This bolt had a bypass, which looked like a giant screw head and was designed to enable staff to access a bathroom from outside in an emergency.

Oli put his coin in the bypass slot and turned it to release the bolt. He looked back at Leon and Daniel, flicking one cheeky eyebrow before charging the door.

The door burst inwards. Abigail screamed as Oli reached into the steamy space and flicked out the light. Oli charged into the little cubicle and gave Abigail an almighty shove through the shower curtain. As she slammed tiles at the back of the shower and lost her footing, Oli scooped her towel and clean clothes from a shelf, whipped the curtain open and threw them all under the running water so they got soaked. As Abigail screamed in pain and shock, Oli backed out of the room and turned the key, leaving his victim screaming in pitch darkness.

'You snitch and I'll come after you,' Oli warned, as he thumped on the door.

Abigail kept screaming as Oli turned back towards the twins, grinning like a loon.

'How cool was that?' he shouted.

*

Three hours later, the hallway was down to a bluish glow of nightlights as Daniel stepped out of his room. Abigail could be heard sobbing a few rooms away and a couple of kids were playing music, even though it was headphones only after ten on a weeknight.

'You awake?' Daniel asked quietly, as he stepped across the hallway and put his head inside Leon's room.

The only light came from a laptop standing on the desk, but it was enough for Daniel to see his brother sat in bed with his phone.

'Show us,' Daniel said.

'None of yours,' Leon tutted. 'I'm talking to Rhea on WhatsApp.'

'Just make sure she doesn't hit you over the head and steal your wallet,' Daniel warned. 'Why don't you invite her over?'

'She's locked up in secure until morning.'

'Can I sit?' Daniel asked.

Leon nodded, and pulled up his legs so his brother could use the end of the bed.

'So what do you make of Oli?' Daniel asked.

Leon shook his head. 'I think the cops were right. He's a massive bullshitter. No way he's connected to any terrorists.'

'Not seeing much potential as a CHERUB agent, either,' Daniel said.

'Nope,' Leon agreed. 'CHERUB recruits a lot of kids who are messed up and rough around the edges, but I don't think Oli has a sympathetic bone in his body.'

'He started on Wes the Weed again after we brushed our teeth.'

'Hard punches,' Leon nodded. 'Wes had tears in his eyes. Before this is over, I might have to accidentally break the little shit's nose.'

Daniel laughed. 'You bust his nose, I'll break his thumbs. And that story about winning a trip to see the Taj Mahal in a poetry competition.'

'He didn't even know what country it was in,' Leon grinned. 'Talk about Captain Bullshitter.'

'Thing is, bro, if we're completely honest . . .'

Leon finished his brother's sentence. 'If we tell James what we really think about Oli, we'll be back on campus doing heavy drill by Monday.'

'So we lie to him?' Daniel asked.

'Not lie exactly,' Leon said, giving a conspiratorial smile. 'We just need to be economical in how rapidly we deliver the truth.'

Daniel smiled. 'String this thing out for at *least* two weeks.'

11. UNIFORM

Two days after arriving at Nurtrust, Daniel came out of his titchy room wearing the uniform of St Andrew's Catholic school. Oli sat in the home's cramped dining area, scoffing Nutella toast.

'Was it today you've got History with Mr Cunningham?' Oli asked. 'Tell the old fart that I said hello.'

'That the guy who got you expelled?' Daniel asked, as he filled a bowl from a giant box of Asda-brand wheat flakes and topped it off with mixed nuts and milk. 'Seen my brother?'

'Saw him disappear with Rhea.'

Leon had spent the previous evening in the TV room making out with Rhea. She was hot stuff, and Daniel was jealous.

'So, you all set for lunchtime?' Daniel asked. 'Bunk

off and head over to our cousin's place?'

'Course,' Oli said. 'I've bunked a million times. Anything to get out of Games.'

'Thought you said you were good at football,' Daniel noted.

'I am,' Oli said defensively. 'I was top scorer on the school team last year.'

A Year Eight girl called Mel sat across the table, big shoulders and purple streaks in plaited hair. 'Top scorer,' she squealed, as she accidentally spat cereal across the table. 'You so full of it, Oli, with them chunky-monkey legs.'

Oli reared up. 'What do you know? You've never been at my school.'

'Seen you run,' Mel said. 'Give us a football, bet you couldn't catch me, let alone tackle me.'

'Am I talking to you?' Oli blurted. 'Is this *your* conversation, hippo?'

Mel looked at Daniel, then pointed a false nail at Oli. 'He's full of shit.'

Wes the Weed chimed in from the next table. 'You know how you can tell when Oli's lying?' he asked. 'He's lying whenever his lips move.'

Oli's chair grated backwards as he stood and yelled. His voice hadn't broken so it was really shrill. 'I'll bust your nose if you don't shut your mouth.'

One of the kitchen staff overheard this and stepped between the boys. 'Cool heads, the lot of you,' he shouted.

Rather than sit down, Oli abandoned the last of his

toast, grabbed his school pack and stormed out. Daniel had wolfed most of his cereal and ignored the kitchen guy's order to come back and clean plates.

'Up yours, losers,' Oli shouted, giving a backwards flip off.

Daniel followed Oli past the admin office, downstairs and along the corridor to the street. He had a fiver and realised there was time to get a McDonald's breakfast before school. But he was distracted seeing Leon up against the shutters of the yet-to-open betting shop, snogging Rhea.

'Get a room you dirty perverts,' Oli yelled.

Rhea stopped kissing Leon and checked the time on her phone. She went to the same Fresh Start unit as Oli, so she gave Leon a goodbye peck.

'Laters, Leon,' she said, before walking off the same way as Oli.

'I love this mission!' Leon told his brother as he picked his school pack off the pavement. 'What a girl!'

Daniel didn't want Leon knowing he was jealous, but the twins knew one another too well to hide emotions.

'Don't worry,' Leon said, as he pulled his phone out of his school trousers and unlocked it. 'I had a word with Rhea. She's gonna fix you up with one of her hot mates. I know your type, she's *perfect*.'

Daniel looked excited. 'Really?'

'Here's a picture.'

Daniel looked at his brother's phone, seeing a police mugshot of a meth addict with sunken eyes and blackened teeth.

'Oh you're *so* funny,' Daniel said, giving Leon an almighty shove in the back. 'And it's pure luck you know. If I'd been sitting by the door when she walked in . . .'

'Nah-nuhh-uh-nuh-nuh-nuh,' Leon mocked, as he wiped lipstick off his cheek. 'So Captain Bullshit's all set for lunchtime?'

*

'I bet he's not coming,' Leon said. 'Chicken shit.'

He was in a side street with Daniel, sitting on a low wall in front of an abandoned exhaust centre. Both boys had coat hoods up, with rain pelting the outsides.

'Better text James,' Daniel said, but Oli came around the corner just as he was about to dial.

'Howdy, partners,' Oli said, stuffing his face from a family bag of Walkers Cheese and Onion. 'Sorry I'm late. Had to wait till lunch was over 'cos they had someone on the back gate today.'

'No probs,' Leon said, as he started a slow walk. 'So our cousin wants this garage cleared out, says he'll pay us thirty each. Take maybe three or four hours.'

'Cool,' Oli said. 'I don't even care about the money, because I've got three grand in my Nationwide savings account. I just wanna get off Games, you know?'

'We've done odd jobs for him before,' Leon continued. 'Sometimes he gives us a bit of weed as well.'

'I love smoking joints,' Oli said. 'I had one that was like, twenty-five centimetres for New Year and I smoked the whole thing myself.'

'Nice,' Daniel said, trying not to meet his brother's

eye because he knew he'd laugh.

They walked a couple of side streets, with the wind whipping rain and leaves. As they turned into a street of two-storey houses, an elderly woman came down an overgrown front path. She clanked her gate and set off at a decent pace towards the boys. When she was a few steps in front of the trio, a set of keys dropped from the woman's coat pocket. She must have been hard of hearing because they made a clatter but she kept on walking.

Daniel picked up the keys and turned to shout after the old lady, but Oli stood in front of him and raised a hand.

'We could go in there,' Oli said urgently, pointing up towards the house. 'Keep your mouths shut.'

Leon and Daniel exchanged glances.

'Old people keep cash in the house,' Oli said, as he watched the lady cut across the road. 'Thousands sometimes. Or she might have antiques, or shit.'

'She's an old lady,' Daniel pointed out.

'*You're* an old lady,' Oli said, as he looked across at Leon.

'He could be right,' Leon told his brother. 'Old people don't trust banks.'

'What if there's someone else in there?' Daniel asked.

'Even if there is, they'll be old, like her husband or something,' Oli said. 'You wanna slave for your cousin for thirty quid when there could be all kinds of valuable stuff to rip off?'

'He's right,' Leon said.

Daniel handed Oli the dropped keys and the three boys glanced about, before dashing up ten metres of driveway towards the house.

The front door was tatty, with a crack in the frosted glass. Oli took a minute, working out which of four keys undid the deadlock and the main lock.

'It's deadlocked, so there's probably nobody else home,' Oli noted, as he stepped into a gloomy house.

It wasn't very warm and there was a smell of damp in the hallway. The living-room had lots of framed photos, an old TV and an ancient video tape recorder with the clock flashing. Leon checked out the kitchen, which had a feeding bowl and a whiff of cats. Oli started opening jars along the counter top hoping to find money, but he only found stale biscuits, flour and gravy powder.

'This isn't worth the risk,' Daniel noted.

Oli laughed. 'What risk? If they catch me they'll put me in a secure care home. But I'm *already* in a secure care home. They might tighten up my curfew or move me back to secure corridor, but who really gives a shit?'

As Oli said this he opened a cupboard under the sink and found a black enamel money-box on a shelf. It was narrow, and the inside was divided into sections with handwritten labels saying things like *gas*, *telephone*, *vet* and *birthday*.

'Ker-ching!' Oli said, rattling coins as he thumped the box on the dining-table. After popping off the lid, he stripped out eighty pounds in tenners, plus a five and a dozen pound coins. 'I bet the old bag keeps more upstairs.'

'We're splitting this three ways,' Leon said, as Oli led a charge upstairs.

Daniel still seemed reluctant. 'She's just an old lady,' he said, as he reached the upstairs landing.

'So what?' Oli said. 'What have old people ever done for us?'

There were two rooms and a bathroom upstairs. There was a jewellery box beside the woman's bed. Oli pocketed a man's sovereign ring and some diamond earrings, while Leon found another seventy pounds under a bar of soap in a drawer full of bras.

Oli ignored the bathroom, then almost had a heart attack as he walked into the other bedroom. The large room was dominated by a hospital-style bed with an electric hoist above for lifting someone in and out, along with a portable toilet.

The man in the bed was in his forties, with lank, greying hair. He snored lightly, but when he breathed, one side of his body seemed completely paralysed.

'Stinks like hell!' Oli whispered, pulling his shirt up over his face. 'But I think we hit pay dirt!'

Besides various pieces of medical equipment, there was a modern flat screen TV mounted on the wall, a laptop on the bed, an Android tablet alongside and an Xbox One with half a dozen games.

'We can't rob this guy,' Daniel whispered, as he stepped in last.

'I know a guy who'll buy this stuff,' Oli said, grinning ear to ear. 'We'll make four, even five hundred quid, easy.'

'We need a bag,' Leon whispered.

'There was a wheeled suitcase under the stairs,' Oli noted. 'Go get it, Daniel.'

But Daniel looked furious, holding up his hands. 'I'm embarrassed,' he said. 'You two should be ashamed of yourselves.'

'This is serious money,' Oli said. 'What's your problem?'

'I don't want this on my conscience,' Daniel said. 'I'm outta here.'

Leon followed his brother out on to the landing, then watched as he stormed downstairs and out of the front door.

As Daniel headed down the front path towards the street, Leon retrieved the wheelie case from under the stairs, and came back to find Oli crawling under the disabled man's bed, unplugging the tablet and laptop chargers.

'He's been pissy all day,' Leon explained to Oli. 'He won't admit it, but he's crazy jealous about me getting it on with Rhea.'

'More money for us,' Oli said, as he slid out from under the bed and swiped dust off the knees of his trousers.

While Leon unzipped the case and started loading up with the Xbox and its accessories, Oli walked around to the far side of the bed, which was barely thirty centimetres from the wall. The disabled guy's laptop was a swanky Lenovo that was probably worth more than everything else they'd stolen. Trouble was, the owner had fallen asleep while using it and the laptop lay open on his thighs, with one arm draped across the keyboard.

Leon felt jittery as he watched Oli slide the laptop towards the edge of the bed. Then he grabbed the man's outstretched wrist and began lifting it away. Oli thought he'd done the job, but as he snapped the laptop shut the man reared up in his bed.

He was a big fellow, more than six feet tall and overweight. 'Who the hell are you?' he shouted, as he shot upwards. 'What are you doing?'

Oli tried scrambling back around the outside of the bed, but the man was only paralysed down his right side and managed to flick his leg, pinning Oli to the wall as the laptop clattered to the floor.

As Oli tried to wriggle free, the man rolled over and swung his fist, hitting Oli hard on the chin. Fortunately for the twelve-year-old, the man was too broad to fit in the narrow gap between bed and wall.

Oli moaned in pain as the punch knocked him back, but he was able to squat down, grab the laptop with its trailing power cord, then scramble under the bed and out the other side.

'You OK?' Leon asked, as he gave Oli a hand up.

'No I'm not,' Oli shouted, clutching at his jaw. 'The asshole hit me.'

Seeking vengeance, Oli grabbed a glass water jug from a bedside table. He threw it at the man's head, but it just clanked off the bedframe and didn't break.

'Scum!' the man shouted as he rolled over and

punched a red emergency button on a cord around his neck.

A voice came out of the necklace inside five seconds. 'GoldAlert emergency. What's the problem, Mr Brown?'

'I'm being robbed in my bed,' he yelled, as Leon and Oli zipped up the suitcase and started scrambling down the stairs. 'Call the police immediately, then contact my mother on her mobile.'

'Bloody hell,' Oli said, clutching his jaw but grinning exuberantly as he followed Leon and the wheeled suitcase out the front door down the driveway. 'We'd better get the hell out of here.'

12. SCARPER

After parting company with Leon and Oli, Daniel passed through the old lady's front gate, crossed the street, walked right for fifty metres and grabbed the rear door of a Mercedes van with a hire company logo on the side. James sat on a folding chair in the cavernous rear compartment, watching video from inside the house on his laptop.

The screen showed the feed from six different cameras. In the top left corner, the disabled man was walking around, apparently cured of his paralysis. The centre of the bottom row showed Oli running down the driveway and Leon behind, dragging the wheeled suitcase.

'Did you get good audio?' Daniel asked.

James made a fake shudder. 'That kid has the moral compass of a sewer rat.'

'I did like you told me, boss. Took the high ground, gave Oli plenty of opportunities to question whether he was doing the right thing.'

'I heard every word,' James said. 'You were great.'

'But it could be trauma or something,' Daniel suggested.

James looked confused. 'What do you mean?'

'Like, Oli's been an orphan his whole life. In and out of care homes. Maybe if he got the opportunity to be in a better environment he'd become a better person.'

James snorted. 'And let me guess, you'd like another week or so to study Oli in great detail and try to unearth this buried potential?'

'CHERUB *is* supposed to be short of recruits,' Daniel said.

James broke into a big grin. 'My cynical side thinks you're just trying to delay your return to campus. As if you had some kind of horrible punishment hanging over your head, or something.'

Daniel gave it a final shot. 'I just think Oli deserves a fuller assessment.'

'So do I,' James said.

Daniel's eyebrows shot up. 'Really?'

'The latest policy is to spend as much time and effort as possible on testing potential recruits, *before* they reach campus and learn the secret of CHERUB. Not like in my day, when you just woke up on campus after being drugged and got warned that nobody would believe if you said anything.'

'Waking up naked was creepy too,' Daniel noted.

'And you're not the only one keen to stay off campus,' James added. 'Every day there's a half-metre stack of paperwork, and John Jones blaring in my earhole. Budget reports, mission briefings, threat meetings, education liaison meetings, ethics committee meetings, post mission reintegration plans. And when I'm out here on a mission, all of that becomes SEP.'

'SEP?'

'Somebody Else's Problem,' James explained.

Daniel cracked a big smile. 'So how long we gonna study Oli for? Two weeks?'

'That's probably pushing it,' James said, smirking. 'But I totally need to finish watching the last three seasons of *Game of Thrones*. And on a serious note, the intelligence service is putting so much effort into infiltrating Islamic State, that I think we can justify a bit more time to investigate the remote possibility that Oli didn't invent the whole terrorist thing.'

'Love *Game of Thrones*,' Daniel said. 'One of the carers made me take my nudie of Emilia Clarke from inside my wardrobe door.'

'Which one's she?' James asked.

'Daenerys, the dragon lady.'

'She's *totally* my dream girl,' James said, before clearing his throat abruptly. 'After Kerry, obviously.'

'Obviously, boss.'

James smiled. 'In the spirit of thoroughly assessing young Oliver, I suppose we ought to test his mettle in a tense scenario, yes?'

Daniel nodded enthusiastically. 'I'll head off now.

With any luck, Oli will get his ass bit.'

James tapped an icon on his laptop screen. 'You there, Michael . . . ? Leon and Oli have left the house. They should be in sight any second now.'

*

'Go left,' Leon told Oli, as they reached a T-junction. 'We can hide out at my cousin's place while the heat dies down.'

Oli was chuffed about the robbery and even more full of himself than usual. 'Screw your cousin and his thirty quid cleaning a garage,' he said. 'I know this guy Trey who buys stolen shit. He'll give us cash. Three hundred at least.'

'But the cops'll be looking for us, Oli. Best be off the street, yeah?'

Before Oli got to answer, a battered Renault SUV squealed to a halt in a disabled bay across the street.

'You thieving little shits,' the man getting out shouted. He was a big guy, dressed in trackies and a paint-spattered hoodie. Even worse, a huge black Rottweiler jumped out behind on a lead. 'Gimme the stuff back.'

Oli froze for half a second, before realising that Leon was already running. The pair scrambled into the road to dodge a woman with three young kids.

'You stop, now,' the man shouted. 'I'll crack your heads.'

Oli was solid, but he wasn't in the best shape. 'Wait up,' he gasped, clutching his side as Leon streaked ahead.

While Leon reached a main road and sprinted past Costa Coffee, Oli found the paint-spattered man and his excited dog closing to within a few metres. Realising that he couldn't outrun his opponent, Oli scrambled through a gate and ripped a windmill ornament out of a neat front garden. It was made of plastic, but weighted with a concrete base.

The big man overshot the gate, then a combination of leaves underfoot and the enthusiastic Rottweiler tugging on its leash sent him skidding into a painful set of splits. Oli was delighted for two seconds, between his pursuer's agonised yell and the moment when he let go of the dog's leash.

'No!' Oli yelled.

The twelve-year-old lobbed the windmill, but it just glanced the eighty-kilo dog in the side. After thinking about doubling back towards the gate, Oli made a run at the hedge leading into the next garden. He got a good jump, and would have scrambled over if the Rottweiler hadn't got a paw on his tracksuit bottoms, dragging him down on to the manicured lawn as a woman stuck her head out of the front door fifteen metres away.

'Help me!' Oli screamed, getting sprayed with saliva as the dog jumped on his chest, ripping off barks.

He had no way of knowing that this was one of the CHERUB campus guard dogs, trained to bark and contain rather than maul. As the dog's writhing weight smeared Oli into the damp grass, he caught a glance of the paint-strewn man struggling to his feet, only to get kicked – fake-kicked – dramatically down by a boy who'd sprinted in from across the road.

Oli realised it was Daniel as the woman by the door ran inside to call the cops. After vaulting the gate, Daniel closed up behind the barking dog and snatched its leash. It took all his strength to haul it back, just long enough for Oli to roll free. As the dog turned to pounce on Daniel, the fourteen-year-old stumbled back and hooked the end of the leash over a fence post.

'Move your butt,' Daniel ordered, hitching Oli up by his trackies and throwing him over the hedge, before grabbing the laptop out of the churned-up lawn and making the dive himself.

Oli was confused by the chain of events, but his pursuer appeared to be unconscious and Leon had doubled back and was waiting on the pavement as they exited through another front gate.

'How slow are you?' Leon jibed, as Daniel gave Oli a shove in the back.

Muddy, shocked and with strings of dog spit in his face, Oli felt Daniel grab his neck and shove him forward. 'The cops are gonna be here, start running.'

Oli got dragged by the twins, feeling warm around his crotch and realising that some pee had leaked out when he thought the dog was about to bite.

13. FENCE

The reality had been Oli snivelling and peeing his pants, but he'd rewritten the story before the mud dried on his clothes. The three boys were in a tatty chicken shop, with Cokes and a jumbo chips on the plastic table in between.

'I almost made it, man,' Oli smiled. 'That massive pit bull grabbed me, but I was all ready to kick up with both feet. Cane that thing in the head, but the dog got lucky when Daniel pulled it off.'

Daniel shook his head. 'You'd have been doggie chow if I didn't come save your ass.'

'That kick in the face was awesome,' Oli said. 'I didn't realise you know martial arts. I used to do Muay Thai, could have got my black belt, but I got moved to a new foster placement before the grading.'

Oli demonstrated his skills with a little jab.

Leon laughed. 'You make a fist like that you'll break your thumb first time you hit someone.'

'I know,' Oli said defensively, as he dipped chips in brown sauce and filled his mouth.

'So if we walk back into Nurtrust with a wheelie case filled with booty, chances are we'll get busted in three seconds flat,' Leon said.

'School will still be open for homework club,' Daniel said. 'There's nothing in my locker yet.'

'Case won't fit in.'

Daniel shrugged. 'Everything else will, though.'

Oli was chomping to say something, but had to swallow his chips first. 'I told you, man. I know this guy, Trey. I've nicked stuff before and he'll pay us in cash. He's a serious dude, like Islamic State terrorism.'

The twins both laughed.

'What's your problem?' Oli growled.

Leon smirked. 'No offence, man, but you're a little *colourful*.'

'What's that supposed to mean?'

'Well, you're almost a Muay Thai black belt, but you don't know how to make a proper fist,' Daniel said. 'You're the top goal scorer for your school team, but you run slow and get out of breath after two hundred metres. You owned a PS4 but you didn't know where the L2 button was.'

Oli started going bright red.

'It's OK, dude,' Leon said. 'We like you. But you don't need to make crazy shit up to impress us.'

Oli didn't know what to say, but broke into a huge

involuntary smile as Leon gave him a shoulder thump, hard enough to rock him off his plastic seat into the chicken shop's front window.

'I never had much in my life,' Oli said. 'I guess I trash-talk sometimes. But Trey is for real.'

Leon smiled. 'You're sure we won't get blown up by a USAF drone strike if we visit his flat?'

'Screw you,' Oli said, giving the finger with his muddy hand. 'I've nicked stuff before and he buys it. And a few times I've done jobs for Trey, like bricks through windows and shit.'

This sounded pretty far-fetched and Daniel snorted. 'Why does Trey want you to put bricks through windows?'

'He runs a protection racket,' Oli said, folding his arms furiously when he saw the expressions on the twins' faces. 'That's god's honest truth, you assholes. If you don't believe me, we'll go see him.'

Leon decided to call Oli's bluff. 'Now?'

Oli scraped up the last few chips and stood up. 'Number eighty-four bus. Ten-minute ride. You coming?'

The trio kept a wary eye out for cops as they waited for the bus and got off by a stop under a railway arch. A cobbled alleyway took them past Asian taxi drivers standing in a noisy circle alongside their parked Priuses and into a cab office under a railway arch.

The receptionist behind the Plexiglas screen looked suspicious when Oli asked to see Trey.

'He knows me,' Oli explained.

'He's in a meeting,' the woman said, as a cynical

eyebrow flickered beneath her headscarf. 'Have a seat.'

An old-fashioned bottled gas heater gave off a sweet smell as the boys squished together on a knackered sofa. Leon flicked through an ancient copy of *FourFourTwo* magazine, while Daniel played with his phone, texting James to let him know what was occurring.

'Just in case there's any argument,' Oli said, as he slid a Samsung Galaxy with a pink cover out of his pocket. 'Everything is split three ways, but the money from this is mine.'

'Where'd you get that?' Leon asked.

'Remember that snivelling girl who I locked in the shower?'

'Abigail,' Leon said.

Oli nodded. 'Gotta pick a pocket or two, eh?'

'Her mother died and you ripped off her phone?' Daniel said incredulously.

Oli shrugged and smirked. 'Life's a bitch, then you die.'

A flimsy door by the service counter came open, and a haze of cigarette smoke along with it.

'Trey's ready,' an old dude in carpet slippers said. All three boys stood up, but he pointed at Oli. 'Just you.'

As Oli vanished inside with the wheeled case, Daniel looked at Leon, shook his head and spoke in a whisper. 'Who robs a girl whose mother just died?'

Leon nodded in agreement. 'Before we go back to campus, I'm gonna bundle Oli into one of the shower rooms at Nurtrust and give him *such* a beating.'

'It's a nice thought, but they'll kick our asses out of CHERUB if we do that.'

'Who's gonna tell 'em?' Leon asked. 'James is cool.'

The pair played with their phones and clock watched. Five. Five fifteen. Five twenty-five.

'Maybe they killed him,' Leon suggested.

'Maybe he took our share and legged it out the back way,' Daniel suggested.

Oli finally emerged, looking unsure of himself and reeking of cigarette smoke. He zipped his jacket and started towards the door.

'So?' Daniel asked. 'What did we get?'

They were out of the alleyway and walking towards the bus stop when Oli finally answered.

'Sixty pounds each,' Oli said, peeling a roll of notes out of his pocket.

'You what!' Daniel shouted. 'That was a twelve-hundred-quid Lenovo laptop. Plus the Xbox.'

'I tried to get it up to two hundred,' Oli said. 'Trey said the market was really tight. Like, nobody is buying stuff.'

'You should have walked out,' Leon said.

Oli shook his head. 'It's the risk you take, OK. Trey's a serious guy. If you walk out, you're gonna offend him. And he's not someone you want as your enemy.'

Daniel gave Oli a little shove back into the bus canopy. 'You'd *better* not be ripping us off.'

'How much did you get for the phone?' Leon demanded. 'Open your pockets.'

Oli bordered on tears as Daniel and Leon stood close.

They unzipped his jacket, went down the pockets inside and out, then made him turn out the pockets in his muddy tracksuit bottoms. All they found were a couple of pound coins and a Fresh Start ID card.

'Where's your share, dumbass?'

'I didn't get one,' Oli blurted. 'It was a hundred and twenty for all three of us. I messed up, OK? I gave you my share because Trey acted like a dick and I felt bad for letting you down.'

A tear welled in Oli's eye and the twins felt sorry for him. He was kinda pathetic.

'I'm sorry.'

'We should go back over the road and beat the shit out of everyone,' Leon said.

Oli raised his hands anxiously. 'They're serious people, you can't mess with them. But there's something else.'

'What?' Leon asked.

'Trey says there's a job that needs doing. I vouched for you two and he said there's a bunch of stuff we can steal. Probably only take a couple of hours, but it needs to be done tonight.'

'What kind of job?' Leon asked.

'And how do you know he'll actually pay us?' Daniel added.

14. FLOOD

'Trey Al-Zeid,' James said. 'He runs a taxi office, possibly involved in a protection racket. My people didn't get to actually see him.'

James was in his flat. The woman on the other end of the phone was Aisha Patel, an intelligence service liaison officer with West Midlands Police.

'The name means nothing to me,' the policewoman said. 'I'm assuming you've already checked his background?'

'Sure,' James said. 'Mid-thirties. His older brother owns the taxi firm, and another one south of the city. He's had a couple of minor traffic violations, and he was arrested in London at a Stop-the-War march back in 2003.'

'Right, right,' Aisha said. 'I'll ask the local beat commander if he knows anything that's not in official police records.'

'What about the possibility of a protection racket?'

'We know it exists,' the officer said. 'There are hundreds of small, mostly Asian-owned businesses in north Birmingham and there's plenty of evidence that criminal gangs extort protection payments from landlords and business owners in return for their *safety*.'

'What evidence?' James asked.

'People turning up at casualty with broken thumbs but refusing to say how it happened, smashed windows, arson attacks on shops and industrial units. But people are reluctant to speak to the police. There's a long history of distrust between police and the Asian community, and people who speak out fear for their family and friends. We can protect an individual and their immediate family, but it's impossible to protect an extended family of parents, cousins, aunties, uncles and so forth.'

'Who's behind the extortion gangs?' James asked. 'Is it a large organisation, or lots of different gangs fighting over territory?'

'Police funding has been cut by a quarter over the past ten years,' Aisha explained. 'We know there's a problem, but we don't have the resources to investigate properly.'

James nodded. 'I hear that a lot.'

'But I certainly have colleagues who'd be very interested to share any information you unearth on Mr Al-Zeid,' Aisha said. 'And I'll get back to you if the local officers come up with anything useful.'

*

Leon pushed Rhea gently against the door of his room, put his hand on the back of her neck and gently nibbled her lower lip. Tongues connected as he moved the hand down her back and she slid one socked foot up the back of his leg as he grabbed her bum.

'Hey,' Daniel yelled, thumping on the door from outside.

'Ignore him,' Rhea whispered, gripping Leon's waist as he backed away.

Leon looked around as Rhea started pushing him towards the bed.

'Ten to nine, dude,' Daniel shouted as he rattled the doorknob. 'Get your butt out here.'

'Don't,' Rhea warned, then looked sore as Leon backed away, wishing that he didn't have to. 'What's so bloody important?'

'Gotta beat nine o'clock curfew,' Leon said, then to the door, 'Come in.'

Rhea scowled as Oli and Daniel strode in, both in shoes and jackets. Leon sat on his bed, grabbing his phone and sliding feet into a pair of Adidas.

'She on board?' Oli asked.

Rhea shook her head and held out her hand. 'Tenner.'

'We said five,' Leon noted.

'Unilateral renegotiation,' Rhea said, waggling her fingers. 'Seven minutes to curfew.'

'Bloodsucking leech,' Leon said cheerfully, wishing he didn't have to leave her as he grabbed two crumpled five-pound notes from his jeans and passed them over.

'Pleasure doing business,' Rhea said, as Leon gave her a quick kiss, then grabbed his school pack and followed the others down the hallway towards the office.

Gurbir heard the three boys coming towards the exit and stepped out of his office, theatrically tapping the face of his watch.

'No, no, no.'

'It's before curfew,' Oli said. 'We're just going over to Morrisons. They're doing Jaffa Cakes for a pound.'

'Three of you?' Gurbir said, as he reached around and thumped Daniel's backpack. 'With luggage? How stupid do I look?'

Oli smirked. 'You always look pretty stupid, Gurb.'

Gurbir smiled and raised one finger. '*One* of you can go over to Morrisons. And you'd better run. Ten past nine at the latest.'

'We're allowed out before nine,' Oli moaned. 'You're violating our human rights.'

'You must think I'm some sort of—'

Before Gurbir could finish, Rhea made a piercing scream from inside the TV room. 'They're fighting. They're fighting! Jono's been stabbed!'

'Stay,' Gurbir said, eyeing the three boys firmly before darting off in a jangle of keys.

The instant he was out of sight, Leon dashed into the office and hammered a green button to unlock the exit door. By the time Gurbir reached the TV room, where a smiling Rhea told him that she was *only joking*, Leon, Oli and Daniel had vaulted the stairs and made it down the long corridor and out on to the street.

'Nice,' Daniel said, as outdoor air hit his lungs.

'Ten more minutes,' Leon moaned, as they started walking towards the main road. 'I was *that* close to getting Rhea's shirt off.'

'Horny toad,' Daniel sneered, as Oli led the way towards a battered Honda saloon with a phone number along the side. The driver looked suspicious as the three boys jumped in the back.

'I booked you,' Oli told the driver, waving a twenty-pound note, as Leon and Daniel looked out the back for any sign of Gurbir or one of the other Nurtrust staff. 'Drive.'

It was a ten-minute ride in the dark. The destination was a little row of shops beneath offices and eight storeys of student accommodation. The twins' eyes followed tattoos and a miniskirt into a busy Chinese takeaway. A convenience shop also seemed to be doing a good student trade, but the third shop in the row was boarded and the final shop was a dry cleaners'. Shuttered for the night, but with a couple working inside.

'There's a side gate,' Oli said, as he led the way around.

The gate was locked from inside, but the brick post alongside had a ledge that made it easy to clamber over and drop into a narrow courtyard. All the trash from the student accommodation dropped down chutes into four giant wheeled bins, and the smell tangled with a sickly aroma venting out the back of the dry cleaners'.

'Does that door even open from outside?' Leon asked,

as he followed Oli up a flight of metal stairs.

'I've been here before,' Oli said triumphantly, as he turned a knob and stepped into a hallway. 'Did some errands for Trey in the summer holidays.'

The lights blinked on with a motion sensor, showing off a bare concrete hallway with pipes and ductwork along the ceiling. The rumble of the dry-cleaning machine below mingled with thumping music from a student party above. Oli seemed to know his way, and pulled a key from his pocket as they approached a plain grey door. A cheap plastic sign read *Sunray Travel Agents*.

'Trey gave me the key,' Oli explained. 'He knows the building manager.'

Oli took half a minute to figure that you had to turn the key one way, then the other to open the deadlock. A burglar alarm chimed as the door opened, but Oli silenced it by tapping a plastic fob against the control plate inside the door.

There was a bank of lights, but Oli just flipped one switch, as Leon crept across the carpeted floor and peeked through a Venetian blind at the street out front.

'What's our job?' Daniel asked, as he studied three desks set up with MacBooks and a fourth with a giant hi-res monitor connected up to a Mac Pro. There was a toilet and kitchenette off to one side, and a glass partition, behind which stood a huge Xerox printing machine, and metal racking stacked with packets of large-format printing paper.

'Guess they print holiday brochures and stuff,' Leon

said, as he leaned into the print room.

There was a stack of A2-sized posters just inside the door, depicting the Arabic alphabet along with the logo of a local mosque. Another poster showed illustrations of Muslim prophets, printed for the same organisation.

'So Trey wants this place trashed,' Oli said. 'I'm gonna bung up the sinks in the kitchen and bathroom and run the water full blast. You guys smash up the big printer. I'm told it's worth over fifty grand. Then we throw all the papers and shit on the floor so they get soaked.'

'Can we steal stuff?' Daniel asked, as he eyed a swanky Wacom graphics tablet and a shuttle controller used for video editing.

'Steal it or smash it,' Oli said, as he headed for the kitchen. 'That's what Trey asked.'

To emphasise the point, Oli picked a wilted spider plant off a desk, spewed soil over a desk top and then lifted one end of the desk so that everything slid on to the floor. As Daniel stuffed MacBooks and computer gear into his backpack, Oli started blocking the kitchen sinkhole with a bin-liner weighed down with a packet of paper and Leon went for the printer.

He didn't fancy getting electrocuted, so Leon ripped the plug out of the wall. The printer was a metre deep, shoulder height and almost three metres from where paper got sucked in to the point where it shot out the other end. He opened a bunch of plastic flaps around the machine and launched a couple of kicks, but it was a sturdy beast so he went to the kitchen.

'Quicker and quieter if we just pour water over it,' Leon told Oli.

Leon made several trips, pouring buckets of water over the printer, before pulling all the toner cartridges and paper off the shelves. Daniel had fun flipping desks and tipping the contents of drawers out over the floor. Oli seemed to have expertise in flooding, and not only got the kitchen and bathroom sinks overflowing, but also removed the lid of the toilet cistern and wedged the inlet valve so that water kept running into the blocked toilet bowl too.

A dozen minutes after they'd entered, the office was trashed and the puddles emerging from kitchen and bathroom had merged into one and were working their way across the carpet tiles.

'Someone's gonna be pissed when they get to work in the morning,' Daniel said, as he wedged the cylindrical Mac Pro into Leon's backpack.

'Half-ten,' Oli said, as he headed back out into the hallway.

'What about the stolen gear?' Leon asked. 'Will Trey give us cash?'

'Trey won't want anything that links him to this,' Oli said, as the trio set off back towards the rubbish chutes. 'I know a dodgy pawn in town that'll probably take most of it.'

'But where will we keep it overnight?'

'Stop worrying, you chicken,' Oli said. 'Gurbir will have finished his shift. It's all agency staff on nights, and none of them give a shit.'

15. GAMES

Last lesson the next afternoon was Games. Leon pulled his blazer over his school football shirt and headed out of the changing room in shorts and muddy hooped socks. Daniel had decided to put tracksuit bottoms over his kit and came out a few seconds behind.

'Nice goal, man!' a big kid told Daniel. The twins had only been at the school for a week, so they barely even knew names of guys in their own class.

'Cheers,' Daniel answered.

Changing meant they'd emerged from school after kids in regular lessons had cleared off. The twins crossed a paved yard with nothing but a few Year Eight girls standing around an outdoor ping-pong table. As they moved through a gate on to the pavement, they were surprised to spot the old man who'd beckoned Oli into the taxi office the previous afternoon.

'You boys,' he shouted, beckoning them towards a seven-seat VW parked across the street. 'Get here.'

The twins were curious as they waited for a break in traffic before jogging across. If they'd had their com units inside their ears they could have alerted James, but they'd taken them out before playing football in a soggy field.

The car was arranged so that the front passenger seat had been swivelled to face in towards the rear seat. 'You know who I am?' a stocky, olive-skinned man asked.

The old dude urged the boys to climb through the van's sliding door, but the boys stood their ground.

'What's this about?' Daniel asked.

'I'm Trey,' the stocky man said, as an even bigger dude in the driving seat turned around to eyeball the boys. 'Been looking for your smartass friend Oli. He got detention or something?'

The twins shrugged and exchanged nods before Leon said, 'He's not at this school. He goes to Fresh Start, over somewhere . . . I don't know exactly.'

'Got expelled from here,' Daniel added.

The old guy kept urging the boys into the van, but Leon knocked his arm away when he gave him a shove.

'Don't touch me,' Leon growled.

'We're outta here,' Daniel added.

But as he took a step back, Trey pulled out a pocket revolver and cocked the trigger. 'In,' he ordered.

Leon wondered if there was some way he could get his com from his backpack and alert James as he settled on a rear bench with stained blue covers stretched over it. The old guy slammed the sliding door, and didn't get a chance to jump in before Trey signalled his driver to pull out.

'What do you know about my print shop?' Trey asked, pocketing the gun as the van accelerated. 'I'm told Oli left Nurtrust with two older boys last night. Must be you, right?'

Trey clearly had a source, so the twins both nodded. 'Sure.'

'What in the name gives you the balls to think you can rip off my print shop? You think you'd get away with it?'

'Little dirt bag stole that key from under my nose,' the driver added.

Leon and Daniel's jaws dropped. 'The print shop was *yours*?'

'My father's,' Trey said. 'How dumb are you?'

'Oli told us you run a protection racket,' Leon explained. 'Said we had to trash the joint. Owner hadn't made his payments or something.'

'I paid that weasel Oli four hundred,' Trey said, looking at his driver. 'But he threw a strop 'cos I said the pink phone wasn't worth much because it's a couple of years old.'

'Four hundred,' the twins gasped.

They'd searched Oli's pockets, but money could have easily been stashed inside his underwear or down a sock. 'He gave us sixty each.'

Trey leaned right to the edge of his seat as the VW took a corner. Close enough for the boys to catch garlic on his breath.

'You'd better not be lying,' Trey warned. 'Got a nice wrench for breaking thumbs back at the wood shop. But I'll go easy if you help us find golden boy. You got his number?'

Leon had few qualms about dropping Oli in it. He grabbed his mobile from his blazer and explained that it had to be switched off in school. In actual fact, his phone was modded and he swiped in using a special combination that meant all calls and messages would also be relayed via campus to James.

'Oli man, where you at?' Leon began. 'You bunked school . . . ? Right . . . When's your bus get in? You wanna meet up, get fish and chips or something . . . ? You know the car park behind Morrisons? Come round there when you get off the bus . . . ? I've got something to show you.'

Trey scowled as Leon ended the call and took a breath. Back at his flat, James got an emergency alert on his phone and listened in, impressed that Leon had the presence of mind to fix a meet right on his doorstep.

'Twenty minutes,' Leon said.

*

Rather than risk being seen with binoculars, James leaned out of his bedroom window and positioned a couple of tiddly wireless cameras so that he got a clear view over the car park. He grabbed a Taser and a Glock semi-auto pistol before heading downstairs to the car park and moving the Focus into a disabled bay with a decent view.

As James listened to muffled audio coming via the monitoring function on Leon's phone, an attendant in an orange vest started writing him a ticket.

'Hoppit,' James growled, as he opened the driver's window and flashed a police ID.

The VW van came into the lot a couple of minutes later and parked a few spaces down. James zoomed one of his remote cameras so that he could see in the vehicle's back window. The twins looked OK. Trey and the driver were having a conversation about a birthday present.

Daniel was allowed out of the car, and gave James a slight wave as he crossed into Morrisons' rear entrance, presumably to go out front and meet Oli as he got off the bus. James hopped out of the car, followed him through the back door of the little supermarket and quickly caught up.

'OK, mate?' James asked.

'Trey's got a gun, but he's not waving it around or anything. Says Leon will get it if I don't come back.'

'You're sure?' James asked, as the pair kept walking towards the street exit at the front of the shop. 'I can move in and get Leon out if you want.'

'Trey just wants to get hold of that lying bastard Oli,' Daniel explained. 'Wouldn't mind knowing what he's up to myself. Little rip-off merchant . . .'

'Take this,' James said, passing over a lipstick-sized tube of pepper spray. 'Bear attack formula,' he warned. 'Don't stick around if you spray it in the car, 'cos the fumes alone can blind you.'

'Nice one, Q.'

'Keep safe.'

As Daniel headed out the automatic front door to a bus stop right outside, James grabbed vitamins off the nearest shelf and paid at the self-checkout so that he looked like a regular shopper as he strolled back into the car park.

16. STAPLES

James checked things were still calm inside Trey's VW, before using a bus tracker app on his phone to work out when Oli would likely arrive. The app said seven minutes to wait when Oli and Daniel came out the back of the supermarket.

'What's back here?' Oli asked, clearly having second thoughts.

Ten metres away, Trey was emerging from the VW. Oli tried doubling back inside the supermarket the instant he saw.

'You get over here,' Trey roared, as Daniel grabbed Oli by the back of his coat, then got an arm around his chest and started marching him.

'Let go you prick,' Oli shouted, backpack sliding down his arm. 'You don't know what you're doing.'

'I know you ripped us off,' Daniel growled. 'And you

lied about doing the print shop for Trey.'

After a few stumbled paces, Oli got shoved to Trey, who dragged him into the car.

'Door,' Trey ordered, as Daniel stumbled in.

The driver moved off, with the VW protesting against the half-closed sliding door with bing-bong sounds. Once he'd slammed it shut, Daniel got back on the rear bench next to Leon. Oli tried to get between them but Trey shoved him face down in the half-metre gap between front and rear seats, then pinned him under a rigger boot.

'You think I wouldn't realise it was you that stole the key?' Trey shouted. 'I've been good to you, Oliver. Gave you jobs when others said you were too young to be trusted. And this is how you repay me?'

Trey had one boot on Oli's back, and used the other one to deliver a kick to the side of his head. Not full strength, but enough to make him gasp.

'You lack respect,' Trey roared. 'Messed up big time.'

Back in the Focus, James felt his heart speed up as he started the engine. He didn't want to stay back too far, but Leon and Daniel's phones were trackable, so losing sight of the VW wouldn't be a calamity.

A Fiat coming in blocked James for a bit, then a man with a buggy crossing the street. Leon's tracker signal seemed to have stopped moving. James guessed it was a traffic light, but after three hundred metres and a left on to a service road he saw the VW parked on a cobbled driveway, leading up to a tatty little mews building. Trey's thug/driver was just shutting the front door.

As James parked across the street and took a laser microphone out of his surveillance kit, so that he'd be able to listen in, Trey shoved Oli against a chewed-up woodwork bench inside.

'See this vice?' Trey shouted, holding Oli's head right up to it. 'One lie, one smart word and I'm gonna use that to crush every bone in your hand. Understand?'

The twins watched, breathing a touch of sawdust and looking around at a big table saw, a lathe and a bunch of other woodworking equipment. Rusted paint cans and partially completed window frames gave the impression that nobody had worked here in some time.

'Where are the laptops?' Trey demanded.

Oli looked scared, but shrugged like he wasn't. 'Sold 'em.'

'To whom?'

'That's for me to know,' Oli said.

Trey grabbed Oli by the back of his neck, lifted him one-handed and slammed him hard on the workbench. Leon and Daniel couldn't communicate, but both sized the situation up: Trey's driver was big, but they both thought he could be taken down if they surprised him. Trey was trickier because of the gun, but he'd have a hard job getting the gun out quickly while he was manhandling Oli.

'You wanna mess with me, brat?' Trey roared. 'I'll kill you.'

'If you do, you'll never find your laptops. And what'll Uncle say when he finds out that you let a schoolboy steal a key to his print shop and trash the place?'

Trey tightened Oli's wrist behind his back with one hand, while another grabbed a gas-powered framing stapler from a shelf under the bench.

'Last chance, Oliver.'

'What's on the laptops, Trey?' Oli teased. 'What's Uncle gonna say when he finds out you've lost 'em?'

The gas-powered stapler had a cartridge filled with heavy-duty staples, strong enough to drive through the thin board that you might find as the base of a drawer, or backing a kitchen cabinet. When Trey pulled the trigger, there was a little explosion and a 10mm staple shot into the back of Oli's hand.

'Tell me now or I'll crucify you,' Trey roared.

Oli screamed in pain as Trey lined up the stapler to take another shot.

'Nooo,' Oli begged, tears streaming down his face. 'There's a pawnbroker's.'

'Where?'

'Booth Street, near the station.'

Trey turned towards his driver. 'Look it up. See if we can get there before it closes.'

'How dare you rip me off?' Trey roared, his attention back on Oli.

Trey fired a second staple into the back of Oli's hand. As the twelve-year-old screamed, Leon saw that the driver was focused entirely on Googling with his phone. He glanced at Daniel, who made a slight nod towards Trey.

'Gotcha,' Leon murmured.

Leon launched himself at the driver, using a pivoting

high kick that caught him in the temple and knocked him cold. As the big man crashed, Daniel grabbed a length of wood resting against a wall and made a lance, driving it hard into Trey's stomach.

As Trey gasped, Daniel felled him with a kick behind the knee and ripped the stapler out of his hands. CHERUB agents are trained to use minimum force, but Daniel didn't have much time for people who fire staples into twelve-year-olds. Even if the twelve-year-old in question was a horrible lying shit . . .

'See how you like it,' Daniel roared, as he put the stapler against Trey's butt and fired three staples through his jeans.

'Dude!' Leon said, jangling the keys to the VW as he gave Daniel a shove. 'We're in enough trouble already.'

Daniel knew his brother was right, so instead of shooting another staple, he swung a punch with the tool, catching Trey in the head and knocking him cold. Then he crouched down and took the pocket revolver, instinctively checking inside the barrel before dropping it into his front tracksuit pocket.

'One measly bullet,' Daniel noted, showing his brother.

Oli had been bawling his head off the whole time and as the twins closed in, they realised that while one staple hadn't done much damage, the second was lodged deep in the bony part of his index finger.

'Gruesome,' Leon said.

On some level, both twins felt sorry for Oli. For all his faults, Oli was a mixed-up kid who'd had tough breaks. But they had to stay in character for the sake of the mission, and Oli had lied and cheated them.

'Where's the money you made today?' Leon demanded.

Oli had tears streaming down his face. 'In my shorts,' he sobbed.

It took Leon a couple of seconds to work this out, but when he lifted Oli's jacket, he realised that Oli wore shorts with pockets under his jeans.

'Money's ours,' Leon said, as he ripped open a Velcro pocket and pulled out several hundred pounds in twenties.

'All of it,' Daniel added.

'Please,' Oli sniffled.

'There's six hundred quid here,' Leon said brightly. 'Any complaints?'

Oli flickered with anger, then sighed. 'It's yours. I'm sorry. OK?'

Across the room, Trey's driver was coming around and making a move towards the door.

'One more move,' Leon warned, brandishing the stapler and making his point with a couple of shots at the ceiling.

Oli groaned as Daniel helped him off the table.

'Suppose we'd better take you to hospital,' Daniel said, as he tore white tissue out of a dispenser. 'Wrap this around your hand.'

'I'll drive,' Leon added, rattling the keys to the Volkswagen.

17. PAWN

Freja was a Dane by birth: witchlike grey hair and somewhere in her early sixties. She moved like she was younger as she opened the door of her small shop. It was in a side road, close to Birmingham New Street station, and a customer in a suit wanted to get in as she stepped out, carrying a freestanding sign that read, *We Buy Gold for £££*.

The customer wanted a watch battery. Freja opened dozens of tiny plastic drawers behind the shop counter until she found the right size. She charged four pounds and offered to fit for free, but the man was in a hurry and said he'd do it himself. As she put the day's first takings in the till, Freja heard the bell over the shop door jangle, and saw two large men reflected in a glass cabinet full of second-hand camera equipment.

'Good morning, gentlemen.'

Trey had spent much of the previous evening in casualty. There was bandage under his tracksuit bottoms where three staples had been removed. His big hands drummed on the counter.

'Kid came in yesterday,' he began. 'Stocky lad. Four MacBook Airs that belong to me. Don't want no fuss, I'll pay back whatever you paid the kid.'

In the background, Trey's driver pulled a roll of fifty-pound notes.

'Six hundred, wasn't it?'

Freja stiffened up, giving the impression that she'd dealt with plenty of situations like this before. At the same moment, the driver bolted the shop door and flipped a sign to *closed*.

'No laptops or other high-value items are kept on these premises,' Freja said. 'I wasn't working yesterday. But if my colleague purchased a computer, it will have been passed on to our reseller. They either strip the equipment for parts or wipe all the data and sell them on eBay.'

'Can you get them back?' Trey asked. 'There's data on those machines that is important to us. I'll even give you an extra two hundred pounds for your trouble.'

Freja smiled slightly at this prospect. 'Let me check.'

The elderly Dane had yet to boot up the ancient Windows PC behind the till.

'You often pay money to kids bunking off school?' Trey said, trying to sound vaguely threatening. 'You're lucky I didn't go to the cops.'

Freja gave a stiff smile, as she logged into the

computer and started going through a database of invoices for the previous afternoon.

'I've worked in this store more than a dozen years,' Freja said coyly. 'In my experience, people either go to the police first, or not at all.'

Trey looked sore, but kept fingers drumming and his mouth shut.

'Six hundred pounds, four times thirteen-inch MacBook computers,' Freja finally announced, as she swivelled the monitor so that Trey could see. 'I can call our reseller and see if we can get them back before the data is erased.'

Trey nodded, then looked tense as Freja grabbed an old-fashioned phone with a long curly lead. There was a brief conversation.

'You gentlemen are in luck,' Freja said. 'The equipment takes a couple of days to process. Our reseller can bring the laptops back when they make their collection run this afternoon. Eight hundred pounds will cover what we paid, plus our handling costs. I'd suggest you drop in just before we close at six. Or first thing tomorrow.'

Trey looked frustrated, but was more concerned with speed than with paying an extra two hundred. 'Is there any way we could get them sooner?'

'The reseller is based in Watford,' Freja said. 'If you leave your mobile number, I'd be more than happy to call as soon as they arrive.'

Trey tutted, before jotting his mobile number on a *We Buy Gold* flyer. Once the big men had left, Freja took the piece of paper into a back room, separated from the rest of the shop by a bead curtain.

Besides a kettle and sandwich toaster, the space was crammed to the ceiling with junk, from old paperwork to cardboard boxes filled with broken electrical gear and shelves of musical instruments.

There was a tiny desk in the corner, at which James Adams sat with four open MacBooks. Each one was locked and encrypted, so he had the backs off and was using his own laptop to make bit-for-bit copies of the hard drives.

'You handled that really well,' James said warmly.

Freja smiled. 'Twenty-five years in this business. You get used to cops asking questions and guys demanding their stuff back. So how long will it take to copy the hard drives?'

'Couple of hours,' James said.

'Why not just take the laptops?' Freja asked.

James smiled. 'Information tends to be more valuable if the bad guys don't know you've got it.'

'So who are they, Detective?' Freja asked. 'Should I be worried?'

'I'm on to something,' James explained. 'But at this stage, I have no clue what that something is.'

*

Trey got his laptops back just after 4 p.m. CHERUB's head mission controller, John Jones, arrived in Birmingham ninety minutes later, and met with James, Leon and Daniel around the dining-table in the flat over Morrisons.

'Two sugars,' James said, as he put a chipped *World's Best Auntie* mug on the table in front of his boss.

'So what was on the laptops?' Leon asked.

'The encrypted data has been transferred to the GCHQ Decryption Bureau in Cheltenham,' James began, as he took a seat next to Daniel and pulled a chocolate digestive from a pack. 'Judging by the unencrypted data, two MacBooks were used around the print shop for designing leaflets, e-mailing and general office duties. The other two are more interesting. One had quite a lot of poster and brochure designs for Islamic groups, leading us to believe that the printworks were used to produce leaflets and banners used by extremist groups. There was also web design software and evidence that the computer had been used to design and update websites for extremist organisations.

'The fourth laptop is a higher specification than the others. The login and e-mail details lead us to believe that it was used for similar purposes around the office. The hard drive has been partitioned and one partition set up with 512bit encryption key. There are several hundred megabytes of data in that partition and I suspect that this is the data Trey was so keen to get back.'

'How long will it take to decrypt?' Daniel asked.

Leon liked knowing more than his brother. 'You can't decrypt 512bit, Dumbo.'

James nodded. 'A brute force decryption of the data on the hard drive would take decades, even using the fastest computers. But the key vulnerability of very complex encryption systems is that someone somewhere has to know what the encryption key is.'

Now John began speaking. 'While James has been concentrating on the laptops, I've been doing more research into Trey Al-Zeid. Local community police have been interviewed. They backed Oli's suggestion that Trey is involved in some sort of racket that makes threats and extorts money from local taxi companies, shops and landlords. What they're less clear on is where this money goes.

'There's talk in the community that the money goes to support militant Islamic groups in North Africa and the Middle East. Others say this is all smoke and mirrors and that Trey is part of a regular organised-crime-style extortion racket.'

'You're much less likely to mess with your local extortion racket if you think they might have links to serious terrorists,' James explained, before John continued.

'Trey's father owns one of the biggest taxi businesses in Birmingham and is believed to have something to do with the extortion racket, but the real kingpin is a man who everyone seems to call Uncle. He has been photographed at community events over the past few years, but he does a good job hiding his name.'

Leon nodded knowingly. 'Oli said something to Trey about upsetting Uncle when he stole the laptops. So whatever info is on that laptop must give us a clue about who Uncle is and where the extortion money goes.'

James and John both nodded.

'I think we can safely say that the recruitment element

of this mission is dead,' James said. 'Oli is clearly smart enough to be a CHERUB agent, but he's just . . .'

James couldn't think how to phrase it correctly in front of his boss, so Daniel finished the sentence for him.

'Oli is the most loathsome kid I've ever met.'

James nodded in agreement. 'You rescued Oli from Trey's grasp, but I think we can assume that Trey might come after him again. So, we're going to arrange for him to be given a new surname and moved to a foster home at least a couple of hundred miles from here.'

'Can't we just do the world some good and shoot him?' Daniel suggested cheekily.

'I wish,' James grinned. 'Especially as I've got to find a good foster home and do all the paperwork for his transfers.'

'So we're staying for at least a while longer?' Leon asked.

James nodded. The twins smiled because it meant that they got out of more heavy drill back on campus. But Daniel had another realisation.

'I put staples in Trey's leg and stole his gun.'

'And we took the six hundred Oli made from the laptops,' Leon added.

Daniel nodded. 'So we're not exactly flavour of the month.'

James and John both erupted in smiles.

'We've gotta do a bit of work on getting you back into Trey's good books,' James said. 'Don't worry, I have a few ideas.'

18. BROTHER

Gurbir yelled as Rhea strode past his office, long legs and a school uniform that violated at least ten regulations.

'What I do now, Gurby-kins?' Rhea asked, contemptuously popping bubble-gum as she leaned in the doorway. But her expression turned for the better when she saw a handsome seventeen-year-old, sat in a plastic chair with a bright yellow North Face pack resting between his legs.

'This is Ryan,' Gurbir explained. 'I have a few calls to make, would you mind showing him to room thirteen?'

'Oli's room?' she asked.

'Oli has been placed with a foster family some distance from here,' Gurbir explained.

Rhea flicked an eyebrow. 'Good riddance to the little shite.'

Gurbir half smiled as Rhea beckoned Ryan with a purple fingernail. 'You coming then?'

Ryan slung the yellow pack over his shoulder and grabbed a duffel bag. He eyed Rhea as she led him through the dining area, slightly put off by her cigarette smell.

'Like your jeans,' Rhea said.

'Cheers,' Ryan said. 'Diesel. Bought 'em with my birthday money.'

'I like it when they're tight enough to see a crotch bulge,' Rhea said, then as Ryan looked down at himself in a state of panic, 'Joke!'

'Been here long?'

'Too long and still another three months on secure,' Rhea said, as she kicked the half-open door of Oli's old room. It had been vacuumed and clean sheets put on the bed, but Oli's Aston Villa posters had stayed on the wall.

The bed bounced as the big pack hit the mattress.

'Maybe I'll show you around the neighbourhood,' Rhea said, as she stepped closer. 'If you like, that is.'

'For sure,' Ryan said, smiling.

'Wanker!' Daniel said, as he barged through the door and gave his big brother a friendly shoulder punch. 'Train OK?'

Leon came in behind and got a jolt. He was conscious that Rhea was a year older and stood the same height as him if she wore heels. Ryan was almost a head taller, making Rhea look like perfect girlfriend material for his older brother.

'Missed you,' Leon said, stepping past his brothers and marking territory by giving Rhea a kiss. She accepted it grudgingly, before taking a step back.

'You missed me since breakfast?' Rhea said disbelievingly, tutting. Then she smiled at Ryan. 'So you guys are brothers? I *totally* see the resemblance now.'

'I got the full share of brains and looks,' Ryan explained. 'The twins got half each.'

'Kiss my ass,' Daniel smirked, but Leon was too jealous to join the smiles.

'I'll leave you bros to catch up,' Rhea said, enjoying Leon's discomfort and giving Ryan a wink as she edged out.

'You wanna go to my room?' Leon asked, but Rhea didn't bother answering.

'Smooth,' Ryan grinned, not wanting to cause trouble, but unable to resist teasing his little brother.

'I saw her first,' Leon said, once Rhea was way down the hallway.

'Give over,' Ryan said. 'She just started flirting with me. How could I possibly know what was going on?'

'If I looked like Leon *I'd* be worried,' Daniel said.

'Huh!' Leon snorted. 'When did you last make out with someone, stud?'

It had taken Ryan less than two minutes to be reminded that while he loved his twin brothers in theory, actual time in their presence was pretty irritating.

'So I spoke to James before I came over here,' Ryan said, trying to take charge. 'I'll unpack, grab some food. Then we'll go see Trey.'

Ryan had been set up with a tatty Peugeot 208 and drove his brothers a couple of miles south, to Edgbaston. The house was detached, with a mossy paved drive. A BMW M3 Coupe sat next to a seven-seat Citroen with a pair of child seats in the back. It wasn't luxury, but it was good digs for a guy whose only official job was as a part-time controller for his father's taxi business.

The woman answering the door looked harassed. Two little kids running round half naked, bottles being sterilised in the microwave, washing machine running and something on the stove.

'We don't want overpriced cleaning products,' the woman said wearily, pushing shut the door before she'd even finished opening. 'Read the sign: *No Cold Callers*.'

'We're here to see your husband,' Ryan explained politely. 'You are Mrs Al-Zeid?'

'He's expecting us,' Leon added.

The woman grunted, swiped the back of her hand against a greasy forehead and yelled up the stairs. 'Trey, there's three lads here.'

'What lads?' Trey shouted. 'Tell 'em to sling their bloody hook.'

'Say you're expecting them.'

'I'm not expecting—'

The rest of Trey's sentence got drowned out because one of the kids slipped on the kitchen floor and started bawling.

'Just get down here,' the woman screamed, leaving the door ajar as she rushed in to comfort a distressed toddler. 'Like I haven't got enough on.'

The boys took the opportunity to step into the hallway. It smelled of bleach, and a toddler craned around a doorway to see who'd arrived. Daniel took the opportunity to stick a tiny listening device to the wall behind a radiator.

'What the hell?' Trey snapped, as he came around the top of the stairs in a Sonics basketball shirt and one hand holding his butt. 'This is my home! I'm not a man to be messed with.'

Trey saw Ryan first as he began limping down the stairs. He'd not seen him before, but he recognised the twins and his eyebrows shot up furiously.

'You've got some blasted nerve!' Trey shouted. 'This is my private home. How did you find out that I lived here?'

'It's not hard if you're smart,' Ryan said, but deliberately avoided details. 'I thought it was better to corner you here than at the taxi office surrounded by your pals.'

As Ryan spoke, he took out the pocket revolver, keeping it pointed at the floor, with the barrel swung open so that it couldn't be fired.

'An expensive item,' Ryan noted, as Trey snatched the outstretched gun.

'Where are the bullets?'

'That's a gesture of goodwill,' Ryan said. 'But do I look stupid enough to hand a potential enemy a loaded gun?'

Trey grunted. 'So, why are you here?'

'I just moved into Nurtrust with these two,' Ryan explained. 'You're an influential man in these parts. My brothers and I don't want you as an enemy.'

'We helped you find Oli,' Daniel added.

The brat in the kitchen had finally stopped screaming and Trey pulled shut the kitchen door so that his wife couldn't hear.

'That prick,' he hissed, pointing at Leon. 'That prick put three staples in my ass. I can't sit down and my driver has a broken nose.'

'Through your jeans and pants,' Daniel scoffed. 'Not into bone, like Oli.'

'You took my brothers hostage,' Ryan said calmly. 'They acted the way they did because they were scared. But it was Oli that caused all the trouble.'

'So why isn't *he* here apologising?'

'Oli's gone,' Daniel said. 'Foster placement.'

'Where?'

The twins both shrugged.

'We're young and fit,' Ryan said. 'My brothers don't want to live in fear of retribution.'

'We'll work,' Daniel said.

'Errands, jobs. Like you used to give Oli.'

Trey paused to think, running a hand through stubble on his chin.

'Fine mess you made,' Trey said thoughtfully. 'Not just the print shop. Water flooded into the shop below. Whole lot's gotta be stripped.'

'What about insurance?' Leon asked.

Trey snorted. 'The flooding was a criminal act, so the

insurance will want a police report. And I don't want cops nosing around in there.'

The brothers nodded knowingly.

'So it all needs clearing out,' Trey said. 'Upstairs and the shop below. I'll get you a truck. You come after school tomorrow and start clearing out anything that's damaged. I guess it'll take a couple of evenings, maybe part of Saturday. Got new carpet tiles coming Monday, so it's gotta be done by then.'

'Sounds fair,' Ryan agreed. 'I'll help my brothers. And then we'll be even?'

'Thereabouts,' Trey said. 'And of course, I want the six hundred you took from Oli as well.'

Ryan smiled as he pulled an envelope out of his jacket.

'Your bullet and six hundred quid.'

Trey snatched the envelope. 'Tomorrow after school,' he said firmly, wagging a finger. 'And you'd better not be spreading word about my address. Next time you wanna see me, you call the taxi office and you make an appointment like everyone else.'

19. SQUELCH

Monty was barely out of his teens, greasy hair and stick thin.

'Fine mess you boys made,' he said, as he unlocked the door marked *Sunray Travel Agents* and flicked on the lights.

The trashed office hummed with the noise of two dehumidifier units, sucking moisture out of the air, down long pipes and draining into the toilet. Ryan's first couple of steps were OK, but his trainer squelched carpet on the third.

'You gotta clean all the damaged stuff out,' Monty said, as he crossed the wet floor and pointed into the print room. 'All this soggy paper's gotta go downstairs to the rubbish, then the carpet tiles gotta be taken up.'

Dumping the paper didn't take long, but the carpet tiles were hell. Crawling around the damp floor on their knees, each lad started in a corner with a Stanley knife and a wallpaper scraper. Some tiles came up with a hard tug, but where there was a lot of glue the tiles ripped apart and had to be scraped off piece by piece.

After twenty minutes, Ryan had lifted nine tiles out of more than four hundred. His jeans were soaked, knees and elbows hurt, and his fingers were all gummed with the brown paste used to stick the tiles to the floor.

'You boys better pick up the pace,' Monty noted, as he opened up to let in a smartly dressed service engineer.

Ryan worked along the edge of the partition separating the desked area from the print room and watched as the engineer stripped down the giant printer.

'They're not designed to have water thrown on them,' the engineer told Monty. 'This machine is a wreck. You'll be better off buying a new or reconditioned machine.'

'No,' Monty said. 'We have a big job for early next week. The machine has to be up and running.'

The engineer nodded sympathetically. 'We have a demonstration unit in our showroom, which we'll be more than happy to make available to you for your printing needs. Then we can have the new 950L model shipped in by the end of next week.'

Monty sighed and thumped the machine. 'We need *this* machine working by Tuesday. I'll pay you cash to work through the weekend.'

'You'll also get fluorescent printing and full two-year warranty on a 950L,' the engineer continued.

Monty looked panicked as he pointed at the door.

'My boss wants this place cleaned up and running smooth when *his* boss comes through that door on Tuesday afternoon.'

The engineer stepped back, wiping toner dust from his fingertips on to a rag. 'I'd love to help, but I could work on this machine for a week with no guarantee it'll run again. These things just aren't designed to have water poured inside them.'

The boys kept ripping carpet as Monty showed the engineer out of the building.

'So the mysterious Uncle's gonna show his face here on Tuesday,' Daniel whispered.

'Sounds that way,' Ryan agreed.

Like most things, there was a knack to pulling carpet tiles and by nine the boys had cleared more than half the floor. Monty worked at the back of the room using the Mac Pro to design new menus for a local restaurant.

As the boys worked, they placed listening devices under all the desks, including specially designed low-frequency microphones that were ideal for recording keystrokes. Although tapping any key on a keyboard sounds the same to a human ear, sophisticated listening software can detect a slightly different sonic signature for every key and then use simple decoding techniques to work out what is being typed.

It was past ten and the Sharma brothers had done three-quarters of the carpet tiles when Monty sent them to the shop downstairs.

'Are we getting off soon?' Leon whinged. 'My knees are screwed from crawling around.'

The answer was no. A caged flatbed truck had reversed on to the pavement out front. An overalled man had unlocked the shop's metal shutters, and the boys were shocked by the mess as they stepped inside.

It had been a convenience store, filled with scruffy metal shelving racks, for food, magazines and stuff. At the rear there was a big empty space where there had once been fridges selling milk and beer.

The ceiling bulged where floodwater had collected from the floor above. To the left, part of the ceiling had collapsed completely, leaving a hole big enough to climb through and a run of dangling strip lights. Water had drained from the vinyl floor, but it had filtered through concrete and plaster to get here, leaving a layer of pinkish silt over everything.

The overalled man was a giant, with knockout body odour and *BEAST* tattooed across his knuckles.

'If it's metal it goes on the truck,' Beast explained, illustrating the point by pounding a metal shelf so hard that it buckled before crashing to the floor. 'Wanna get home before one. So I'm working hard and you're working hard. Dig?'

'Dig,' Leon said, earning a scowl for daring to grin slightly.

The noise was mad as the three boys and Beast tore into the shop fittings, ripping out shelves and bashing ones that wouldn't budge with rubber mallets. By the end the brothers had little cuts all over their hands and sweat-soaked clothes smeared in plaster dust.

'Need one lad to help unload at the other end,' Beast

announced. 'Other two can piss off home.'

Ryan was the oldest and, since he'd not yet registered at the local college, he didn't have school in the morning. It was close to midnight, so there was little traffic as the truck headed north out of the city. The metal shelving up back crashed over every bump, and even though Ryan was past smelling like a rose garden himself, he gagged at the stale sweat smell coming off Beast's filthy overall.

'You know Trey?' Beast asked.

'Met him once,' Ryan said, as the truck pulled on to the A41, heading east out of the city.

Beast grunted. 'Trey thinks he can pull the wool over Uncle's eyes. Better to own up in my book.'

'Sure,' Ryan agreed.

'Specially since Uncle's tight with Trey's dad. Worst Trey will get is a kicking.'

'Don't know all the ins and outs,' Ryan said, looking out as a motorbike shot by, doing at least a hundred. 'He'll kill himself.'

'Son's got a bike,' Beast admitted, smiling slightly. 'I said to him, if you crash and break your legs, don't come running to me.'

It was a bad joke but Ryan laughed, because Beast knew stuff that he wanted to hear.

'What does Uncle do exactly?' Ryan asked.

'Fingers in a lot of pies,' Beast explained. 'If you're loyal he's a top man. I'm not the sharpest, but I've been alongside him twenty years, man and boy. Started at the scrapyard straight out of school, 'bout a month after me.

Now, Uncle owns the joint and I'm still out in the truck, picking up scrap.'

They turned off the ring road and hurtled down a rutted track that set all the metal in the back rattling and jarred all the bits of Ryan's body that hurt after six hours' graft. Inside was like the scrapyard scene from *Breaking Bad* and every other thriller Ryan had ever seen, with stacked-up cars and red London buses awaiting their last ride.

'Got the biggest car shredder in Europe down there,' Beast said proudly, as he pointed out left into darkness. 'Have to shut it down at night 'cos the estate lot what lives behind moan about the noise. Back in the old days we used to smack down anyone who complained to the council, but Uncle makes us behave ourselves these days.'

Beast roared with laughter as he stopped abruptly, then reversed up to a mound of random scrap. The pair climbed in the back cage and spent ten minutes throwing out the metal shelves.

'Is there a toilet?' Ryan asked.

Beast laughed. 'Don't stand on ceremony, son.'

As Ryan peed on scrap, Beast headed towards a pair of cabins and unlocked a door. The first cabin was some sort of site office, filled with staff lockers and safety gear. The second was more modern, with blinds at the window and an air conditioner on the roof.

'Is that Uncle's office?' Ryan asked, as Beast came out and started locking the other hut.

'Never stays in one place for long,' Beast explained,

as he handed Ryan a half-litre bottle of cola. It was cold to touch.

'Worked hard,' Beast said, as Ryan downed half the bottle in four gulps.

'Got any jobs here?' Ryan asked. 'Anything that pays? I'm young, but I'll pull my weight.'

'No chance,' Beast said, as he locked up his truck before setting off towards a battered BMW. 'Besides, a lad your age should be studying.'

Ryan moved to get in the passenger side, but Beast shook his head.

'I ain't your taxi service,' Beast grunted. 'You'll pick up a night bus from the stop at the end of Savoy Crescent. And don't hang around, 'cos there's a few guard dogs on the loose in here.'

Beast floored the gas, spinning up his back wheels and flailing Ryan with grit. Ryan had been hot all night, but now the breeze caught sweat-soaked jeans and hoodie. He considered investigating the huts, maybe even picking a lock and having a rummage. But CHERUB teaches you never to act without preparation.

Ryan batted a clump of mud off his cheek, and double-tapped his earlobe to activate the microphone on his com unit as he set off at a jog.

'You there, James?' Ryan asked. 'Did you catch all that?'

James laughed. 'Sounded like progress to me, pal. You OK?'

'I'm trashed,' Ryan said. 'Can you pick me up?'

'Last time you rode on the back of my motorbike you

said it was the most terrifying experience of your whole life,' James noted. 'And that you'd never ride with me again.'

Ryan reached the electronic gate and realised that Beast had shut it behind him. Glancing around, he found a tear in the fence close by.

'Well *you're* still alive,' Ryan noted. 'So I guess your riding isn't *that* deadly.'

20. BAGS

It was past 3 a.m. by the time James dropped Ryan back at Nurtrust and filed a detailed report so that staff on campus could start doing background research. He still looked tired the following noon, as he walked into a Costa Coffee in central Birmingham and spotted an Asian woman. She had tight-cropped hair and wore dayglo Nikes and leggings, like she'd be heading towards the gym.

'Tanisha?' James asked, as he approached holding freshly squeezed orange and a triple espresso. 'Can I get you something?'

'I'm good,' Tanisha said.

'Thanks for meeting at short notice,' James said, as he settled on a leatherette bench and laid a document pouch on the table. 'Are you good friends with Inspector Patel?'

Tanisha smiled. 'Aisha started off as a community support officer, back when I was a junior scribbler for the *East Birmingham Echo*. We got to know each other quite well.'

'Inspector Patel said you're the person to talk to if you want to know about Uncle. She said you wrote articles about him, most of which weren't published.'

Tanisha raised a hand and sounded blunt. 'Who are you?'

James pulled a credit-card-sized ID out of his wallet. It showed him as a detective inspector with the Metropolitan Police.

'And who are you *really* with?' Tanisha said, smirking.

'That's a genuine ID,' James said defensively. 'Look at the hologram.'

'I know they fast-track graduates in the Met, but how old are you? Twenty-five, tops.'

James snatched back his Met Police ID and swapped it for his real one.

'Her Majesty's Intelligence Service,' Tanisha read. 'So you want to know if Uncle is a radical, sending all that racketeering money back to Islamic State in Syria or wherever?'

'Is he?' James asked, before glugging his orange juice.

Tanisha laughed. 'The answer is complex.'

'Story of my life,' James grinned.

'Uncle – or Martin Jones to use his proper name . . .'

'Is that his *real* birth name?'

'Uncle was born in 1968, when racism was far more out in the open than it is today,' Tanisha explained.

'Welsh mother, Pakistani father. They decided to give him an English first name and use his mother's surname.

'There's not much remarkable about his childhood. Parents ran a shop in North Wales, and moved to Birmingham when Uncle was ten. He was a tough lad. Got in trouble with the law. Spent time in borstal, two kids by the age of nineteen.'

'Religious?'

Tanisha shrugged. 'Not until he married his second wife, who was Muslim. He built up a little crew that hit the big time during the taxi wars in the eighties.'

'Taxi wars?' James asked.

Tanisha nodded. 'There were more than a hundred private-hire taxi firms in Birmingham back then. Price cutting, fare poaching and nobody making any money. Then rival firms started sabotaging one another. Started off with fake calls, and blocking radio signals – this was before everyone had mobile phones. Then windows got smashed, cars vandalised. People started getting their legs broken and their houses burned down. After a few years, Uncle's crew got the upper hand and you wound up with three big taxi firms for the whole of east Birmingham. All owned by Uncle, or his close friends.

'He also made money in the scrap business, set up taxi firms in London and Manchester, and when the taxi business took a downturn, he started extorting money from shopkeepers, landlords, restaurant owners.'

'And the law just let him?' James asked.

'There's a lot of politics involved,' Tanisha explained. 'First off, when Uncle started, there wasn't a single dark-skinned officer in the Birmingham police force. And how do you report a crime when you don't even speak the same language as your local cops? By the time Birmingham started getting Asian police officers, Asian councillors, Asian Members of Parliament, Uncle was so ingrained in the system that most of them were his people. They'd condemn him in public, but behind closed doors they'd talk him up.

'*Uncle keeps the drug dealers out of Asian neighbourhoods. Uncle paid for repair work on the mosque. Uncle stops the developers moving in and closing down Asian-owned businesses.* And when it came to election time, they'd be lining up to ask for campaign donations. Labour, Conservative. Uncle would donate to both sides, as long as they didn't rock his boat.'

James was fascinated. 'And Uncle's influence extended to your newspaper?'

'God yes,' Tanisha nodded. 'We knew his name, but we were never allowed to publish it, to preserve the great mystery. If you published an article about some charity donation made by one of his taxi firms, you'd have the phone ringing off the hook with advertisers. But if you published anything critical, Uncle would send out an edict. Any business that dared to advertise in your newspaper would get a petrol bomb through their letterbox, and no newsagent would dare to sell the paper with the article inside.'

'Clever,' James admitted.

Now Tanisha narrowed her eyes accusingly. 'And you know what really pisses me off?' she said, wagging a finger. 'People have known about Uncle for years, but the police always claim not to have resources to investigate. *Your* intelligence lot are only interested in a tiny number of radicals, while a massive crook sits in the background pulling levers for half of Birmingham.'

James smiled. 'I'm here to help.'

'You're young and idealistic,' Tanisha said. 'But the system is rigged against ordinary decent people. I even know what your next question is going to be.'

'You do?' James asked.

'You're going to ask me if Uncle turned into some crazy radical, and if he's donating profits to radical groups.'

'That's what I need to know,' James admitted.

Tanisha snorted. 'Uncle has grandparents, cousins and a half-brother in Pakistan. He sent money to them over the years, enabling them to become quite influential in their region. In 2013 there was an American drone strike close to the family compound. Two of Uncle's nephews and his eight-year-old goddaughter were killed. I'm also told that some of his cousins were arrested and beaten by Pakistani troops who were hunting for Taliban in the area.'

'How do you know this?' James asked. 'You don't work for the newspaper any more, do you?'

'When classified advertising went online, the *Echo* went under, like most local newspapers,' Tanisha admitted. 'I have two office cleaning jobs and I volunteer in a women's shelter. But I still live in the community and I still hear things.'

'So your source on this was reliable?'

'My source was a housekeeper who worked for Uncle's third wife. I don't know her well, but she had nothing to gain by lying to me.'

'So Uncle turned radical?'

Tanisha looked slightly irritated by this comment. 'Uncle drinks alcohol and holidays in Las Vegas, his latest wife and four of his six children aren't Muslim. So he's not about to grow a beard and start living under the principles of Sharia Law. But after the drone strike, he *is* violently opposed to western interference in the Middle East and North Africa.'

'And is he active?' James asked. 'Does he donate to causes?'

'Uncle has the morals of a sewer rat. He's had drivers run over by their own taxis, blackmailed local planning officials, petrol-bombed family businesses that don't pay his protection fees and beaten two of his ex-wives into the hospital. He now makes four or five trips a year to the Middle East. I have no idea what he's up to, but if I were you, I'd be looking for something that's unsavoury and highly profitable.'

21. JUDO

Ryan met the twins as they headed out of school. They grabbed McDonald's, then drove to the Sunray Travel office. Monty and a guy with a hipster beard were doing design work in the office, as the three brothers ripped up carpet tiles in the print room.

Just before six, Monty went out and got coffees for everyone. The quintet sat around having their break when a key turned in the main door. The new arrival was short, sunburnt skin peeling off his nose, and ten years older than in police surveillance photos. But it was unmistakably Uncle.

He was accompanied by a broad-shouldered Asian woman, dressed in canvas pumps and a jogging suit.

'Uncle,' Monty said, trying to sound warm, but obviously cacking himself as the little man looked around at the whirring humidifiers and glue patches where the carpet had been ripped up.

'What's all this then?'

Monty looked sheepish. 'We had a flood.'

Uncle gave his accomplice a nod. She gave Monty a brutal punch in the mouth, followed by an expert knee in the ribs. Then she ripped his arm up behind his back and splayed him face first over a desk.

'Did you just lie to me?' Uncle said calmly, as hipster-beard and the three CHERUB agents looked on warily.

'No,' Monty said, then as Uncle stepped closer, 'OK, yes . . . Trey told me to.'

'Who do you work for?' Uncle demanded. 'Me or Trey?'

'You, sir,' Monty begged, as the woman tightened the wrench on his arm.

'Who is the manager of this print shop?'

'I am, sir,' Monty snorted.

'I'm told I need a 950L printing machine, for the princely sum of seventy-two grand,' Uncle said. 'And I'm not paying for that, Monty. *You* are.'

'I don't have that kind of money,' Monty begged. 'There's no way . . .'

'Your parents own their house, don't they?' Uncle teased. 'And the bakery? I'm sure they can get another mortgage.'

'My parents worked all their lives,' Monty gasped. 'They're in their sixties.'

'I don't give a shit how you get my money,' Uncle shouted, then looked at his female bodyguard. 'Give him another taste, sweetheart.'

She moved ruthlessly, a knee in the kidneys, then flipping Monty on to his back and boxing him with a barrage of head shots.

'You have one week to come and tell me how you plan to pay for my new printer,' Uncle said.

Blood streamed from Monty's mouth as the kickboxer yanked him up and shoved him out into the hallway. Hipster-beard looked terrified as Uncle approached, pulling something out of his back pocket.

The bearded designer was relieved by the sight of two twenty-pound notes.

'Taxi Monty to the hospital,' Uncle ordered. 'Keep your trap shut.'

The designer trembled as he scrambled out, half expecting the kickboxer to sprawl him with a kick up the arse.

This just left Uncle, bodyguard and the Sharma brothers, still holding their drinks.

'I hear you boys are a bit tasty,' Uncle said, raising his fists like a boxer. 'Messed up Trey and his idiot driver. Any of you prepared to show my girl Mya what you've got?'

Ryan figured it was his job, since he was oldest. 'I'm game if she is,' he said, putting his coffee on a desk and stepping forward.

Expecting a cocky teen who'd probably done a few judo classes, Mya kept her hands low as she stepped forward and launched a vicious thigh kick. The blow hurt, but Ryan was taller and lunged with his right arm.

Ryan caught Mya under the chin with his palm, then

took her by the throat, driving her backwards across a desk top. He narrowly avoided a kick in the face as he let go, and rather than take the opportunity of a knockout blow, he flipped the desk.

Mya crashed off the back, accompanied by pens and a tape dispenser. Then Ryan leaned on the underside of the desk, pinning his opponent between the desk top and the wall behind.

'You can't do that,' Mya protested, arms flailing as she tried to break loose.

'You kept your arms low,' Ryan said, matter of factly. 'You showed me a lack of respect.'

Uncle was smiling as Ryan took his weight off the table. Mya furiously launched herself back at Ryan. He went low and used Mya's momentum to roll her over his shoulder, judo style.

'*Enough,*' Uncle yelled, stepping between as Mya hissed.

Mya got up in such a fury that she caught her ankle on a cable, tugging a lamp off a desk top. The twins smirked as Ryan and Mya eyeballed furiously.

'How old are you?' Uncle asked.

'Seventeen,' Ryan said. 'My brothers are fourteen.'

Uncle smiled. 'You like hurting people?'

'Only if I have to,' Ryan said.

'How's your moral compass?' Uncle asked.

'What do you mean?' Ryan asked.

'I mean, if I pay you a hundred quid to go smack someone into next week.'

Ryan shrugged, so Leon answered. 'If he won't, I will.'

'I know potential when I see it,' Uncle smiled, looking at Mya and wagging a finger. 'You're living at Nurtrust, right?'

Ryan decided to push his luck. 'I asked Beast about a job at the scrapyard. Full time, part time. He'll tell you I'm a hard worker. I just moved into the neighbourhood and I'm flat broke.'

Uncle shrugged. 'Come by my office at the yard tomorrow morning. I'll see what we can do.'

'Awesome,' Ryan grinned. 'Thank you so much.'

'Now I need some quiet,' Uncle said, as he made to sit down at one of the desks. 'You boys better clear out.'

'But Trey said we should—' Ryan began.

Uncle laughed as he sat in an office chair. 'Trey's lucky that his father is one of my oldest friends. He can get down on his knees and pull up carpet tiles for himself.'

As the boys headed out, Uncle opened a MacBook and the microphone under the desk recorded his login.

22. ROCKY

It was Saturday morning. With no school, kids at Nurtrust were pottering around in nightwear and grabbing breakfast to eat in bed. Ryan hated his cramped room with tiny escape-proof window, so he settled on a sofa in the TV lounge with bacon and hash browns. Rhea sat alongside, tucking her feet under her bum and smiling as she sipped hot chocolate.

'We could do something tonight,' Rhea said. 'You got an ID? There's a club called Passenger, not far from here.'

Ryan raised his hand. 'What about my little brother?'

Rhea shrugged. 'Leon's cute, but he's just a kid.'

'I can't,' Ryan said. 'I like you, but I'm not gonna start some huge row with Leon.'

Ryan was in shorts and he found Rhea's hand touching just above his knee.

'I can be very persuasive,' she purred.

Daniel picked that exact moment to step in from the hallway.

'A word, brother,' he said, taking a superior tone.

Ryan apologised to Rhea as he ditched breakfast and headed out into the hallway.

'Leon's not gonna like *that* if he finds out,' Daniel said, smirking as he led the way to their rooms.

'I just got a text,' Daniel explained. 'James wants the three of us to drop by the flat in half an hour.'

They knocked on Leon's door, and found him towelling off after a shower.

'Nice zit on your back,' Ryan teased. 'Want me to splat it?'

'So what does James want?' Leon asked, as he dropped the towel and went for jeans, which still had yesterday's briefs lined up inside.

'Probably wants to tell me how great I am,' Ryan suggested. 'How the whole mission was going nowhere, until my magnificence stepped in and saved the day.'

'You don't half talk some crap,' Leon said, as he realised that the trousers he'd just pulled up were gummed with carpet glue and went to his locker for a clean pair.

'You heard from Rhea?' Daniel asked his twin, stirring it.

Leon instinctively glowered at Ryan. Then shrugged and acted all defensive. 'I'm not that bothered.'

Daniel smiled. 'So Ryan can take a run at her?'

Leon ground his teeth as he sat on his bed, pulling

on socks. Ryan flicked Daniel's ear and said, 'Need to get my shoes,' as he backed out.

*

James looked cheerful when the brothers arrived at his flat twenty minutes later. They gathered around the dining-table with mugs of tea and a stack of bacon sandwiches.

'You got mayo?' Daniel asked, as he lifted the top off a sandwich.

'I won't have that filth in my house,' James said, shuddering. 'So it took about an hour for the microphone to record enough keystrokes to get Uncle's password. We've unlocked the backup I made at the pawn shop and a couple of support staff have spent the night going through the data . . . Oh balls.'

The three brothers laughed as a rasher fell out of James' sandwich and hit the floor between his legs.

'So what have we got on the laptop?' Ryan asked, as James grated his chair back and grabbed the bacon.

'Business accounts mostly,' James began. 'Taxi firms, scrapyards, Sunray Travel. Plus classic money-laundering outfits like dry cleaners, web cafes and of course the print shop. There's also personal stuff in an encrypted e-mail account, lots of e-mails between Uncle and his current wife, telling her how much he misses her when he travels. Hospital bills for his mother's care home.'

'Is any of it incriminating?' Leon asked.

'There's some detailed information about the protection racket,' James said.

'What about the trips to the Middle East?' Ryan

asked. 'Isn't that what we're here for?'

'We can now access Uncle's encrypted e-mails but there's thousands to go through,' James explained. 'We know where he's been and the names of some of the people he's met. But there are dozens of sets of accounts on the laptop and thousands of documents and e-mails in the cloud. I've got four intelligence analysts and a forensic accountant working on this, but it will take a good while to get through it all.'

'So what do we do in the meantime?' Daniel asked.

'For now, I don't think there's much for you and Leon to do. Since it's the weekend, go see a movie or something.'

The twins smiled. 'Can you give us money?' Leon asked, cheekily holding out beggar hands.

'Scroungers,' James said, tutting, then smiling. 'You two have worked hard this week. Just stay out of trouble.'

'I assume I'm still going for my meeting with Uncle?' Ryan asked.

James nodded. 'You'll hopefully get inside Uncle's cabin at the scrapyard, drop a few listening devices if you can, but no stupid risks.'

'What about his car?' Ryan asked. 'You want me to put a tracker on it?'

James shook his head. 'Any tracker worth having is bulky, so I don't want you taking that risk. I'll get an adult from MI5 to handle the job.'

*

Ryan pulled up at the scrapyard gate in his battered Peugeot. The giant car shredder made the ground rumble, while teams of overalled men drained fuel tanks and stripped valuable parts from cars before they met their doom.

'Uncle wants to see *you?*' the guard on the gate said suspiciously. 'He's out of the country.'

Ryan shook his head and sounded firm. 'Uncle said to meet me here this morning. I saw him in town *last night.*'

The guard backed off and spoke into a radio. A car transporter came out as he waited for a response.

'Straight ahead,' the guard told Ryan finally.

Mya stood guard at the door of Uncle's air-conditioned cabin. She eyed Ryan furiously, as he noticed fingertip bruises on her neck, where he'd thrust her backwards.

'Is he in?' Ryan asked.

Mya narrowed her eyes. 'Give me a shot and I'll beat you into next year.'

Ryan smirked. 'I'll spar with you anytime.'

'I don't spar with children,' Mya grunted.

'Nah,' Ryan teased. 'You just get beaten up by them.'

'He's on the telephone,' Mya barked. 'Wait.'

Ryan waited eight minutes. Thinking about the tiny listening devices in the pocket of his hoodie. Thinking about his best escape route if something went wrong, and imagining Rhea, all made up pretty for a night of clubbing. Maybe Leon really had stopped caring about her . . .

The cabin door crashed and Uncle vaulted the three metal steps, clattering gravel as he landed and giving

Ryan a friendly jab on the shoulder.

'Oi, oi, handsome boy!' Uncle said cheerfully.

The man behind was chubby, in a spotless version of the orange scrapyard overall that Beast had worn the night before.

'Gotta walk and talk,' Uncle explained. 'Just back from a trip so busy, busy! What do you think of my yard, Ryan?'

'Machines and trucks, like every five-year-old boy's dream,' Ryan answered, earning a big laugh as they set off briskly down a gravel path.

A truck honked and Uncle gave the driver a thumbs-up as they walked a couple of hundred metres.

'I like this business,' Uncle told Ryan, holding his arms out wide. 'You start with junk, you end with money. No branding, no advertising, no smartass San Francisco start-up building an app and taking half your passengers.'

Ryan nodded. 'You said you might be able to fix me up with some work?'

Uncle looked over his shoulder at the man in the overalls. 'What do you reckon, George? Good strong arms on him.'

'Next spot that opens up is his,' George said. 'Gimme your mobile, it'll probably be a few weeks.'

'And maybe I can find some tasks more suited to your skills in the meantime,' Uncle said, throwing a couple of punches to make his point. 'Eh, son?'

Ryan smiled as Uncle explained to George.

'Mya takes down guys weighing three hundred

pounds. But this lad had her pinned under a table.'

George smiled. 'Maybe he can visit that woman on the estate who calls Environmental Health every time we run the shredder after seven . . .'

Ryan smiled as they rounded a corner into a section of the yard with a high wire perimeter around it. Inside was a large aluminium hangar, three storeys high, with sliding orange doors which were raised at the bottom.

After ducking under, Ryan found himself in a room full of machinery. Most dated from the seventies or eighties with beige control cabinets fitted with LED displays and tiny amber-screen monitors. There were several huge cylinders and mechanical arms. At the far end was a workshop where three men seemed to be disassembling some kind of ancient pump.

'Are these fairground rides?' Ryan asked.

George and Uncle roared with laughter.

'Engineering parts,' Uncle explained. 'We break them down for spares and scrap what's left. If you get it right, it's extremely profitable.'

As George and Uncle began a conversation with one of the guys working on a pump, Ryan studied the equipment and recognised a couple of major oil company logos. Lots of the gear had gauges with measurements in barrels or gallons and he realised that the giant posts which he'd initially imagined were spokes from a fairground ride were drilling rods. In the far corner there were four giant drill heads.

As he stepped in further, Ryan realised that close to half of the hangar was lined with control consoles and tatty spare-part boxes bearing the tartan logo of a company called Offshore Marine Exploration. It seemed significant, because he knew that Uncle was up to something in the Middle East, and that the region's economy was dominated by oil. He'd have liked more time to explore, but Uncle was on the march after his conversation.

'So I'll need your number,' George reminded Ryan, as they ducked back under the door. 'You can find your way back to your car?'

Ryan tapped his number into George's iPhone and Uncle shook his hand.

'Be in touch,' George said, making a phone with his fingers before striding off after his boss to inspect some other area of the yard.

Ryan sauntered back to his car and got sworn at by a crazy guy who almost mowed him down in a dump truck. When he neared the cabin, he saw Mya sat on the steps out front wearing a big smile. Then he noticed a broken wing mirror on the ground beside his Peugeot.

'What the hell?' Ryan shouted, as he picked up the mirror and stormed over to Mya. 'Did you do this?'

Mya half smiled. 'There's some pretty big rats around the yard. Maybe one of them bit it off.'

'Bitch,' Ryan hissed.

Mya shot up. 'You want a piece of me?' she shouted. 'You made me look weak in front of my boss.'

This time she had her arms up. Ryan had no idea if he could beat Mya again, but he didn't have anything to gain by fighting and the car belonged to CHERUB, so he didn't much care about the mirror either.

'I'm too much of a gentleman,' Ryan said, bowing sarcastically as he got into the car.

Mya flipped him off with both hands as he drove away.

23. SKY

'Yo!' James said, as he let Ryan into the flat.

James had gone full slob, dressed in shorts and his lucky Arsenal shirt, watching Soccer Saturday with a bottle of beer and a half-eaten Domino's.

'Pepperoni,' James said. 'Gone a bit cold, but you can zap it.'

'Plates?'

James opened a cupboard over the sink and passed Ryan a plate.

'So how'd it go?' he asked, as Ryan grabbed two slices and set the microwave for ninety seconds.

'Mixed,' Ryan admitted, as the pizza rotated. 'I didn't get inside Uncle's cabin, but I might have a lead. There was a shed with a whole bunch of oil pumps and drilling equipment. And these consoles, all manufactured by a company called Offshore Marine Exploration.'

'Did you ask Uncle what they were?'

Ryan nodded. 'He said they strip the equipment for parts. I just found it interesting that half the hangar was full of oil stuff.'

'Definitely interesting,' James said, as he grabbed his laptop from under pizza boxes. 'I had a preliminary report from the forensic accountant. The scrapyard is Uncle's biggest earner by far, but it's reported big losses for the past three years. He said it was because they'd been purchasing a lot of gear at auction, but only realising a small fraction of its cost at resale.'

'Money laundering?' Ryan suggested.

'That was my first thought,' James said. 'Channelling profits to an overseas subsidiary to avoid UK tax. I'll give the accountant a call and see what he can find.'

As James grabbed his mobile, Ryan opened his phone, Googled *Offshore Marine Exploration* and began to read a Wikipedia entry.

Offshore Marine Exploration (OME) was an Aberdeen-based company, specialising in the design and manufacture of oil drilling equipment . . . OME was a technology pioneer during the development of deep-water oil fields in British and Norwegian waters in the late 1970s . . . Company expanded aggressively in the 1980s, with over 300 employees producing oil drilling and extraction control systems for oil markets throughout the world . . . Floated on the London Stock Exchange 1986.

Shares hit hard in the Black Monday crash of October 19th 1987. OME was declared bankrupt in 1991 and assets bought by Texas-based rival GeoPump Inc . . . GeoPump

moved production of OME equipment to Mexico . . .
Manufacture of OME-designed equipment ceased in 1995,
when GeoPump filed for bankruptcy.

'Hey, Georgiou,' James told his phone. 'I want you to run a search on the accounts of Uncle's scrapyard. Any invoices related to oil drilling equipment, especially if it says it's manufactured by OME . . . Really . . . ? Really . . . ?'

Ryan looked round at James, who seemed properly excited.

'So?' Ryan asked, when the call ended.

James was grinning. 'I think you've lucked into something on your little tour, mate. Georgiou says he'd already noticed that Uncle's yard was making large purchases of surplus equipment from oil exploration companies in Scotland and Norway. In 2015 almost two million pounds went out, but then all the equipment gets written off as scrap in the company accounts.'

Ryan looked baffled. 'Which means?'

'No idea,' James said. 'But Georgiou did give me a number for a company called OME911. Apparently they were paid to do some repair work on OME equipment at Uncle's scrapyard about two years back.'

Ryan found a link to the OME911 website through Google, but the link bounced to a domain registry: *Buy this and thousands of other domains from just $99.*

James was peering over his shoulder. 'Use Wayback Machine.'

Ryan quickly found a 2012 version of the OME911 site on Wayback and read aloud, 'OME911 is the leading solution for onsite repair and maintenance of Offshore Marine pump and control systems. Our three engineers are former OME employees. We are the only company with full access to OME schematics and software diagnostic tools.'

James tried a phone number on the site's contact page, but it rang dead.

'Looks like they shut up shop,' James said. 'Print off the contacts page.'

James took his laptop and logged into the security service database. This gave him back door access to company, tax and banking records for most EU citizens. It took a few minutes for James to interrogate tax databases and make a Word document containing the names and last known addresses of the UK employees of OME911.

Ryan grabbed a printout of these details from an inkjet in James' bedroom, settling back on the sofa as James began checking out the names, hoping to find someone who might have a clue why Uncle was buying up OME equipment.

'Holy crap,' James said, as he turned the laptop to show an article from an Aberdeen newspaper.

Oil man Chris Carlisle dies after drug overdose in Birmingham Airport Hotel.

Ryan realised Carlisle was one of the three engineers pictured on the OME911 website, as James started Googling the other two.

'Birmingham airport's only a couple of miles from Uncle's scrapyard,' Ryan noted.

James nodded excitedly as his fingers tapped keys. 'Big coincidence, or what?'

Ryan grabbed a tablet and started his own Google hunt, as James used the MI5 database to access tax and mobile phone records for the other two engineers.

'Gordon Sachs, Kam Yuen,' James said, as he looked at a pair of Vodafone bills on his laptop screen. 'Neither filed their personal tax return this April. Both stopped making calls on their mobile phones – Gordon in October last year, Kam stops a few weeks earlier. And that's around the time Chris Carlisle was found dead in his hotel.'

'You think all three got murdered?' Ryan asked. 'I've got a phone number for the fourth employee.'

James looked confused. 'There were three engineers.'

'And a company secretary,' Ryan said, as he rattled James' own printout. 'Morag Henderson.'

James grinned. 'Good Scottish name. You think I should call her?'

Morag was in her seventies and it took several minutes for James to convince her that he wasn't trying to sell life insurance, or no-win-no-fee legal services. He explained that he was a police officer, doing some routine paperwork related to the death of Chris Carlisle, and that he wanted to fill in some blanks relating to his career with OME911.

'The company was set up by myself and a group of maintenance engineers who worked for OME,' Morag explained in a thick Scottish accent, as James set his phone to record the call. 'When OME went under, there was still a lot of their equipment installed at oil wells around the world. We bought software and spares from OME and sent engineers all over the world to keep the pumps and control panels running.

'When we started in '95, we had six engineers, but the three senior engineers retired, leaving Gordon, Kam and Chris. Over the years most OME equipment was gradually replaced. Even the newest OME gear is now more than twenty years old.'

'So the business just dwindled to the point where it shut down completely?'

Morag laughed. 'That's what we always expected to happen. But the US placed export sanctions on Libya, Iraq and Iran. That stopped them buying new pumping equipment for their oil wells. So the OME equipment stayed in place. And it's good stuff, some of it's forty years old and still going strong.'

'So Gordon, Kam and Chris were the only guys who could fix these oil pumps if they went wrong?' James asked.

'Not so much the pumps,' Morag said. 'The OME equipment was solid and simple, not like modern kit which is all computerised. Most mechanical things can be fixed locally, but the control consoles do require specialised knowledge. And if you're losing twenty thousand dollars a day because your oil well has shut down, it's worth paying the best engineers a few thousand to fly in and fix it properly.'

'So why did you shut down?'

'Age and politics,' Morag explained. 'Chris was sixty-four when he died. Kam and Gordon are well into their fifties. And with the Arab uprisings, the climate the guys were working in was getting more dangerous all the time. When Gaddafi ran Libya, the guys got three thousand dollars a day, stayed in good hotels and were escorted by armed police. After the regime collapsed, oil industry workers started getting kidnapped and held for ransom. Even guys who had mercenaries guarding them and the political backup of a big oil company were getting murdered in Iraq.'

James nodded. 'So it just got too dangerous?'

Morag sighed. 'It wasn't a question of *if* one of the guys got kidnapped. It became a question of *when*. I was getting phone calls with guys offering us fifty thousand dollars to go fix control consoles in Libya, but it was just too dangerous for a Scotsman to set foot over there. The guys decided to retire after we got a very good offer for our diagnostic equipment and spare parts inventory.'

'Who from?' James asked.

'My memory's not what it was,' Morag said. 'Stocky little Asian fellow with a Brummie accent. God, what was his name?'

'Martin Jones?' James suggested.

'Yes,' Morag said. 'Lovely fellow. Most of his people called him Uncle. He took us all out for *wonderful* Thai food after we signed the deal.'

'Cool,' James said. 'So when did you last see Kam and Gordon?'

'Chris's funeral, I suppose. They'd both moved down south, because they were always flying in and out of

Heathrow. We'd courier parts to their hotels from our warehouse in Aberdeen, but I'd only see them in the flesh a couple of times a year.'

'Did they have family?'

'Chris was the family man. Three kids, seven grandkids. Lovely wife, who I still play bowls with twice a week. Frankly, I was stunned when Chris turned up dead in a hotel room.'

James wondered if she suspected foul play, but he was posing as an officer linked to the investigation, so he'd blow his cover if he asked.

'And the other two, Kam and Gordon?'

'Kam was divorced. Two daughters, but the break-up was horrible and I don't think he sees much of them. Gordon, well . . .' Morag paused for a sharp intake of breath. 'I'm fairly certain he was homosexual.'

'Right,' James said, grinning at the un-PCness of her tone. 'Well you've been very generous with your time, Mrs Henderson. I'll try not to bother you again.'

'Oh, I'm a lonely old bird,' Morag said cheerfully. 'You can bother me all you like.'

'Did you follow that?' James asked Ryan, after he'd hung up.

'Most of it,' Ryan said. 'So Uncle bought up all the spare parts and a bunch of OME equipment. One of the three guys who can fix the control consoles is murdered in a hotel a few miles from here. The other two are missing, presumably murdered too.'

James shook his head. 'What use are two dead engineers?' he asked. 'What use are all those OME control consoles to Uncle if there's nobody alive who can fix them?'

Ryan nodded thoughtfully. 'So what then?'

'They say Islamic State is the wealthiest terrorist group in history. You know why?' James asked.

'Oil?' Ryan guessed.

'Exactly,' James said. 'Black market oil is a billion-dollar business. Islamic State-controlled areas of Syria, Libya and Iraq are full of oil wells. So I would guess that Uncle has hoovered up the supply of spare parts to keep OME equipment pumping, and has control of the only two guys who can fix things fast.'

'Kidnapped?' Ryan asked.

'We'll need more evidence to be certain,' James said. 'But that's what it looks like from where I'm sitting.'

24. SMART

Five days later

James had spent the night at Kerry's thirtieth-floor apartment in London's Canary Wharf. She'd complimented him on his suit, helped pick his tie and told him he had nothing to worry about, before kissing him good luck. But James wasn't a suit person. He hated the tie clamped around his neck. Smart shoes scraped the back of his ankles and the trousers itched.

It was peak rush hour as James came off the tube at Westminster. He made the short walk to the Ministry of Defence building in Whitehall, picked up a lanyard at reception and got a security guard escort to an office on the seventh floor. The narrow room had one-way glass, looking over a large conference table in the next room.

'You look the business,' John Jones said, as he got out of an armchair and gave James a handshake, followed by a little man-hug. 'Nervous?'

'A little,' James admitted. 'First time I've presented an intelligence briefing. Feels like my first day at school.'

'What's to worry about?' John teased. 'It's just the intelligence minister, the defence minister, a full colonel from the SAS, the heads of MI5 and MI6 and a few experts on the oil industry and Radical Islam. Coffee?'

'Water,' James said, clutching at his throat.

James shook a few hands as he stepped into the conference room, then practically swallowed his tongue when the intelligence minister came into the room accompanied by the deputy prime minister. It felt like he had a voice in his head yelling, *This is a big deal*, over and over, but he got a grip once he started speaking.

Since everyone in the room was senior enough to know that CHERUB existed, James gave a brief rundown on his mission in Sandy Green. He then explained how he'd spent the last few days researching the disappearance of Kam Yuen and Gordon Sachs.

'The pair haven't been sighted in the UK for over six months,' James explained. 'Over the past week I've pieced together evidence that Martin Jones – more commonly known as Uncle – paid to have Yuen and Sachs smuggled out of the UK on a privately owned launch and then transferred to a cargo vessel carrying recyclables to North Africa.

'An electronic monitoring request to GCHQ and the CIA has enabled me to track down several e-mail references to faults at oil installations using OME equipment and controlled by Islamic State. Yuen and

Sachs weren't named in any of the communications, but it does seem that there is a network of engineers working for Islamic State who are capable of sourcing spare parts and repairing equipment at oil wells in Islamic State-controlled areas. Some of these people may be working willingly. Some, like Yuen and Sachs, appear to have been kidnapped and are being forced to work against their will.

'I then worked with Morag Henderson. We made a list of eighty-three active oil wells that are controlled by groups affiliated to Islamic State, and are still believed to use OME pumps and control systems.'

The deputy prime minister cleared his throat. 'Oil wells are large facilities that stick out of the ground, yes?'

He got a few nods.

'So, why can't we use air strikes to disable the oil wells?'

The head of MI6 answered. 'US and UK policy with regard to Islamic State and illegal oil exports has been one of containment. Namely, stopping the oil being smuggled to refineries, either by sea or by pipeline. Destroying hundreds of oil wells with aerial bombing would be highly destructive, lead to thousands of casualties amongst civilian workers. It might also lead to retaliatory attacks on oil wells by Islamic State groups, and potential disruption to the global oil supply.'

The deputy prime minister nodded, then looked at James. 'So we can't bomb the oil wells, and I assume we can't move in and arrest this "Uncle" character until the two British hostages are safe?'

James was about to continue, but the defence minister spoke over him. 'Might I remind you that the current government has a strict non-intervention policy with regard to ground-based operations against Islamic State. Even if we *can* find Yuen and Sachs, we will not send British special forces in to rescue them.'

The deputy prime minister sat forward. 'But we'd look very weak as a government if news of this became public and we didn't act to help two decent men who appear to have been kidnapped on British soil.'

'But it *isn't* public,' the intelligence minister noted.

One of the oil industry analysts said exactly what James was thinking. 'First off, I'd like to think that some kind of attempt to rescue these two men is a good thing. Second, OME equipment is twenty to forty years old and probably goes wrong quite frequently. If we remove two critical personnel who are repairing the control consoles, chances are we'd degrade the amount of oil IS is able to put on the black market with minimal casualties.'

There were a few nods around the big table.

'How much would we degrade the capacity of Islamic State?' the deputy prime minister asked.

The analyst rocked her head uncertainly. 'Let's assume that a third of the eighty-three oil wells stop working within a year. If each one produces five hundred barrels a day, at a black market price of thirty dollars a barrel that's—'

'A hundred and forty-nine million, four hundred and sixty-two thousand one hundred and eight dollars that

IS groups won't be getting their hands on,' James said.

'You did that in your head?' the deputy prime minister asked, smirking.

'I'm good at arithmetic,' James said modestly, as laughter rippled around the table.

The special forces colonel eyed James. 'So what kind of operation would you propose?'

James smiled uneasily. 'That's more your field of expertise than mine, Colonel. Obviously we need to know where Yuen and Sachs are before we can rescue them. If we found a large well and sabotaged the control systems – perhaps with a small drone strike – there's a good chance Yuen and Sachs would be sent out to fix it. As long as we don't arouse suspicion, a small commando-style team on the ground should be able to deal with whatever security team has been put around them.'

'And your method of escape?' the colonel asked.

James smiled. 'Sir, I'm a mission controller at CHERUB. This is your field of expertise.'

The colonel seemed flattered by James' show of respect. 'You'd have to pick a well close to the sea, or near a border with a friendly country,' he explained. 'As long as you met that criterion, escape would be far from impossible.'

The defence minister cleared his throat. 'Escape may not be *impossible*, but the government is in a fragile state and the policy on military intervention on the ground in Islamic State-controlled areas is not about to change.'

The deputy prime minister thumped on the desk angrily. 'These are British citizens, kidnapped on British soil. Are you really telling me that you intend to do nothing to assist them?'

'The policy is clear,' the intelligence minister shot back.

'The policy is an ass,' the defence minister roared, as James found himself with another reason to hate politicians.

'Gentlemen,' the head of MI6 said firmly, as he got to his feet. 'It's not essential that we send in British soldiers, with British uniforms and equipment. What we need is a small force of trained operatives with no links to the British military. If the operation goes wrong, we can deny all knowledge.'

The colonel bristled at this idea. 'What's the point having British special forces if we're afraid to use them?'

But the three politicians instinctively liked the idea of a mission where their asses would be covered if things went wrong.

'The team can be assembled and trained using British resources,' the MI6 head said, smiling as he sensed that the politicians were with him. 'We'll need someone to lead the operation. It'll be better if they're up to speed on the situation and have both combat training and significant experience of working under cover. Of course, they'll have unofficial assistance from UK special forces, and MI6 can source further expertise from ourselves and the intelligence services of our allies in the Middle East.'

James shuddered as he realised that the head of MI6 and several other pairs of eyes had settled on him.

The deputy prime minister smiled. 'I'm told your record as a CHERUB agent was outstanding, and you seem like a very bright young man.'

James felt like his tongue was ten times normal size as he looked around at John for support.

'Can you spare your boy to run this one, John?' the colonel asked jovially.

John looked at James and cracked a big smile. 'I think I'll manage without him for a few weeks,' he said. 'So, James, do you think you can pull this off?'

'I guess,' James said, half hoping that he was about to wake up and find that he was still in bed next to Kerry.

25. TEETH

John seemed proud as they headed out of the conference room. 'Good stuff,' he told James. 'I'm glad they're not just gonna abandon Sachs and Yuen.'

'I don't know where to start with this,' James admitted.

But John was glancing at his watch. 'I've got another meeting over at MI6. Chat later!'

Then James found the deputy prime minister shaking his hand. 'I'll need progress reports,' he said. 'I have every confidence in you.'

James wanted to speak with the special forces colonel, but these were important people and they all dashed off, leaving him alone in a hallway. He loosened his tie and felt shaky as he stumbled into a bathroom, slammed a cubicle door and made a dry heave over a toilet bowl.

James had a pain down his side and realised he

needed to sit still for a moment, so he put the toilet lid down, sat and took a slow deep breath. He pulled his phone and tried getting his head around the problem he now had to solve. When the screen came on, he spotted a forty-minute-old message from Kerry.

You'll knock 'em dead in the meeting. X.

James erupted in a big smile. Thinking how much he loved Kerry. How empty his life would seem if she wasn't around. He called Kerry's number.

'Hey you,' Kerry said, sounding like she was walking fast.

'You OK?' James asked.

'My boss just dumped on me from a great height,' Kerry said, her voice all high and stressed. 'There's a mistake in a contract I'm working on. Two hundred pages and I've got to go through marking up all the mistakes before the lawyer comes in tomorrow. So I'm sorry, but there's no way I can meet you for lunch today.'

James sighed, but wasn't surprised. He rarely stayed with Kerry in London during the week, because it was all work and sleep.

'So how was *your* meeting?' Kerry asked, and then she sounded angry after he'd explained. 'You agreed to do what! Are you nuts?'

James had no way of knowing who was outside the toilet cubicle, so he spoke in a whisper. 'It was *so* much pressure,' he admitted. 'My boss, a full colonel covered in medals, the intelligence minister, the deputy prime minister. All smiling at me and I'm like, *OK, yes sir, I'll do it, sir.*'

'Islamic State chop people's heads off,' Kerry said. 'This is no CHERUB mission. This is off the chart dangerous.'

'You think I should pull out?' James said.

Kerry's voice calmed down. 'Only if you really want to.'

'Are you pissed off at me?'

Kerry sighed. 'If I sounded that way, it's because I was shocked. But I'll support you if this is what you *really* want.'

'I want to help those guys,' James said. 'But if I get this wrong, people will die.'

'Then you've got to build the best team you can,' Kerry said. 'Plan carefully, get good advice and good people working with you.'

'Do you think I'm a lightning rod?' James asked. 'Like, nobody senior will take this on because if it goes wrong it's a career killer.'

Kerry laughed slightly. 'If this goes wrong, your promotion prospects are the least of your concerns.'

'GRRR!' James moaned, as he thumped the tissue dispenser. 'Why didn't I just say no?'

'You're *brilliant* at your job, James,' Kerry said. 'You're just overwhelmed right now. Once you start breaking the problems down and you've got decent people around you—'

James interrupted. 'Kerry, do you *really* want to spend your life working sixty-hour weeks going through two-hundred-page contracts with lawyers?'

'I'm not going to do this forever,' Kerry said.

'Quit,' James urged. 'You're smarter than me. If we planned this thing together . . .'

'James . . .' Kerry said, giggling.

'You're only doing the job for the big bucks,' James said. 'But who really cares about money?'

Now Kerry sounded a bit pissed off. 'You only say that because you inherited plenty from your mother.'

'I'll look after you.'

'I want my own career,' Kerry said. 'Not your charity . . . And you're just saying this stuff because you're stressed.'

James heard someone speak, and Kerry mouthing, 'OK, OK.' Then into the phone, 'My meeting is about to start and my boss is glowering at me through a glass partition. I'll call you later, OK?'

'I love you,' James said.

Kerry laughed. 'I love you more. And don't worry. Everyone will support you and you'll do great.'

James heard a sound like a door opening, then the speaker went dead. He felt warm, imagining Kerry in her black business garb, pulling her close and smelling the top of her head. Then he started thinking about what Kerry had said.

She was right that he'd feel less overwhelmed once the shock had worn off. He started breaking the rescue mission down into manageable chunks and thinking about who he'd want alongside him in a situation where his life was on the line.

James hit the contacts button on his phone and scrolled down as far as B before dialling.

'Yo, dumbass!' Bruce Norris answered.

James smiled, as someone in the next cubicle ripped a huge fart. 'Hey,' James said. 'Are you still on campus, helping out with combat training?'

'For a few more days,' Bruce said. 'How's Birmingham? How's the mission?'

'It's taken an interesting turn,' James admitted. 'Is there any chance you'd be up for something violent and highly dangerous?'

'Always,' Bruce said.

'Cool,' James said. 'Because I need people I trust. So I'm gonna try getting the old gang back together, for one last mission.'

*

The twins had school, but Ryan had nothing to do but kill time at Nurtrust. He'd spurned Rhea's advances, out of respect for Leon, and spent all day Monday and Tuesday in his room, doing Skype sessions with a maths tutor on campus.

Like most CHERUB agents, Ryan had taken his exams at weird times, enabling his studies to fit between missions. This meant Ryan already had enough qualifications for university, but he was now studying some extra modules to give himself an advantage when he got there.

He kept checking his phone, but James had vanished and there had been no job offer, either from Uncle, or the site foreman. It was Thursday morning when he finally got a call from campus.

James Campus flashed on his caller ID, but it

was a girl's voice.

'Ning, is that you?'

'Who else, dear boy?' Ning said, putting on a posh English accent. 'Where you at?'

'Bored off my head,' Ryan said. 'I've done so much math, I'm seeing imaginary numbers in my dreams. Now I'm out, picking my car up from the repair shop.'

Ning sounded amused. 'You crashed?'

'Nah, just someone messed with a wing mirror. So how come you're at James' desk?'

'I help out in his office sometimes,' Ning explained.

'Is he coming back here, do you know?'

'That's why I'm calling,' Ning explained. 'You and your brothers have been reassigned.'

'What?' Ryan gasped. 'I've unearthed all kinds of stuff up here.'

'I don't know all the details,' Ning said. 'But apparently an MI5 team has planted more bugs in Uncle's cabin and home. And they've recruited informants. A cleaning lady and some dude at the scrapyard whose immigration status is dodgy.'

'*CHERUB agents shall only be placed at risk in scenarios where adult agents cannot perform equally well,*' Ryan said, quoting from the CHERUB training manual. 'So I guess my ass is heading back to campus. The twins won't be happy if they're back on heavy drill.'

'You won't be on campus for long,' Ning said. 'James said you need to head over to his flat and meet a guy called Joffrey from MI5. Hand over all the receivers for the listening devices and pack his stuff up in the Ford

Focus. Then you've gotta drive back to campus and pack your swimming trunks and suntan lotion, because we're all heading off to the summer hostel. Me included.'

'I'm confuzzled,' Ryan admitted. 'If you don't know what's going on, can I at least speak to James?'

'You'll be lucky,' Ning said. 'He's just got back to campus, but he's buzzing about like an over-caffeinated bluebottle, planning some kind of secret mission.'

'*All* CHERUB missions are secret,' Ryan pointed out.

Ning shrugged. 'Yeah, well this one's even more secret than usual.'

26. HOSTEL

James hadn't been to the CHERUB summer hostel in five years. Although it was autumn, the first sunlight caught the water around the Mediterranean island as the fifteen-seat executive jet made a banked turn and aligned with a short landing strip.

'Happy memories,' Bruce said, from the seat across the aisle, as he looked at the giant outdoor pool and rows of accommodation huts. These housed over a hundred CHERUB agents for twelve weeks between June and September, but out of season the population dwindled to a husband and wife caretaker and a small security team.

Besides James and Bruce, the little jet carried five agents. Ryan, Ning, Leon, Daniel and Ryan's chunky best mate, Alfie. There was also a chef, a cleaner, training instructors Capstick and McEwen and two assistant instructors.

Alfie, Ning and the twins had a slide-out table between their seats and a rowdy game of Cards Against Humanity on the go. James was more interested in the fact that he had mobile reception for the first time in two hours.

He picked up three voicemails. The first was from Amy Collins, who'd been James' mentor when he first arrived at campus thirteen years earlier.

'Good to hear your message, James,' Amy's recorded voice said. 'But I'm with the FBI now, so I've got my own undercover stuff going on and there's no way I can get out of it.'

'Amy's out,' James told Bruce, his seat juddering as the jet touched down.

The landing strip was short, so everyone got thrown as the pilot used wing flaps and reverse thrust to slow down.

'Pity,' Bruce said, as he braced hands against a bulkhead. 'She'd have been perfect.'

'I've put some other calls in,' James said.

'What about the twins, Callum and Connor?' Bruce suggested.

'Final year of their masters degrees,' James explained. 'They can't take time out. Gabrielle's busy. Rat damaged his neck in a racing car last year.'

'Shakeel?' Bruce suggested.

James shook his head and laughed. 'He's in Brisbane, running some Internet start-up with guys he met at uni. Plus, the last time I saw Shak he'd totally let himself go. Must have weighed more than a hundred kilos.'

'Really?' Bruce said. 'Unbelievable!'

The plane U-turned at the end of the landing strip and taxied back towards a dilapidated hut. A ground attendant in Royal Air Force uniform ran out to place blocks in front of the wheels as the exit swung open.

James was out behind the two instructors and stepped on to the tarmac just as his sister came jogging out of the hut, dressed in shorts and her *Rathbone Racing* team hat.

'Thanks for coming,' James said, as he gave her a hug.

Lauren smiled. 'Thought I'd come and save your ass one last time.'

James' mate Kyle was behind and shook Bruce's hand. 'Your employers were OK?' Bruce asked.

Kyle laughed. 'It's a charity. They've never got any money. My boss wasn't keen to lose me, but when I mentioned six weeks' unpaid leave, the finance department practically bit my arm off.'

As Bruce kissed Lauren, James turned his attention to an austere, dark-eyed woman. She was petite but muscular, with black hair curling down her back, and clad in combat shorts and a white vest.

'Tovah?' James said, offering a handshake. 'Thank you so much for coming at short notice.'

Thirty years old, Tovah spoke with a deep Israeli accent. 'Excited to finally meet you, Mr Adams.'

'Call me James,' he said, as Ryan led the rest of the youngsters out of the jet. 'I can't thank you and your government enough for your help.'

'No problem,' Tovah said, as Bruce closed in.

'My very good friend Bruce,' James said, as he shook hands. 'Bruce, this is Tovah, who absolutely *isn't* from the Israeli intelligence service.'

Tovah smiled and shrugged innocently. 'I barely even know where Israel is.'

'So why *are* you here?' Bruce asked.

Tovah cracked a huge smile. 'I'm here to teach you guys to fly.'

*

Kerry left her apartment at 6 a.m. She took a ten-minute taxi and forty-storey elevator ride to visit her bank's legal department. The walnut conference table was set up with coffee, juice and breakfast pastries. She'd been through thirty pages of a contract with a one-eyebrowed lawyer and her two assistants when the phone in the centre of the table rang.

'My apologies,' the lawyer said, as she grabbed her coat and briefcase and beckoned the assistants. 'I've been called to a meeting in Amsterdam. They're setting up a jet at London City.'

Kerry rattled the two-hundred-page document in front of her. 'Will you be back to finish this today?'

'Unlikely,' the lawyer said. 'Call my office when my secretary gets in. I'll try and get you some time tomorrow.'

'Is there anyone else . . . ?' Kerry asked, as the trio steamed out, grabbing smartphones and scooping documents off the table. 'Shit.'

Kerry thumped on the table. Her boss, Doug, would chuck his toys out of his pram when he found out. She drained tepid black coffee and scoffed a mini-cinnamon Danish, before grabbing a phone off the table and calling her boss. Doug wasn't at his desk yet, so Kerry left the building and strode fifteen minutes to her bank's other tower at the opposite side of Canary Wharf.

Doug erupted the moment she got out of the twenty-second-floor elevator.

'Why aren't you with Doreen?'

'She had to go to Amsterdam.'

'You what?' Doug shouted, as he beckoned Kerry. 'My office.'

'I couldn't help it,' Kerry said. 'I was there, she got called away.'

They'd reached Doug's corner office, with river views and a giant TV showing the Bloomberg channel.

'Why did you use Doreen on legal for this contract?' Doug roared, as he sat behind the desk. 'You know how busy she gets.'

'You said it was important. You told me to get the best person.'

'She's always super busy,' Doug roared. 'I need this contract for the meeting at eleven. Do you think the Korean consortium will arrive with a half-assed, half-finished proposal?'

'I could call around,' Kerry said. 'See who else is free. Or get outside legal in to look at it.'

'Not in two hours, Chang,' Doug moaned, as he reached out for a phone. 'Why didn't you sit down with Doreen last night?'

'I didn't leave this office until nine,' Kerry said, tempted to add *two hours after you.*

Doug dialled someone on his desk phone, but got an engaged tone and slammed it down. 'You don't seem to get things done, Chang,' Doug snapped. 'And if you can't, I'll source people who can.'

Kerry's boss was always moody. It wasn't usually a good idea to talk back, but she was determined not to cop all the blame.

'Doreen and I had the contract drafted ten days ago,' Kerry pointed out. 'You were the one who sat on it for a week and only noticed the errors yesterday.'

'I'm busy, in case you haven't noticed.'

Kerry snorted. 'You left early to play golf two afternoons this week. I've been here until eight every night, trying to sort this leasing deal.'

Doug stood up and roared. 'How dare you speak to me like that in my own office. You've worked here less than two years. I've had unpaid interns who are more effective than you.'

'You're a bully,' Kerry told her boss, as he moved around the table and faced her off.

'Sweetheart, if you can't take the heat . . .'

'Do you want me to try and find someone from another law firm, or not?' Kerry asked. 'And I am *not* your sweetheart.'

'Whatever,' Doug said. 'You made the problem, *you* solve it.'

Kerry made a little grunt as she spun on high heels and left her boss' office.

'You OK?' a colleague asked, seeing a tear in Kerry's eye as she strode twenty paces to her windowless office.

'I'll live,' Kerry said unconvincingly.

But the tears kept welling when Kerry reached her desk. Besides the contract her boss was yelling about, there were files for three more deals on her desk: finance for a soft drink bottling plant in Chile, a deal to lease trains in Russia and a Spanish billionaire who was planning to buy a Welsh furniture maker, fire all the workers and move production to a giant factory he was building in Romania.

If nothing happened, she'd get through all of her work by 7 p.m., but something always happened. Kerry groaned as her mobile buzzed, but smiled when she saw a picture message from James on the screen. It showed the peeling frontage of accommodation hut 32 at the CHERUB summer hostel.

Just landed. Remember what we got up to in here, back in Summer 08?

Kerry zoomed the picture message as Doug walked by, bawling out someone else. She could see a tiny James, reflected in the hut's front window, with his camera phone in front of his face and the black skinny jeans that made his bum look good. She'd never wanted to hug him so badly and her fingers hovered over the keyboard on her screen, before typing:

2 late 2 join the gang?

James was online and replied instantly. Heck no!!! RU serious?

Deadly serious.

Kerry trembled as she opened her briefcase. She tipped all the work papers on to her desk, took out her work phone and laptop. Then she replaced them with a framed desk photo of James and the bobble head Elvis and Jesus figures stuck to the top of her monitor.

She spent a couple of minutes stripping a few compromising pages from the file on the furniture factory takeover. She dropped them into an envelope, did a quick Google search and addressed it to the editor of a local newspaper based close to the Welsh furniture factory. It wouldn't stop the takeover, but at least the bank and the billionaire wouldn't be able to lie about the takeover benefiting the workers and local community.

Kerry stripped the ID badge from around her neck and hooked it over the monitor before stepping into the hallway. There was a photocopier at the end and Doug was there, looming over a curly-haired graduate yelling, *I need those figures by yesterday!*

Part of Kerry wanted to take a short run, sweep her boss' legs and flatten his nose. Part of her wanted to say goodbye to some co-workers she considered friends. But mostly, she just wanted to be out of here.

She handed the envelope to a receptionist. 'That needs to be sent by urgent courier,' Kerry explained. 'Tell Doug I've found an outside lawyer and I'm heading there now to sort the Kobyashi contract.'

Kerry's brain churned as the lift took her down. Thinking about the salary she'd given up and six-figure bonus due in January. Was it crazy to quit a sought-after job for some high-risk mission halfway around the world?

The weird thing was, she'd never felt more sure of anything in her life.

27. DRAWL

'G'day,' Capstick shouted, in his annoying Aussie drawl. 'I've got good news.'

The squat instructor stood by the summer hostel swimming pool. Ning, Ryan, Leon, Daniel and Alfie faced him in their CHERUB uniform, while two assistant instructors stood at a console nearby, working out how to retract the electric pool cover.

'Normally, my job is to persecute you kids and get you into the best shape possible,' Capstick continued. 'But this is a different situation. I have twenty-eight days to prepare former CHERUB agents for a highly dangerous mission. They left CHERUB more than five years ago, and most of them now spend their days sat on fat lazy asses behind a desk. Your job is to motivate the grown-ups by showing them how far they've fallen off the pace. You're gonna go on training runs with them.

You'll spar with them, play sport with them and study with them. It's old CHERUB versus new and I want you to show no mercy.'

'Current versus Crusty,' Ryan suggested.

Capstick wagged a finger and laughed. 'I like those names. So go get your swimmers on, 'cos we're gonna start with some fun in the pool.'

*

'Look at that,' Bruce teased, poking the ripple of flab over the waistband of Kyle's swim shorts. 'And when did that skin last catch some sun?'

'Screw you,' Kyle said, as the pair followed James down a curved path running between the accommodation huts and the main pool. 'Just because I haven't spent the last year bumming around on some beach in Thailand.'

'Bumming around!' Bruce snorted. 'Six hours' training four days a week, plus I was teaching Muay Thai classes.'

Lauren was waiting for them. Sat on a low wall, in pool shoes and a Lycra one-piece. She had a decent tan for someone with a pale complexion. Her shoulders and arms were ripped, because motor sport puts massive strain on the neck.

'I see a dividing line,' Bruce told Lauren, as she stood up. 'Those who respect their bodies, and those who gave up.'

Lauren smirked when she saw Kyle. 'You're *actually* chubbier than James.'

'Hey!' James yelled. 'Mission controllers have to train.

184

I'm not *that* unfit.'

'I hate all of you,' Kyle noted, as they rounded a line of trees and reached the edge of the pool.

'Aww crap,' James said, as soon as he saw what was about to happen. 'I *hate* this game.'

The Olympic-size pool had been set up with a hundred coloured balls floating on the surface. A dumpster at either end would serve as a goal.

'You're two minutes late,' Capstick said, glancing at his huge plastic diver's watch. 'Do that again and I'll give you push-ups. Red balls are worth one point, yellow three, blue five and green ten. You're only allowed to carry one ball at a time. Barging is allowed, but no holding, no hitting and instant disqualification if you hold anyone's head under the water. Each round lasts twenty minutes, or until all the balls are cleared. The first team to win three rounds wins the match. The losing team has to run the twelve-kilometre circuit of the island before they get dinner.'

'There's five of them and four of us,' Lauren pointed out. 'That's not fair.'

Capstick scoffed. 'Blame your brother for his slack recruiting skills. Fair is for fairy tales. Now get to your end of the pool.'

The four Crustys and five Currents lined up, fifty metres apart at opposite ends of the pool. A training assistant with his legs dangling over the end of a high board blew a whistle and everyone dived in.

Although wind and currents had blown the balls around, most were clumped in the middle of the pool, close to where they'd been released. Everyone wanted the ten-point green balls first. Bruce and Ning were the fastest swimmers on their teams and each scooped a green.

Alfie tried using his bulk to stop Bruce, but Lauren was close behind. Bruce flipped the ball across, giving her a simple shot into the mouth of the blue dumpster.

'Ten nil,' Bruce shouted, as he quickly grabbed a three-point yellow and flung it at Lauren as Alfie locked arms around his waist.

'Holding!' Bruce protested.

Alfie was twenty centimetres taller than Bruce and fifteen kilos heavier. But Bruce was super strong. He ripped free, then drove Alfie hard into the poolside, leaving him badly winded. With Alfie temporarily disabled, Bruce and Lauren linked up, with Bruce throwing balls across and Lauren making the short final throw into the goal.

But while Team Crusty's healthy duo racked up the points, things were going less well at the other end. With a man over, Ryan and Leon played a tactical game, lobbing dozens of balls down towards their goal, allowing Daniel and Ning to scoop and shoot.

Kyle threw balls back and batted Daniel's throws with some success, but Ning was a fish and James couldn't get within two metres as she rattled a stream of plastic balls into the dumpster. Rather than a losing battle with Ning, James decided to break along the edge of the pool. He scooped several balls and flipped them up to Bruce as he swam. But as he neared the middle, James found himself double-teamed by Ryan and Alfie.

As Alfie gave James a powerful shove, Ryan dived and whipped down his shorts.

'Hey!' James shouted, grabbing frantically as Ryan surfaced and resumed lobbing balls down towards Daniel and Ning.

Five minutes into the twenty, more than half the balls had been cleared. Those that remained tended to be low-value reds and yellows, scattered along the edges of the pool. Bruce and Ning were sharks amidst dolphins, scoring consistently with the opposition getting nowhere near. At the other extreme, Kyle was red-faced as he clambered out of the pool and lay flat on his back, breathing rapidly.

'Are you hurt?' James shouted, looking around after hitting the dumpster rim with the last five-point blue.

'Stitch,' Kyle gasped. 'So painful.'

'It's the first round,' James said. 'And I thought *I* was unfit.'

With Kyle out it was five against three. The Currents made their numbers count, with their two fastest swimmers – Ning and Ryan – collecting balls and feeding them to Alfie's long arms near the goal, while the twins did what they could to harass the opposition.

There were four and a half minutes on the countdown when the last single-point reds clattered into the dumpsters at either end. Kyle had made it to a sunlounger and was still clutching his side as the others climbed out of the pool and the training assistants tipped up the dumpsters and started tallying points.

'You're bright red,' Lauren noted, as she gave Kyle a look of concern.

'Heart attack material,' Bruce teased. 'I thought you belonged to a gym.'

'Didn't say he actually went though,' James noted.

'Just gimme a couple of days,' Kyle moaned. 'I'll be fine once I've blasted off the cobwebs.'

'We have a winner,' Capstick announced, as one of the assistants handed him a piece of paper. 'Current Agents, two hundred and forty-three. Crusty Old Agents, one hundred and thirty-two.'

'Hah!' Leon shouted, as he high-fived Ning. 'That's almost two to one.'

Lauren and Bruce looked at each other, shaking heads as Capstick approached, smiling and thumping James on the back.

'How's my training so far, boss?' he asked.

Since James was in charge of the mission, he was technically Capstick's boss. Though he'd have to follow orders during physical training, if he didn't want to lose everyone's respect.

'I'm grand,' James lied. 'Fine and dandy.'

'Looking forward to that run around the island?' Capstick asked, as he eyed Kyle. 'My youngsters have you whipped, and you might end up having to give this fellow a piggyback.'

As the training assistants poured balls back into the pool ready for round two, James saw Tovah coming down the path from the huts, dressed in a black bikini.

'I could bury my face in that cleavage,' Bruce noted quietly.

'Misogynist pig,' Lauren growled, as she thumped him.

'Hey,' Tovah said, peering at James over the top of her sunglasses. 'This looks like fun. Can anyone play?'

28. BUNKS

The hut slept eight, so James, Kyle and Bruce got a set of bunks each.

'Oh, glorious day!' Bruce said brightly, as he came from a slightly grungy bathroom dressed in shorts. 'Sun is shining and life is good!'

'Sod off,' Kyle moaned, pulling a pillow over his face. 'My body hurts.'

'What bit?'

'All of it,' Kyle said, as he sat up. 'I'm old.'

'You're twenty-six,' Bruce noted. 'Jesus.'

Kyle saw a tangle of sheets in the next bunk across. 'Is James up?'

Bruce smiled. 'Kerry arrived on a boat around three a.m. They were all over each other.'

'I wish I had that,' Kyle said.

'What?' Bruce asked.

'James and Kerry,' Kyle explained. 'They're like an institution. None of that messing around trying to find my perfect guy. You just meet someone when you're twelve and it all goes great.'

Bruce laughed. 'They've broken up a hundred times.'

Kyle nodded as he pulled up a set of tracksuit bottoms. 'But did we ever doubt that they'd get back together every time it happened?'

'I dated Kerry,' Bruce pointed out acidly.

'No offence,' Kyle said, clutching his ribs and groaning as he stood up.

'So over it,' Bruce said. 'Thai girls are awesome! How's your love life these days? You still seeing that quantity surveyor with the nose ring?'

'He dumped me for an Indian PHP programmer,' Kyle said, sighing as he checked his iPhone and slid feet into Adidas. 'Breakfast?'

'Bloody right,' Bruce said. 'I've got a crazy appetite.'

The main kitchen and dining-room was undergoing an off-season refurbishment, so the chef had made do with a domestic kitchen in a staff flat. She'd cleared sofas out of a living-room and found odd chairs and fold-out tables to make a dining space.

'Ahoy, mateys,' James crowed, as Kyle and Bruce joined him at a buffet table.

'Look at that grin,' Bruce teased, as James loaded his plate with bacon, eggs and sausage. 'Someone got lucky last night.'

'Where is Kerry?' Kyle asked.

'Shower,' James explained.

Lauren was eating with Capstick at one table, while a rowdy crowd of current agents sat at the next.

'Why you holding your back, Kyle?' Alfie shouted. 'Need a walking stick? Or maybe a Zimmer frame?'

Bruce narrowed his eyes. 'How's them ribs I smashed into the poolside, Alfie? Nice and bruised, like Daniel's eye?'

'You guys should probably take things slow today,' Leon added, as he stuffed scrambled egg into his mouth. 'People your age gotta think about your blood pressure.'

'Or popping your haemorrhoids,' Alfie added, as his table erupted in laughter.

Friendly whoops went up as Kerry rolled in. Lauren and Kyle gave her hugs.

Kerry turned sharply and looked at Bruce. 'So, when do we get to smack these sarcastic brats around the dojo?' she asked.

'Soon enough,' Bruce said, as he took a seat next to Lauren. 'See how smart they are tomorrow morning, when they've got no front teeth.'

'I'm not scared of you,' Alfie told Bruce. 'I've found bigger objects than you up my nose.'

Laughter roared around the current agents' table. James gave Kerry a kiss as they passed in opposite directions. James with his plate stacked, Kerry heading to the buffet. As James settled between Lauren and Kyle, Tovah darted out of the kitchen, holding a fruit plate covered in cling film.

'What?' James asked, as he poached a hash brown on his fork.

'Bad news,' Tovah told James. 'I did some calculations. If you want to fly on this mission, you need to lose four kilos.'

James gawped as Tovah swapped his bacon and eggs for sliced melon, garnished with two red grapes.

'You're kidding me,' James said, pointing at Kyle. 'He's fatter than me.'

'Hey!' Kyle yelped.

Tovah shook her head. 'Kyle may be overweight for his body size, but he's shorter so he's still only sixty-four kilos. *You* need to be under seventy-five.'

Everyone apart from James started laughing.

'Who ate all the pies?' the teens at the next table started singing. 'Who ate all the pies?'

'These sausages are dee-licious,' Kerry teased, as James glowered at his melon. 'Is it every meal, or just breakfast?'

'Every meal,' Tovah said. 'Serious calorie restriction is the only way James can drop four kilos in five weeks.'

'Hey,' James growled, as Lauren snapped a pic with her phone. 'What are you doing?'

'Had to, bro,' Lauren explained. 'Your expression right now is priceless!'

*

While CHERUB had blown its investment budget on the swanky new Campus Village, the summer hostel had been neglected. The gym was no exception, with creaky floorboards, cracked glazing and fighting mats patched up with duct tape.

Capstick led the training session, starting with laps and stretches. Kyle hadn't sparred for ages, but triumphed over aches and put on a decent show sparring with Leon. Daniel got outclassed by Tovah. As the two biggest, James paired with Alfie, and their session got red-faced and bad-tempered as it progressed. Bruce and Kerry had been sparring since they were nine years old, but since Kerry hadn't trained intensely since leaving uni, Bruce had to go easy.

After ninety minutes and a few partner swaps, Tovah, the five Currents and the five Crustys lined up breathlessly in front of Capstick and McEwen.

'Yawl worked hard,' Capstick said, smiling. 'Especially you, Kyle, blowing off a lot of cobwebs.'

Kyle smiled as Bruce slapped him between the shoulder blades.

'But,' Capstick said dramatically. 'Since Currents and Crustys are in competition, I want each side to pick their three best fighters for three bouts. Winners get first dibs at showers and lunch buffet. Losers run ten laps and wipe down sweaty mats.'

Since Ning and Alfie were mates and Leon and Daniel were his little brothers, Ryan had assumed a leadership role amongst the Currents, and led the quintet into a circle by the back wall.

'Bruce is going to beat whoever,' Alfie began. 'Ning's too fast for James, Kyle's a wreck and I reckon Ning can take Kerry or Lauren, because they're both out of practice.'

Ryan nodded in agreement. 'So if Bruce wins his bout and Ning wins hers, it'll all be down to the third match-up.'

'Hang on,' Ning said. 'I'm the best, Bruce is the best. We should fight each other.'

The four lads shook their heads. 'Nah, we have to be tactical,' Ryan said.

Ning smiled. 'I've been hearing about the legendary Bruce Norris since my first dojo session on campus. I've *always* wanted to fight him.'

'But then we'll be a bout down,' Ryan said. 'What's the point?'

Ning put indignant hands on hips. 'Who says I can't win?'

The boys laughed and shook their heads.

'Ning, for god's sake,' Alfie said. 'Bruce won the All-in Campus Fighting Championship every year from when he was *thirteen*. He's been training some of the best young fighters on campus.'

Ryan nodded. 'Bruce has been living in Thailand. He teaches Muay Thai boxing to *Thai* people.'

'I can take him,' Ning said, pounding a fist into her palm. 'I'm fighting Bruce, that's all there is to it.'

29. TAPES

Lauren Adams faced Ryan in an even first bout. Ryan's height and speed, versus Lauren's technique and low centre of gravity. After a lot of circling, Lauren suckered Ryan into overreaching on a punch. She went low, tripped, flipped and won with an arm bar.

Alfie and James repeated their sparring from earlier. Bulky and slow, they grunted, turned red and wound up on the floor in a stalemate. Capstick declared Alfie a narrow winner, mainly because he wanted the third bout to count for something.

Bruce Norris was a few centimetres shorter than an average bloke. Slim, muscular and so fast that opponents often found themselves on the floor and bloody-nosed before they got to make their first move. Ning was the same height. Her broad back and muscular arms made the Chinese state pick her as a future Olympic boxer when she was a little kid and you could see why as she went eye-to-eye with Bruce.

'Fight,' Capstick snapped, as the sweaty onlookers hummed with excitement.

Bruce did what he did. He swept in fast and brought Ning down with a leg hook. It looked like it was over inside three seconds as Bruce dived on Ning's back and tried to wrench her arm. But her powerful shoulders didn't yield the way Bruce expected and there was huge power in the flying knee that slammed him in the ribs and sent him off balance.

Now Ning rolled on top. Bruce writhed as Ning got a knee across his chest and started pounding his face with her gloved fists. If more was at stake, Bruce might have taken the pain and tried to throw her off, but he didn't fancy doing the rest of his mission prep trying to breathe through a broken nose, so he thumped on the mat to submit.

The crowd seemed delighted by Ning's shock victory. Even the Crustys, who now faced gym laps.

'Losing it, Bruce!' Alfie shouted.

Ning's own celebration was muted. She knew Bruce had made a tactical surrender as she gave him a hand off the mat and strolled towards an equipment bin, peeling her gloves.

'You hit *hard*,' Bruce said, grinning.

Ning had beaten enough boys over the years to appreciate the ones who didn't bitch and make excuses when they lost.

'You've never seen me fight,' Ning said. 'I've seen

videos of your campus championship bouts. You always did the same thing against fighters in the early rounds, when you thought it would be easy.'

'My mistake,' Bruce said, smirking as he ripped off a boxing glove and lobbed it into a canvas bag. 'I certainly respect you now. And I've broken my nose too many times down the years to push that one too far.'

Ning shrugged. 'You'd beat me every time if you knew my fighting style.'

'But you played me,' Bruce said, unable to contain a huge smile as he eyed Ning. 'Gotta admire that. You heading straight to uni when you leave CHERUB?'

'Can't decide,' Ning said.

'I'm good mates with the owner of the dojo where I work in Thailand. If you wanted a gap year, I could probably get you work as a trainer. Maybe even earn something on the side from professional bouts, if you're that way inclined.'

'It's a thought,' Ning said brightly. 'I came out of China penniless, so I could certainly use some funds.'

'Pay's not great,' Bruce admitted. 'But the lifestyle's cool. You can find yourself a nice Aussie surfer boyfriend.'

Ning looked awkwardly at her feet and grunted. 'All guys ever want is skinny girls with giant boobs.'

Bruce laughed. 'Don't be so down on yourself. Loads of guys would go for you.'

Ning snorted. 'Like who?'

Bruce smiled. 'Like me.'

Ning was flattered and erupted in a big smile,

but it was also weird because she couldn't work out if Bruce was flirting, or just being kind. Bruce felt just as awkward, because he'd realised that he *was* flirting. But he wasn't on some Thai beach. He'd been working as CHERUB staff, and Ning was a seventeen-year-old agent.

As the pair flushed red, they were both relieved to see Instructor McEwen coming their way, pointing at Bruce.

'Join the other Crustys,' McEwen shouted. 'Ten laps. And Ning, get your sweaty ass out of my gym and into the shower.'

*

James lunched on hummus and carrot batons while everyone else got pizza, but he cheered up when he took charge of fifteen 450cc Honda bikes.

'Who's ridden a motorbike before?' James asked, as the two teams and four training staff gathered.

Lauren, Bruce, Alfie, Ryan and one of the training assistants raised their hands.

'These are 450 CRF dirt bikes,' James explained. 'Almost indestructible. Top speed is only around a hundred and thirty kph, but they're built with high ground clearance and fat tyres that make them good on the kind of terrain we'll encounter in northern Syria. These are stock Hondas for training purposes, but for the mission we'll be making a few adaptations so that they're better able to carry equipment, and a custom gear setting to give us a higher top speed on open roads.

'To begin, I'd like those of us who've ridden before to help me get motorbike virgins used to the controls with a few gentle runs. After that, we'll take a little cross-country ride out to meet Tovah, who'll be taking the second leg of the afternoon's training.'

As the most experienced riders, James and Lauren took the lead, showing the others how to fit protective clothing and use the voice-operated microphones inside their helmets, before sending them off for an experimental ride back and forth along the single-track road that ran between the hostel's main admin building and the dock where supplies got landed.

With clear skies and a mid-afternoon temperature touching twenty degrees, James led riders with varying degrees of confidence along a dirt track. Kyle moaned that his shoulders hurt, and almost inevitably Leon, Daniel and Alfie earned James' wrath, first by starting a race, then by charging across a stream and soaking Kerry and Capstick.

The last kilometre took them down a steep dirt footpath to the edge of the strip where their plane had landed the day before. James opened his throttle and there was a deafening wail as the other bikes and their dusty riders took off in a plume of exhaust. After turning a gentle arc, they stepped off bikes on the part of the landing strip that jutted into the sea.

Tovah was waiting. She had a bright yellow pick-up filled with equipment, and a strange contraption on the ground. It looked like a two-man bobsled, but it had rubber wheels set wide apart at the back and a third directly below its bullet-shaped nose.

'Gather round,' Tovah said, as she thumped on the

carbon fibre tub. 'Here's a question for all of you. Imagine that you've driven or parachuted into enemy territory under cover of darkness. But getting away won't be so easy, because you've blown up the local oil well and rescued a pair of engineers. There's only one road in or out of the area, and there are half a dozen Islamic State-controlled checkpoints between your butts and the Turkish border. The question is, how do you get away?'

As Tovah spoke, she hit a plastic catch, opening up the tub. Within a few seconds she'd reached inside, pivoting and telescoping various carbon fibre struts. She clipped a Plexiglas screen to the outside of the tub, flipped out a control stick, and finally pulled a cord, activating a compressed-air cylinder that rapidly turned sagging nylon into an eight-metre aerofoil wing.

'The PX1 was jointly developed by US and Israeli special forces,' Tovah explained. 'It has a range of two hundred kilometres with a payload of a hundred and fifty kilos. It flies at around a hundred kilometres per hour if there's no headwind, makes less than eighty decibels of noise from a distance of fifty metres and since it's small and mostly made of carbon fibre, it's invisible to all but the most advanced forms of radar. Now, who wants to come for a ride with me?'

James stepped up and Tovah nodded.

'I thought he was too heavy,' Alfie noted.

Tovah smiled. 'He needs to be lighter for a hundred-kilometre mission flight,' she explained. 'But we'll get him off the runway for a little demo.'

James took a helmet and went to sit in the rear

passenger seat, but Tovah told him to go up front before helping him fix the five-point harness.

'This one's a trainer,' she told James, as she straddled a seat close behind. 'I've got duplicate controls in the back.'

James was looking at three smartphone-sized instrument screens and a dozen switches and buttons.

'Where are the rocket launchers?' he joked.

Tovah's voice came through a microphone in his helmet. 'Guess which one you press first?'

James saw a circular red button marked *start* directly in the control stick between his legs. When he pushed it there was a barely perceptible whirr from the engine above his head.

'Now go to menu, launch, take-off and set parameters to three and weather to good.'

James followed the instructions until the left-hand display flashed up a green *go* sign.

'Now gently raise the throttle lever, which is down on your right.'

The little propeller behind Tovah's head grew noisier as the microlight plane started rolling.

'Good,' Tovah soothed. 'Now all the way up, full throttle. And when you see sixty kph on the speed dial, you need to gently pull the control stick towards yourself.'

James wasn't exactly sure where the speedo was, but the microlight had been designed for special forces rather than professional pilots and the screen started flashing yellow as soon as he hit sixty.

'Is this too much?' James asked, feeling the control stick shudder as the nose began to lift.

'All good,' Tovah said. 'Now watch your altitude. The island rises, so unless you want to hit a hillside, you need to bank gently left once your altitude hits seventy metres.'

James had been on plenty of passenger planes, but the microlight was completely different, with the ground vanishing below, windscreen almost touching his face, open sides, tiny engine between his legs and the barest thrum from the propeller.

'This is *so* cool,' James said, banking the tiny plane as he looked down at the others and their motorbikes shrinking to insignificance.

'Now throw the stick left as hard as you can,' Tovah said.

'Seriously?' James asked.

'Do it,' Tovah ordered.

As James threw the stick a red square flashed on the screen and the words *Input Modified*.

'The PX1 has the same kind of avionics you'd find in a large airliner,' Tovah explained. 'If you aim for the ground, or try and do a barrel roll, the computers will override the input. You'll be taught how to fly in override mode and do things like emergency landings, but for regular flying, you take off, program your destination into the GPS, then sit back. The only time pilot input is needed is for landing, and take-offs from short or uneven runways where you need to correct for bumps.'

'It feels so natural,' James said, marvelling at the sunlight catching the ocean, but also feeling vulnerable in a way he never had in a regular plane.

'Now let's finish the circle and take her back to the strip.'

'Can I land it?' James asked.

Tovah laughed. 'We'd normally spend six weeks training special forces to fly PX1s. I've got to do you guys in four, but I still think it's best if *I* land until you've had a few goes in a simulator.'

'Can we master these in four weeks?' James asked.

'At least one hour in the air every day,' Tovah said. 'Double that with the simulators, and there's a fair bit of book learning and maintenance to learn too. So it won't be easy, but you seem like a smart bunch so I'm fairly confident.'

30. STRUCTURE

Four weeks later

James and Kerry had taken off from Gibraltar at sunset and flown a hundred and thirty kilometres east over the Mediterranean. A hop in a microlight was fun, but two hours were gruelling. Harnessed to an unpadded seat, blasted by wind and with nothing to do but occasionally check fuel status and confirm their positon to Tovah back at the summer hostel.

Dark came soon after take-off. Driving rain and lightning had the decency to wait until they were ten kilometres from the island. Having started with their flight computer predicting sixty kilometres of reserve fuel, unexpectedly strong headwinds had put this down to eighteen by the time Kerry sighted the glow of the hostel landing strip through her rain-pebbled visor.

'Shall I radio?' James asked, from the rear seat.

'Go for it,' Kerry said, as a great flash of lightning lit the sky and turned their fragile air-filled wing electric blue. 'The rain's worked through my suit and it's running down my neck.'

'Be glad to see the back of these tubs,' James said, then he pressed his communication button. 'Control, this is Golf Echo Five. I have visual on landing strip, approximately four and a half thousand metres. Are we clear to land, over?'

Tovah's voice came back through the headset, as James thought he glimpsed Ryan and Kyle's distinctive yellow wing a few hundred metres ahead through the rain.

'Negative, negative, Golf Echo Five. Your landing site has been redesignated. You are clear to proceed to landing site 4B. Can you confirm that you have coordinates?'

'Shit,' Kerry moaned to James. 'In this weather!'

Besides the giant tarmac runway, Tovah had selected several sites on the island, enabling crews to practise the kind of rough-terrain landings they could expect on the actual mission.

'Fuel coverage is down to fifteen kilometres,' Kerry blurted. 'Tell Tovah.'

James did what Kerry said, but Tovah gave the answer he was expecting: Fifteen kilometres' fuel was more than enough to make an attempt at landing site 4B, then circle back to the main landing strip if it didn't work out.

'She's taking the piss,' Kerry snapped.

To keep up competition, Tovah consistently ranked the pilot skills of the five Currents and five Crustys. Kerry consistently came up fourth or fifth in the rankings, but site 4B was her jinx. The first time she'd landed there, she'd had to make three attempts. First she'd come in too high, and on the second attempt a gust knocked her off course. The next time she'd had no problems on approach, but one of the rear wheels had hit a rock, ripping the tyre off its rim, causing jarred spines and minor damage to the underside of the carbon fibre tub.

'Just land on the main runway,' James suggested. 'Tovah will moan, but I just wanna get dry ASAP.'

But Kerry didn't share James' rebellious nature. 'I don't back off,' she told James. 'Program the coordinates.'

James wiped moisture off the little screen in the back of Kerry's seat and used gloved fingers to dial up the coordinates of site 4B.

'Can you see that on your screen?' James asked.

'Roger,' Kerry said, as she flipped a switch to take manual control for landing.

The microlight swept over the brightly lit main landing strip, close enough for James to envy two gliders already safely on the ground. James had never had to make so much as a second pass on any of thirty-plus landings, and suspected Tovah would have let him skip this extra challenge if he'd been at the controls.

Kerry gained height as the microlight banked right over the hill at the island's centre.

'Visibility's horrible,' Kerry complained, wiping her

visor for the thousandth time that night.

It was too dark to see anything other than the outline of the ground. 4B was a kilometre from the main landing strip. Less than a minute at flying speed. They skimmed over the hostel buildings at seventy-five metres. Kerry flipped on a xenon landing light in the nose as the unlit grass strip came into a view cut up by streaking rain.

James thought Kerry was a touch low as they approached. But the speed and angle were good and the wind – which could cause problems for even the most experienced pilot in a plane weighing less than its passengers – had temporarily died down.

'Forty metres,' James said, as he watched the strip come into view.

He leaned over slightly so that he could see Kerry's hands on the controls, and she seemed calm. It was only when they were thirty metres from touchdown that he realised that Kerry was too low, perhaps overcompensating for previous attempts where she'd landed hard.

He thought they'd ridden their luck, but five metres from touchdown, James heard a sharp crack. He glanced behind, realising that they'd clipped tree branches. The microlight pulled violently to the right. Kerry had to make a split-second decision, between throttling up and flying around or risking a sideways landing.

She chose full throttle, but the shattered branches had splintered the inflatable wing over their heads.

'It's ripped,' James shouted. 'You've gotta land it.'

The ground happened before James finished his sentence. The combo of Kerry applying power and uneven lift from the ripped wing caused the plane to jolt violently sideways. The undamaged portion of the wing caught the ground, ripping off the main strut holding the wing in place and sending the carbon fibre tub into a pirouette.

James' back jolted as the now wingless plane did a 180 before finally touching down. His neck snapped back and his knees banged the seatback. Kerry screamed as the tub hit the ground sideways, tearing up the grass strip and ripping off two landing wheels.

'Kerry,' James shouted, squeezing his intercom button. 'Mayday, mayday, mayday. Hitting hard!'

Sodden grass got ploughed up, acting as a natural brake. One of the carbon fibre wing struts snapped, showering James with shards. The screen in front of him went dark and he lost all sense of orientation until he felt a crash of shrubbery, followed by the tub smashing brutally into a tree stump.

'James, what's going on?' Tovah shouted.

When he opened his eyes, James realised that the carbon fibre tub had come to rest against a tree. He was strapped in, facing the ground. There wasn't any pain, but when he looked around the back of Kerry's seat, he saw her slumped unconscious, with her legs trapped inside the microlight's deformed nose.

'Get someone out here,' James shouted, as he fumbled with his safety harness. 'Kerry's hurt and I think it's bad.'

Down at the landing strip, Kyle and Ryan were just hopping out, high-fiving after a textbook landing. Lauren and Bruce had landed a few minutes before and stood under a canopy, folding their deflated wing, as Tovah charged out of the control hut.

'Mayday up at 4B,' she shouted. 'James and Kerry.'

Looking shocked, Lauren went for one of the dirt bikes and almost set off, before realising that Bruce was trying to mount behind her. While Lauren and Bruce bolted, Kyle hurried inside the hut and grabbed an emergency medical pack.

'You want me to come with?' Ryan asked, as Kyle pulled the pack up his arms and straddled the nearest bike.

'Secure the wings,' Kyle shouted.

A strong gust had already caught their ultra-light plane and Ryan charged over to stop it tipping as Kyle set off.

Bruce clutched Lauren's waist for dear life as the pair sped helmetless up a gravel path. They skirted the perimeter of the Olympic pool, then blasted up a narrow dirt track with only a small headlight showing the way. Bruce tried to console himself with the idea that Lauren was a professional driver, but kept getting horrible mental images of his skull smashing on trees she was missing by centimetres.

When they reached 4B, Lauren saw a gouge where the plane had landed. There was only moonlight and she had to pull up and aim her headlight to spot the tub resting against the tree, nose first.

'You OK?' Lauren asked, as she approached her brother.

James was stuck a metre and a half up. He'd got his helmet and harness off, but one of the wing struts had bent across his lap, stopping him from dropping out.

'I'm pinned,' James explained breathlessly.

Lauren reached under the tub, opened a flap and pulled a lever designed to shut off fuel supply to the engine. The buckled strut was detachable, but Bruce realised James would fall face first and his first-aid training kicked in.

'Before I release you, can you move your fingers and toes?' Bruce asked.

'I'm not paralysed,' James shouted anxiously. 'Just release the damned thing and start helping Kerry.'

'What about your neck?' Bruce asked. 'Do you have full movement?'

'She's unconscious,' James shouted. 'I'm fine.'

A second light came from Kyle's bike, and a Land Cruiser driven by Capstick was approaching via a wider path a couple of hundred metres off to the side. Bruce released the collar holding the strut in place, then worked with Lauren, helping James slide out, lowering him to the ground and helping him stumble away from the remains of the plane.

James was ghost white and panic breathing. He moved to help Kerry, but Lauren wagged her finger.

'Sit down until you've been looked at,' she ordered.

The tub rested nose-first against a shattered tree, with

Kerry slumped sideways in the pilot's seat. Bruce and Kyle decided it would be easiest to attend to Kerry if she was flat on the ground, so the pair grabbed the propeller mount and gently lowered the tub to the ground.

'Tree's a goner,' Kyle said warily, as he looked at a huge gash in the trunk and roots sticking out of the ground. 'But if it falls it'll fall away from us.'

As Kyle knelt down and unzipped the medical kit, Bruce leaned over Kerry and gently flipped up her visor.

'Is she breathing?' James asked desperately, as he tried to stand up.

'Sit,' Lauren ordered.

Kyle had found a big battery-powered lantern in the medical case and Bruce was delighted to see Kerry's eyelids squeeze as the light hit.

'Kerry, can you hear me?' Bruce asked.

'Yeah,' Kerry moaned.

'She's dazed but conscious,' Bruce shouted, as the Land Cruiser arrived at the other end of the strip. Alfie and Ning had also run all the way from the main strip. Only Tovah stayed back, because the twins were still up in the air.

'She's in a lot of pain,' Lauren said. 'You got oxygen in that case, Kyle?'

As Kyle prepared an oxygen mask and Bruce asked Kerry if she could feel her fingers and toes to make sure that she didn't have a spinal injury, Lauren clambered in the back of the tub and removed James' Styrofoam seat. They'd all been trained in assembling and disassembling the microlight planes and Lauren reached for a catch that would let Kerry's seat slide loose.

'Shall I free it?' Lauren yelled, as James disobeyed orders and stood up to watch.

Bruce squeezed Kerry's trembling hand, as Kyle gave her a few breaths of oxygen.

'It really hurts,' Kerry sobbed. 'I'm sorry I messed up.'

Bruce smiled. 'Don't be daft. Lauren's going to release your seat. You let me know if you want to stop, OK?'

As Capstick and McEwen ran in holding a stretcher, Lauren hit the catch. Kerry's legs were crushed inside the nose and Lauren was shocked as the seat shot back, catching her forefinger in a plastic seat runner.

'Shit,' Lauren shouted, grasping a pair of bloody fingers as she scrambled out of the tub.

While Ning rushed across to help Lauren, Kerry moaned gently as Bruce and Kyle raised her out of the tub and lowered her on to a padded stretcher. Capstick was a trained medic and he took control.

Once Kerry's helmet and boots were gently removed and an oxygen mask fitted, Capstick asked where it hurt.

'Cracked ribs I think,' Kerry said. 'And my right knee.'

Capstick took a pair of scissors and sliced Kerry's sodden flight suit from ankle to thigh. A couple of people gasped when they saw a gory mess around a badly displaced kneecap.

'I don't understand,' Capstick said, as he eyed a piece of black metal protruding from underneath the kneecap. 'Her suit wasn't punctured.'

Bruce shook his head. 'She injured her knee when she was ten,' he explained. 'They put metal pins in the joint. I guess they ruptured in the crash.'

Kerry craned her head up to look, and felt queasy seeing all the blood. 'I'm sorry I crashed,' she told everyone.

With Lauren busy getting her cut finger dealt with, James was free to move across and take Kerry's hand.

'You'll be OK,' James said, smiling slightly.

'No I bloody won't,' Kerry said indignantly, but she squeezed James' hand at the same time. 'Mission's in two days.'

'Everyone back off,' Capstick said indignantly, as he realised that Kerry was now encircled by people gawping at her wound. 'Kyle, see if there's something in that med case we can give Kerry for the pain. Bruce, you call Gibraltar coastguard. Tell them to send the nearest chopper for a medevac.'

31. MEDICAL

It was sunrise as James stepped out of a motor launch, wearing the bottom half of a flight suit, a baby-blue hospital-issue T-shirt and a precautionary foam neck brace. After thanking his Spanish captain, James yawned for a night's lost sleep as he strode up a gentle hill.

He sighted Tovah on her morning run, but she was beyond shouting distance. Everyone else was apparently sleeping off the drama of the night before. Too agitated to sleep, James stepped into the hostel's admin building. The bloodstained stretcher Kerry had been carried on and the medical pack had been abandoned just inside the door. He crossed to a large, slightly shabby office which he'd been using to plan the upcoming mission with Tovah.

A big map of northern Syria and its four-hundred-kilometre land border with Turkey was spread across two desks pushed together. Stickers had been applied, showing IS-controlled oil wells and green dots indicating possible locations of the two kidnapped oil technicians, based upon electronic chatter picked up by the UK–US-controlled Echelon electronic communication monitoring system.

But James was more concerned with his girl than his mission. He flipped his laptop open and placed a video call to the British military's medical emergency centre, which was based at RAF Northolt, west of London. He was pleased to recognise the duty lieutenant he'd spoken to several times overnight.

'What's the news?' James asked.

The lieutenant tapped at a keyboard for a few seconds. 'Patient Chang landed at 0607 hours. Taken under sedation to the Harlow military hospital where she's scheduled for surgery at 1100.'

'Great,' James said. 'Did you get all the scans and X-rays from the Spanish hospital?'

The lieutenant made a few more keyboard taps. 'Imaging's all here, along with some very detailed notes. Much better than you'd get from a British doctor.'

'Good stuff,' James said. 'What about her ward and stuff, so I can contact her, or send flowers after the op?'

'That will be assigned after surgery. If it comes through before my shift ends, I'll email you the details.'

'Fab,' James said, stifling a yawn as he hung up.

He spun his office chair and looked at the map, wondering how they could reconfigure the mission to deal with the loss of Kerry. But Tovah was a former

Israeli commando and microlight aviation expert, and Capstick was ex-Australian special forces. So while James was officially in charge of the rescue mission, he'd taken their advice at every stage and decided to set up a meeting with the pair after breakfast.

Missing a night's sleep was never a good thing, but based on past experience James found staying awake and toughing it out for a day a better option than sleeping half the day and throwing out his body clock. And if he was going to stay awake, he'd need caffeine.

There was a filter coffee maker in a staff lounge across the hall, but as James was about to step out, he heard a grunt and a sound like stuff falling off a table in the next office along. Since all the hostel buildings were dilapidated, he thought maybe a rat or fox had found a way inside. But the moan he heard next was entirely human and he leaned into the hallway to investigate.

The door of the next office was pushed shut, but the glass in the top half was only lightly frosted and James could see the outline of a couple kissing. Both about the same height, girl with long black hair.

'Mmm,' Bruce moaned, as he kissed the girl's neck.

James was intrigued. She was too tall for Tovah, the caretaker's wife was sixty and had grey hair and the female training assistant was practically a skinhead.

'Aww, shit,' the girl gasped.

James gasped too when he realised it was Ning.

'What happened?' Bruce asked anxiously.

'Your watch strap caught in my hair,' Ning said. 'It's fine.'

'Sorry,' Bruce said, as Ning started kissing him again.

James was torn. On one hand, Bruce was his mate, Bruce was a decent guy and he never seemed to have much luck with women. On the other, Bruce had been teaching martial arts on campus, which meant he was CHERUB staff, and since Ning was seventeen and an agent, this broke all kinds of rules.

James watched as Ning backed up and sat on a desk in the middle of the room. Bruce leaned over, kissing her, while running a hand through her hair. James wondered if Bruce would kick his ass if he burst in and told him to stop.

'I don't mind,' Ning said soothingly, as she clenched Bruce's bum. 'I *want* you to. I'm seventeen. I'm not a kid.'

Bruce backed off, running a tense hand over his face.

'I want to know what it's like,' Ning begged. 'I want you to be the one.'

Bruce sounded frustrated. 'It's not that I don't want to,' he said. 'But staff and agents is a big no. I shouldn't even be *kissing* you.'

'*Temporary* staff,' Ning said. 'You're going back to Thailand straight after this mission. Which isn't even a CHERUB mission.'

'Temporary staff is still staff,' Bruce noted sadly.

Ning seemed a bit upset, but then stood up and gave Bruce a kiss. 'Trust me to fall for the only guy on campus who *wants* to keep his dick in his pants.'

'It's not that I don't want to,' Bruce said. 'You're smoking hot.'

Ning laughed as Bruce held her wrist and looked into her eyes.

'You'll leave CHERUB early next year,' Bruce said. 'I'll sort you a job in Thailand and then we can be together without breaking *any* rules.'

'I'm gonna miss you *so* much when you leave,' Ning said. 'I could quit CHERUB.'

'You're still not eighteen,' Bruce reminded her. 'And besides, what's the rush? You've got the rest of your life to *not* be a CHERUB agent.'

'We'll have to Skype.'

'Every day,' Bruce agreed. 'I'm not going anywhere. I *really* like you.'

Ning smiled coyly. 'Since you're still refusing to deflower me, I suppose I could go for some breakfast.'

'We'd better not be seen together,' Bruce said. 'I've already had a few sly comments from the twins about the chemistry between us. You head off first.'

James ducked back into his office as Ning made a swift exit. As soon as she was out of sight, James stuck his head around the frosted glass door and found Bruce picking up the stuff he'd knocked off the table.

'Caught you!' James shouted.

'What do you mean?' Bruce blurted, shooting upright and looking mortified.

James smiled. 'Mate, I'm *bloody* impressed that you took the moral high ground.'

'Rules are there to protect kids from abuse by adults,' Bruce sighed. 'My pre-CHERUB years were no bed of roses, so I respect them.'

'Fair play,' James said.

'Are you gonna tell on us?' Bruce asked. 'I think technically, my employment contract with CHERUB expired when I flew here and signed up for an off-the-books mission.'

'Nah,' James said. 'You're one of my best mates and one of the nicest guys I know. Ning has worked as my assistant in mission control. She's clever, funny and I totally get why you like her. Plus, you're both nuts about beating people up. So basically, it's a match made in heaven.'

'Six-year age gap,' Bruce said, smiling awkwardly. 'You won't be the only one who calls me a cradle snatcher.'

'Screw the lot of 'em,' James said, smirking. 'I'll come visit you in Thailand when you're all settled down with four kickboxing brats and a family dojo.'

32. WEIGHT

James tried to stay awake by keeping himself occupied. Nobody else was around to clean up, so he went into the little sick bay in the admin building and restocked the medical pack. Thoughts turned to Kerry as he scraped her dried blood from the stretcher and nuked it with bleach spray, before setting it to rest against a wall. It was a quarter to eleven, so she was probably getting wheeled into surgery back in the UK.

Before heading out, James sighted a set of scales under a sickbed. He hooked them out with his foot and stepped on. 74.5 kilograms clothed was comfortably inside the target he needed to fly, so he allowed himself a slight grin as he crossed the hallway to the planning office.

Capstick sat at a computer, scanning through a fifty-page Echelon chatter report. Tovah had her feet up on the map table, playing *Monument Valley* on her Galaxy Note.

'So, what's the verdict?' James asked. 'Are we good to go without Kerry?'

Tovah sat straight as she spoke. 'Sickness or injury were always possible, which is why we built redundancy into our plans. Six is better than five, but we'll be OK, as long as we don't lose anyone else.'

James looked at Capstick. 'McEwen weighs over seventy-five kg, but you'd be OK.'

Capstick smiled and shook his head. 'Did my share when I was in Aussie SAS. I've got three young kids and a wife who'd flip if she found out I'd gone on a mission in Syria. And you're *not* poaching my assistants either. I've got twelve kids starting basic training in three days, and we're way behind with the prep work because we've been out here helping you lot.'

'You don't have to tell your wife,' Tovah pointed out, making Capstick shake his head and laugh.

'Done enough death-defying stuff for one lifetime,' he said firmly.

'Fair enough,' James smirked. 'So what's our configuration?'

Tovah looked serious. 'We'll go in with four planes, plus a spare for emergency. Kerry wasn't topping the flight rankings so the pilot roster stays the same. I'll pilot, obviously. Lauren tops the pilot training ranking by some distance, so she'll pilot, as will you and Bruce. Kyle as first backup, which means we now have three empty seats for our two hostages. The other thing to bear in mind is, at the range we're flying, the microlights can take a maximum of one-fifty kilos for two passengers. Yuen and Sachs are big fellows, so one will fly with me since I'm lightest. Since you're heaviest, James, you'll now fly back with an empty seat.'

James scowled. 'So all that dieting was for nothing?'

Tovah laughed. 'Kerry told me you've got a six-pack for the first time in years.'

'Bloody watermelon!' James moaned. 'I never want to see another slice . . .'

Tovah looked at Capstick, who was clicking through the electronic chatter report from Echelon monitoring. 'So we're trained up and Kerry's absence is a blow, but not a critical one. Question is, do we strike as planned?'

Capstick scrolled to a report summary on his laptop screen, and began reading aloud. 'No direct communications related to Sachs and Yuen detected for twenty-six days—'

'No surprise,' Tovah interrupted. 'All Islamic State groups use strong encryption.'

Capstick nodded. 'Which is why they've been monitoring routine Internet and phone traffic in areas close to IS oil wells. Electronic chatter indicates that a well twenty kilometres east of Al Hakasah was out of operation for several days last month. There's even a report of a Facebook message from someone presumed to work at the well saying *Back to work tomorrow. Chinaman came and fixed the console.* Which quite probably refers to Kam Yuen.'

Tovah smiled. 'Every bit of electronic chatter indicates that Sachs and Yuen are alive.'

Capstick nodded. 'UN estimates four million dollars' worth of black oil is being smuggled out of northern Syria every week. Guys who can keep pumps working are too valuable to kill.'

'Is there any indication of the kind of security detail Sachs and Yuen are travelling with?' James asked.

'Nothing,' Capstick sighed. 'They're probably travelling in some kind of lightly armoured convoy. Three to six armed guards. Anything more elaborate would make them conspicuous.'

'What about response time?' James asked. 'If a well stops working right now, how long until Yuen and Sachs reach the scene?'

'On average, we have one to three days from first chatter indicating that a well has gone out of production, to the arrival of the engineers,' Capstick said. 'Obviously, Sachs and Yuen can only be in one place at a time, so if two go wrong at once . . .'

James nodded. 'Presumably they'll try and fix the biggest well first. We're targeting big wells to improve our chances. Speaking of targets, Tovah?'

Tovah leaned across the map. 'The well at Tall Tamar is my suggested target,' she began, as she tapped a spot. 'It's a big well eighty kilometres south of the Turkish border. It's in the heart of IS-held territory, which means the military presence will be light.'

James was no military strategist and looked confused. 'Why light if it's at the centre of their territory?'

'Military forces usually defend the edges of their territory,' Capstick explained. 'There's no enemy to fight in the middle.'

Tovah continued. 'Israeli intelligence tells me that the border with Turkey is open. Main highways are damaged but passable and they can put me in touch with a driver who knows Tall Tamar and can find us a place to hide out until our targets arrive on the scene.'

'Why is Israel so keen to help free two British hostages?' Capstick asked.

Tovah smiled. 'Islamic State wants to destroy the state of Israel. Illegal oil is Islamic State's biggest source of income and taking out Sachs and Yuen will greatly diminish their capacity to keep it flowing.'

'Makes sense,' Capstick said.

James cleared his throat. 'So, just to be absolutely clear, you're both saying we can call in the drone strike on the well at Tall Tamar and get this mission started?'

Tovah and Capstick looked at one another and laughed.

'This is risky shit,' Tovah said. 'But we're as ready as we're ever gonna be.'

*

While James planned, the five Currents and three other remaining Crustys followed breakfast with a six-kilometre run around the island. The end point was a clearing on a seaside cliff, where the training assistants had dropped ten dirt bikes, ready for a ride back.

But as the sweaty runners got to the bikes, they realised that the training assistants had sabotaged them.

Back wheels missing, drive chains removed, and several bikes looked OK but didn't start for less obvious reasons. Race driving had turned Lauren into a reasonable mechanic and she helped to get Bruce and Kyle on the road. As she fixed a locked brake disc on a third bike for herself, she realised that the five Currents were all stumped.

Although the idea was for the presence of the five young agents to motivate the older ones, the teens were learning too and after four weeks, team rivalries had mellowed.

'You haven't got a clue, have you?' Lauren teased, approaching Ryan as the sound of Bruce and Kyle's bikes faded. 'We've had two lectures on bike mechanics.'

Ryan looked sheepish as he held up oily fingers. 'Maybe I didn't pay as much attention as I could have. I can see the back wheel is out of alignment, and the fuel line is loose, but I can't see where this tube goes.'

Lauren laughed as she tapped her fingers under the seat. 'There's nothing to plug it into because the fuel tank is missing.'

'Oh,' Ryan said dopily. 'So I won't be able to get this one going at all?'

Now Lauren was cracking up. 'Without a fuel tank, I don't think so.' She pointed at another bike. 'Take the fuel line from your bike, fit it to that one and put some air in the back tyre. You should be OK after that, but check the brakes just to be certain.'

Alfie spoke as Lauren turned back to the bike she'd just fixed for herself. 'Would you please mind helping out here?'

'Oooh, aren't we suddenly *so* polite!' Lauren said. 'What about when the seat broke in my plane and you said it was because I have *an arse wider than the Grand Canyon?*'

'Just joshing,' Alfie said. 'You know I think you're great, Lauren.'

Lauren tutted as she looked around. 'You're all hopeless,' she moaned. 'Daniel, it looks like the electronic ignition is loose and needs screwing back in. Ning, you need air in your tyres and clean the crap out of the jammed rear brake. Leon, that lightning bolt on the speedometer means your battery is flat, but you'll generate enough charge to start if you roll her uphill and push off from there.'

Lauren moved towards her own bike and gave it a kick-start.

'What about me?' Alfie asked.

'Your problem,' Lauren said, flicking up one cheeky eyebrow. 'My Grand Canyon ass is out of here.'

Lauren hoped Alfie would end up having to run back and was disappointed when she arrived and found Ning close behind, with Alfie riding pillion. Everyone headed into the gym, expecting Capstick and McEwen to be waiting, for some kind of gruelling combat workout. Instead, chef had laid out tables with lasagne, and two ancient rear-projection TV sets had been wheeled in. One was rigged up to a PS4 ready to play *FIFA16*, but Lauren was seriously excited to see the second one, linked to an ancient Sega Megadrive.

'Oh my god, it's *Ecco the Dolphin!*' Lauren blurted. 'I bloody *loved* this game when I was little.'

'The graphics are terrible,' Alfie noted. 'I didn't even realise they had computer games back in your day.'

Lauren turned sharply, hooked Alfie's ankle and dumped his ass on the padded floor. 'Too slow, young man,' she teased.

James clapped to seize attention before Alfie got his shot at revenge. 'Shut the hell up, all of yous,' he yelled. 'I've just had a conference call and I can confirm that the drone strike is set for tonight.'

A few cheers went up, but Bruce and Kyle looked more circumspect.

'Since you've all worked hard for the last four weeks, we're gonna spend the afternoon chilling out with food and video games. Enjoy, people!'

The mood was jovial as Lauren took the controls for *Ecco the Dolphin*, while most of the others went for the buffet table. James was surprised to find himself confronted by a very serious-looking Ryan.

'You OK, pal?' James asked, as he bit into a sausage-stuffed pepper that he'd just picked off the table.

'I was thinking about your mission,' Ryan said. 'I know you've got an empty seat now that Kerry's hurt.'

'Shit happens,' James said, blowing on the hot sausage. 'It's the nature of any mission.'

Ryan nodded. 'I was thinking.'

'Should that be cause for concern?'

Ryan smiled, but was irritated by James' interruption. 'I was ranked second on the flight training, behind

Lauren. I'm sixty-two kilos, so only slightly heavier than Kerry.'

James shook his head. 'I appreciate your enthusiasm, Ryan. But Ewart authorised you to come here and form a training team to help us five old farts get back into shape. The actual mission is off the books. Nobody with links to the British military or adult intelligence. No British-made equipment or identity documents. If we're caught, we'll say we're mercenaries hired by Sachs and Yuen's kidnap insurance. Not that it matters, because IS will scythe our heads off, whatever we say.'

'Kerry was your best Arabic speaker,' Ryan said. 'I'm almost fluent.'

'Tovah's fluent.'

'And if she gets hurt?' Ryan asked. 'And isn't she supposed to stay back and prep the aircraft?'

James seemed to take this on board. 'True. But we'll be packing up later and leaving for Turkey first thing. I'd have to write a mission proposal, get it by Ewart and get approval by the ethics committee. And even if I did all that, they're *never* going to approve the mission.'

'Why not?' Ryan asked.

'Because it can be done by adults,' James said. 'It's an *absolute* rule. CHERUB agents are never put in danger unless the mission can't be performed by an adult.'

'Screw CHERUB then,' Ryan said. 'I'll quit.'

James laughed. 'Ryan, give it up. We're fine with the team we've got.'

'James, *listen*,' Ryan said firmly. 'I want to help.

I've got four months until I turn eighteen. Chances are, I'll spend that time on campus twiddling my thumbs. This could be my last shot at doing something that matters.'

'You might also get killed,' James pointed out. 'This isn't a CHERUB mission. It's a full-on commando raid and you're *seventeen* years old.'

'I know what it is,' Ryan said. 'People younger than me died in the trenches in World War One. You can still join the British Army at sixteen, so if there was a war today I'd *still* be old enough to go fight on the front lines.'

James was torn. He'd worked with Ryan on the massive mission to bring down the Aramov clan. He had no doubt that Ryan was an outstanding agent, and while they could do the mission with five people, a sixth would make life easier and give more of a cushion if things went bad. But it stuck in James' throat that Ryan was still so young.

'I *want* this,' Ryan said. 'Think back to when you were my age. You weren't stupid, were you? You were capable of making your own decisions.'

James felt a tear well in his eye as he remembered his own last days at CHERUB. The sense of going back to being an ordinary person. The feeling that the most exciting part of your life was probably over.

'You'd be an asset to the mission,' James admitted, pulling out his phone as Ryan broke into a smile. 'So, as far as I'm concerned, you're welcome on my team if you quit CHERUB. But while this mission is off the books, the chairman of CHERUB is still *my* boss when I get back to campus. So you've got to speak to Ewart and make sure this is all OK.'

Ryan smiled as he took out his mobile and dialled CHERUB campus.

33. BEST

Instructors Capstick and McEwen were happy to let everyone chill out and play video games, but training had started in the water on day one, and after a PS4 FIFA tournament resulted in comprehensive victory for the Currents, consensus grew that the only proper way to finish training was to tip a hundred coloured balls in the swimming pool.

In Kerry's absence, Tovah joined Bruce, Kyle, Lauren and James on the Crusty team. And James laid down the rules.

'I don't want anyone else getting injured,' he yelled. 'So it's one twenty-minute round only and keep the physical stuff sensible.'

When the whistle sounded, Bruce and Alfie formed a new definition of sensible that involved getting into a massive ruck in the middle of the pool. It had to be broken up by Capstick diving in and, when it erupted for a second time, Capstick yelled, 'That's your lot,' and had both players red-carded from the game.

The eight remaining players duked it for the full twenty minutes. James was in his best shape since leaving CHERUB six years earlier. Kyle had tanned and was now fit enough to keep the pace until the final whistle blew, with a few nice moves along the way.

Bodies dripped as James put his neck collar back on and exhausted players watched the training assistants counting up balls at opposite ends of the pool. Shouts went back and forth as both scores passed 190, with just a few left in each dumpster.

'One-ninety-six, to the Crustys,' an assistant shouted.

At the other end, Leon and Daniel jumped for joy as the assistant counted one-ninety-nine, before adding a final five-point blue ball to make two hundred and four for the Currents.

'Still best,' Leon shouted, as he high-fived his brother.

Alfie couldn't resist getting right in Lauren's face. 'You still lose, Grand Canyon butt.'

As Lauren shoved Alfie in the pool, James grabbed his phone off a sunlounger and saw a message from Chairman Ewart Asker.

'Bad news, guys,' James announced, after he'd read the message. 'I'm gonna have to disqualify the Current team for fielding an ineligible player. Apparently Ryan Sharma is no longer a CHERUB agent.'

Ryan looked shocked, as Ning burst out laughing and told James to get stuffed.

Kyle put a friendly arm around Ryan's wet back. 'You OK there, pal?'

'Nervous,' Ryan admitted, as the twins scrambled out of the pool and approached. 'But I guess I got what I wanted.'

The twins hugged their older brother.

'So, I guess you two won't get kicked out of CHERUB before me after all,' Ryan said.

'Just don't go getting yourself killed,' Daniel said.

Leon nodded and grinned. 'I don't personally give a crap, but Theo will be devastated if you're not around to protect him from me and Daniel.'

Ryan's brain froze, as he realised he'd been wrapped in his own thoughts and hadn't given any consideration to the effect on his youngest brother if something bad happened.

'I'll be fine,' Ryan said unconvincingly.

'All right, people,' James shouted. 'We need to pack and clean up ready for tomorrow. If you're interested, we should have live video from Tovah's Israeli Air Force buddies shortly after eleven.'

*

The PS4 had been swapped for the video output on Tovah's laptop and all the gym lights switched off, intensifying the blurry night-vision image on the big telly. It was close to midnight and the Currents, Crustys, instructors and their assistants all sat on plastic pool chairs or sprawled across the padded gym floor in their nightwear.

'Wish we had popcorn,' Leon said.

A pilot's voiceover came out of the screen in Hebrew.

'He says the drone is one kilometre from target,' Tovah translated.

Controlled remotely from Israel and travelling at sixty kilometres per hour, the metre-long quadcopter drone skimmed over a village at two hundred metres, then tilted forwards and lost height as the outline of an oil derrick came into view.

'Here comes a shit storm,' Alfie predicted, blurting over something from the screen and earning an angry *shush* from Tovah.

James had sent detailed US satellite photos to the Israeli Air Force team controlling the drone. Blowing the well to pieces with a missile would be easy, but no repair team would visit a well that was obviously beyond repair. The trick was to cause minor damage, and to do so in such a way that it didn't raise suspicion of sabotage.

At fifty metres the well's control room came into view. It was a regular prefab site cabin, mounted on a metre-high steel platform in case of flooding. There was a light on inside and a man in the cabin seemed to glance around, as if he'd heard something.

The drone shot up slightly and hovered over the shed's fibreglass roof. The image on the big screen split and Tovah pointed to the right-hand side to explain.

'That's a high-resolution camera, underneath the body of the drone,' Tovah explained.

The right of the screen showed a metal arm sliding out of the drone. There was a slight rocking of the image as the arm dropped a coin-sized listening device on to the cabin roof. Then the drone skimmed a couple of metres along the rooftop, dropping another, as Tovah translated more commentary.

'They're testing the audio. Apparently they're getting a good signal from both devices.'

Ryan looked at James and spoke in a whisper. 'Will we get that audio while we're in the field?'

'That's the plan,' James said.

As the arm retreated inside the body of the drone, its remote pilot steered gently towards an electrical supply box at the side of the hut. It fed from a chunky mains cable and there was a backup diesel generator to compensate for erratic local electricity.

The drone pilot flew as close to the box as he dared and lowered a metal probe, the size and width of a man's lower arm. It was an electromagnetic pulse generator (EMP), capable of creating a super-intense magnetic field that would fry any electrical equipment within a ten-metre radius.

The sabotage would be obvious if the generator got left behind, but the drone's own sensitive electronics were also susceptible to being fried. So the EMP had been jerry-rigged with seventy metres of strong fishing line, which reeled out as the pilot took off.

After stabilising at seventy metres, the pilot activated the pulse. The image on screen flickered for several seconds. Everyone looked anxiously towards Tovah as the two remote pilots babbled frantically in Hebrew.

'What's happened?' James yelled anxiously. 'Did it just crash?'

'The pulse wasn't supposed to damage the drone, but it looks like it did,' Tovah explained. 'They're getting no signal from the drone. They're trying a backup frequency . . .'

Suddenly the image on the left side of the screen came back, showing the view from a healthy drone, hovering several hundred metres off the ground with the oil derrick visible below.

Tovah continued to translate the stream of Hebrew. 'They seem to think the drone defaulted to an automatic self-protection routine when the pulse interrupted their signal. All systems normal, but they're not sure if the cable linked to the EMP snapped.'

The right side of the screen came back to life, showing a length of cable getting wound around a motorised fishing reel. A half minute went by before the silver EMP probe came into view and the pilots started yelling triumphantly.

'They've got it,' Tovah translated unnecessarily, as the probe disappeared back into the drone's belly. 'Now they're going to do surveillance.'

The drone backed up and dropped down to around a hundred metres. From this range it was clear that several lights around the derrick had blown out. When the co-pilot zoomed his night vision on the hut, it showed smoke pouring out the door, while the man who'd been inside was around the back using a fire extinguisher to fight a small blaze in the supply box. A couple of guys in hard hats were running across from the main pumping station, desperate to find out what had gone wrong.

'They're elevating to fifteen hundred metres and switching the drone to autopilot for the ride home,' Tovah said, as she smiled at James.

'Godspeed, Mr Drone,' James said, as he strolled to a wall behind the TV and switched the gym lights on. 'We've got two planes booked for tomorrow,' he yelled. 'Folks going to Turkey for mission mayhem need to be on the tarmac at 0600 ready to load planes and equipment. Take-off is scheduled for 0700. The RAF plane taking the rest of you back to the UK is due at eleven. Chef and the training instructors will need help packing up, so the four remaining Currents need to eat breakfast and have bags packed and asses down by the pool by 0900.'

'Once James is out of here I'm in charge,' Capstick added. 'And I haven't handed out a punishment lap in almost a month, so you'd better not muck me around.'

34. BLACK

It had always been an off-the-books black mission, but up to this point James had been comforted by familiar surroundings: the hostel, old friends, CHERUB agents, training instructors. Now it felt real, strapped into an unmarked thirty-five-year-old Antonov freighter, complete with red-faced Slav pilot and patched-up bullet holes.

They were making a second pass at a dirt landing strip, five kilometres from the southern Turkish town of Viransehir. The first run had been abandoned after the front landing gear failed to drop, and seeing the co-pilot opening a floor plate and winding it down with a manual crank didn't inspire confidence.

Lauren had never had a problem flying, but she grasped Bruce's hand and grimaced as the deafening jet touched down, blasting great trails of grey dust over surrounding fields.

'I'll never complain about Ryanair again,' Kyle joked, as rusted landing wheels squealed to a halt.

After a flight that was windowless, unpressurised and unheated, James, Ryan, Lauren, Tovah, Kyle and Bruce threw off grotty blankets and undid safety harnesses as a rear cargo ramp lowered to the dirt. First sight was a pair of Turkish customs officers jumping out of a Toyota pick-up, while an airport maintenance truck ploughed through the jet dust.

'They hate Israelis,' Tovah told James.

'I don't speak Turkish,' James said, as he unzipped a document pouch and pulled a dozen-sheet cargo manifest.

'Me neither,' Tovah said.

The two officers strolled up the cargo ramp, stubbly beards and guns on hips. False passports were inspected and stamped. James passed a pre-agreed seven thousand euros with the manifest and earned a broad smile.

'Automobile parts,' the officer said in broken English, smiling at his colleague as he stamped and initialled each page of the manifest.

'Get your gear out of here fast,' the officer said. 'Use the side gate.'

Five microlight planes, along with weapons, micro-drones, body armour and everything else needed for the commando-style raid, had been packed into cardboard crates marked with Audi and Citroen logos, before getting vacuum sealed in thick plastic.

The team worked up a sweat, wheeling the crates

down the ramp and lifting them in the back of the truck. James rode with the cargo, while the others crammed into a ratty Mercedes taxi, getting a dust shower as the unmarked plane throttled up to leave.

The drivers deliberately steered clear of Viransehir's centre, speeding past streets of tiny homes and cutting through recently harvested fields. Their destination was an isolated, modern farm building, tall enough to house a giant cotton harvester and equipment used to pack raw cotton into truck-sized bales.

'You won't be disturbed here while you prepare,' the truck driver told James. 'The rest of your equipment arrived last night. I've also brought food and cooking equipment, as instructed.'

After getting everything inside, a scrum over the only toilet and a light lunch of yoghurt, bread and local soft cheese, the team began to unpack and make final preparations. Tovah checked all five microlights for transit damage. The package that had been waiting for them contained new grey inflatable wings, replacing brightly coloured ones designed to maximise safety during flight training.

While the olive-skinned and dark-haired Ryan and Tovah fitted and test-inflated the new grey wings, James and Lauren had to make themselves look more like Syrians. The pair had an uncomfortable – if amusing – experience dying their blond hair, with no hot water and a pressure hose designed to clean agricultural equipment. Then they stripped down to underwear and Kyle gave them a once-over with a spray tan, designed to darken subtly rather than turn them sunbed orange. The final step was disposable contacts, designed to make blue eyes brown.

Ryan didn't have much growth, but James, Kyle and Bruce hadn't shaved and the trio posed for selfies with four-week beards and James' dye job.

The next stage was to try on their kit. Combat boots, tight-fitting stab-proof undershorts and vests, then lightweight bullet-stopping body armour. They didn't want to appear too militarised, so the men got waterproof jackets, plaid shirts, cargo pants with lots of zip-up pockets for storing equipment. There were also combat helmets, only to be worn at the dangerous end of the mission.

Since they were entering Islamic State territory, Lauren and Tovah would have to wear double veils, full sleeves and gloves for their road journey.

'Why did I just dye my hair?' Lauren asked, as she peered out through the tiny slit in her veil. 'You can't even bloody see it. And I can barely see where I'm going.'

'You need to practise walking around in it,' Tovah said seriously. 'You'll stand out if you keep tripping over.'

James couldn't resist a wolf whistle as Lauren walked up and down the concrete floor. 'Man, you so sexy, sistah!'

Lauren snapped her head around. 'Shut up or I'll break your legs, asshole.'

'Not very ladylike,' James teased.

Lauren stripped back down to socks and undies as Bruce found the weapons crate. Since UK- or NATO-issue weapons were off limits, James had sourced East European and Russian weaponry, while Tovah had ordered up a selection from Israeli intelligence's arsenal.

'There's like thirty guns here,' Bruce noted. 'This is my kind of shopping. Oh man, there's Galils in here! I love these babies.'

Bruce pulled the Israeli-made, ultra-compact assault rifle out of its foam packaging, aligned the sight and played around with it for a few seconds to familiarise himself. He then added two pistols, a silenced large-calibre and a tiny .22 that fitted in his shirt pocket. Bruce then clipped on grenades, smoke bombs, an extendable baton, a Taser, several knives and a half-metre-long machete.

'Let's go kill bad guys!' Bruce shouted, as he expertly twirled the machete from hand to hand.

James laughed, but Tovah looked furious and faced Bruce off. 'I was in the Israeli Defence Force,' she said angrily. 'Saw a lot of shit, and it was always boys who liked guns too much who'd end up getting killed. More importantly, some of 'em almost got *me* killed.'

Bruce was startled as Tovah wordlessly stripped his arsenal down and reminded everyone that it was best if they each used the same kind of rifle and handgun, to minimise the amount of ammunition and spares they'd need to carry.

The atmosphere stayed tense as everyone packed up with spare underwear, rations, first-aid gear, and distributed the various electronic items they'd need for the rescue operation. When everything was packed, the final stage was depersonalisation.

Jewellery, mobile phones, wallets and anything else that would enable their identities to be ascertained had to be abandoned. After that, James broke the seal on cheap Casio watches, Chinese in-ear radio equipment and bulky phones with combined cellular and satellite coverage.

'Ten-day battery life, military-rugged, fully encrypted, for emergency use only,' James explained. 'Once you leave this room, you're anonymous. You don't call your girlfriend, check your e-mail or Facebook. And since this is a black mission, there's nobody to call but each other. As far as the British and Israeli governments are concerned, they don't know we're here and this mission does not exist. There's will be no SAS rescue team. No Apache helicopters dropping by to pluck us out of danger. If we die, we're just six unidentifiable bodies in a desert. And if we live . . .'

James dramatically pulled a rack of pills from his pocket. 'This is old-skool spy stuff,' he announced. 'Cyanide pill. Pop one in your mouth, bite it between your back teeth and you'll be dead inside two minutes. It's not pleasant, but neither is being captured, tortured and beheaded by Islamic State.'

Tovah shook her head firmly. Ryan looked anxiously at Kyle and Lauren. Bruce picked up the packet, but put it down without breaking off a pill.

'You're sure?' James asked.

Bruce cracked a big smile. 'Not dying, not getting caught,' he said firmly. 'Don't need suicide pills. We're all gonna be fine.'

35. BORDER

James picked up a final electronic chatter report just after 1400 hours. There were plenty of phone calls, e-mails and texts from workers at the damaged well, indicating that someone was coming to repair the damaged pump controllers within a day or two.

The bad news was that no signal had been received from the two listening devices placed on top of the well control room and the assumption was that they'd been damaged by the unexpectedly powerful EMP generator, or heat from the fire.

The team's ride south was a thirty-seat passenger coach, whose owner/driver used it for an irregular bus service into Syria. It arrived empty and they spent a quarter hour loading packs, microlight planes and partially dismantled dirt bikes into the luggage hold.

They set off with an exhaust plume some way behind

the latest emission standards. Rather than head straight for the border, the coach stopped on the edge of town, collecting four bearded men. A second stop brought a single Arab passenger, dressed in amber-tint sunglasses.

The first stretch south was through smallholdings and recently harvested cotton fields. As they got closer to the border with Syria, shelters made from scrap wood and plastic sheeting began to appear in fields along the roadside. These were occupied by some of the two million refugees who'd fled Syria during the civil war. The closer they got, the more refugees they found, along with wafts from their refuse heaps coming through the air conditioning.

The last stop in Turkey was at a properly organised refugee camp, with lines of identical white shelters marked with the Red Crescent logo. An Arab TV crew boarded the coach, followed by five smartly attired men. They filled most of the remaining seats as a group of porters rammed the cargo area with pallets of food and medical supplies, leaving the driver with a fight to lock down the luggage doors.

The border crossing was heavily manned on the Turkish side. Two dozen troops backed up the customs officers, with tanks parked on either side of the road in case of trouble. The queues of vehicles trying to enter from Syria stretched to the point where the road disappeared into haze, and the land on the Syrian side was a mass of human tragedies. People who'd been refused crossing and had nowhere else to go.

The Turks had less appetite to stop people from

leaving. The four-hundred-kilometre land border had eighty legal crossing points and many hundreds of illegal ones, making it almost impossible to police. James watched a pregnant woman scream at an entry guard as the coach got filtered into a single lane, with high wire mesh on either side. Signs in Turkish, Arabic and English told people to stay in their vehicles, while further along the awkward face of Syria's former dictator had been shot out of a *Welcome to Syria* billboard.

The bus got waved through the Turkish gate. The bearded men on the Syrian side had Kalashnikov assault rifles and tatty camouflage jackets from which Syrian Army insignia had been picked off. The two cars up ahead made no attempt to hide the Turkish lira notes they handed across with their passports.

Expecting the guards to board and inspect, Ryan pulled his green, fake, Turkish passport from his pocket and felt sweat bead on the back of his neck. But the guard gave the driver a friendly smile, then tipped his head respectfully at someone. The journalist? Or perhaps the well-dressed men who'd boarded with the medical supplies?

'Apparently we're in the right company,' Ryan whispered to Tovah, in Arabic.

The coach's hydraulic door hissed shut. The exhaust threw out another plume and they were inside Islamic State-controlled Syria, heading south on a highway built with oil money. Beyond the traffic queuing to get into Turkey, the countryside was deserted. Advertisements had all been ripped up or blacked out.

This was Islamic State territory now, but buildings showed scars from months of fighting and burned-out cars left black trails where they'd been pushed off to the side of the road.

Speeding fines clearly weren't on the Islamic State priority list. The coach's plastic trim rattled and squealed as they topped a hundred kilometres per hour. Cars skimmed past, going much faster than that.

A shambolic roadblock caused brief delay, but fifty euros and some banter from the driver did the trick. Shortly after, they left the highway, taking another modern road. A scary interlude came with a tunnel cut through a rock formation. There was no speed enforcement and no electricity to power the lights inside. The coach had to swerve as it rounded a bend and encountered two cars that had crashed head on and been abandoned in the dark.

Over the space of two hours, passengers came and went, the food and medical supplies got unloaded outside of a large hospital and the sun was failing as James pulled out a little GPS unit which calculated that they were now less than five kilometres from the sabotaged well at Tall Tamar.

The driver pulled into a village that had seen some heavy fighting. Modern concrete houses were sprayed with bullet holes and every metal roof had collapsed.

'This was a Kurdish area,' their driver explained. 'Anyone who wasn't killed would have fled north, and the battle damage means nobody has resettled the area.'

'So we'll be safe?'

'Stay out of sight, keep a man on watch. But you'll be safer here than anywhere else nearby. And most importantly, you have this.'

He gestured out of the window as the coach turned off-road, in front of a strip mall. The layout was like hundreds James had seen when he'd been at uni in America. A medium-sized supermarket, a gas station, a run of smaller shops and a pair of fast-food restaurants at the far edge of a two-hundred-car lot.

Unlike the ones James had seen before, the gas station had exploded, leaving a burned-out canopy and a crater with the exposed remains of underground fuel tanks. The supermarket had lost all its glass and been looted bare. There was a hole where a tank had driven in one side and out the other. The smaller shops had fared even worse, with three completely collapsed. The remaining cars were either burned out, or crushed so thoroughly that a tank crew appeared to have decided to have a little fun driving over them.

'It's perfect,' Tovah told the driver, seeing more than enough uncratered tarmac for the microlights to take off, while the shell of the supermarket made a decent overnight shelter.

Bruce, Kyle, Lauren and Ryan started diving into the cargo bay and dragging out the gear.

'Outstanding,' James agreed, as he shook the driver's hand and gave him five thousand euros. 'The other five will be paid through to your bank in Turkey when we get back.'

'What if you all get killed?' he asked, half joking.

'You'll get paid,' Tovah said. 'My people will see to that.'

As the coach headed off, everyone dragged the equipment inside the corner of the supermarket, to the annoyance of birds roosting in the framework beneath the twisted metal roof. Then James gave out orders.

'Tovah, Lauren, erect a canopy in case it rains. Then start assembling the bikes and planes. Bruce, Kyle, I want you to secure the area. Take guns. Find the motion alarms and spread them around. Also, when you're on the prowl keep your eyes out for a working tap. We've brought drinking water, but it would be nice if we can wash and flush a toilet. Ryan, how's your head for heights?'

'It's OK.'

'Great,' James nodded. 'There's a satellite dish I need rigged up so I can download chatter reports. There's also a UHF aerial, so I can have a go at picking up a signal from the listening devices on the control centre roof.'

'And what are *you* planning to do, boss?' Lauren asked, sarcastically. 'Put your feet up?'

'I'm going to get the generator running,' James said. 'Then if you're *extremely* lucky, I'll plug in the mini boiler and make you all a nice cup of tea.'

36. PUSSY

It was 5 a.m. and Bruce sat on a stack of plastic bread crates, beneath the bird-limed frame of what had once been a supermarket roof. Five screens glowed in the dark, reporting info from night-vision cameras, motion sensors, the unboosted UHF signal James had successfully retrieved from the well control room and a web browser, set to automatically receive chatter reports and any other info British or Israeli intelligence sent their way.

Bruce wasn't the kind of person who could spend long periods with his thoughts, and after checking all screens and refreshing the browser, he stood. The supermarket's floor remained intact, so Lauren and Tovah had created a waterproof shelter by stretching a tarp between two lines of looted metal shelving.

Kyle snored inside a sleeping bag as Bruce stepped

over, using a little black torch to show the way. Lauren clearly liked to be cosy, and Bruce smiled when he saw her snuggled on a bottom shelf with knees almost up to her chin. He crouched in front of their water boiler and rummaged through a box of dehydrated food packets. The writing on the packs was in Russian, so Bruce had to guess based on dodgy photos and feeling the hard lumps inside.

In the end, he tore a pack at random, removed the plastic spork inside and two-thirds filled it using the tap on their water boiler. The steaming packet burned fingertips as he stepped back to his position. He took an experimental sniff when he was back on the bread boxes and was pleasantly surprised by the aroma of chocolate and banana custard.

After a good stir and a few sickly-sweet mouthfuls, he was alarmed by a scraping sound in the next aisle. In theory, nothing human could get past the motion sensors without setting an alert, but something was going on because the birds up on the I-beams were chirping restlessly.

Bruce flipped down a set of night-vision glasses and ripped a silenced pistol out of a holster. He considered waking the others, but the sound wasn't far away, so he figured it was better to act alone.

Another crowd of birds flew up as Bruce rounded a corner. A black object moved just to his right. A powerful shoulder, reaching out to grab. Bruce swung and shot, the gun's muzzle silenced, but a bullet tore bone and flesh before splinters clanked noisily off the metal shelving. James and Ryan woke as hundreds of birds spewed into the air.

'Who's on guard?' Tovah asked, as she shot up and reached for her rifle.

'Bruce?' James hissed.

'I'm round here, I think I shot someone.'

Tovah was first to join Bruce in the next aisle. She shone a torch, lighting up Bruce's back and the body of a wildcat. Similar to a domestic cat, but half as big again, the shoulder Bruce had seen had actually been the back of a creature that had strolled in looking to catch an unwary bird.

'Great smell,' Tovah noted, as she looked at strands of brown and pink goo splattered up the back of the shelf. 'Bullet must have ruptured the bowel.'

'Nice shooting, buddy,' Kyle noted, pulling down the front of his trousers as he walked towards a bucket to take a pee. 'Everybody back to bed.'

'No,' James said firmly. 'Hopefully nobody was close enough to hear the shot, but we'll need at least a couple of extra people on alert just in case.'

'Agreed,' Tovah said, as she glanced at her watch. 'I'm game. I'll not get back to sleep now anyway.'

'Too tense to sleep much in the first place,' James noted, as he checked their cameras and motion sensor readouts. First light had just breached the horizon. 'I have to say I envy Sleeping Beauty here.'

There were a few smiles as James shone his torch on Ryan, who remained blissfully unaware, with his head buried deep inside quilted nylon.

'Bloody hell,' Tovah moaned, as she joined James looking at the screens. 'Bruce got the last chocolate and banana.'

'Tea or coffee?' Kyle asked, as he came back from peeing and wiped hands with a disinfectant wipe.

Lauren nodded as she wriggled off her shelf and sat up, rubbing her eyes. 'Who shot who?'

'Bruce murdered a cat,' Kyle explained. 'Easily mistaken for an armed assassin.'

'Explains the smell of cat mess,' Lauren noted, as she stood up.

James nodded in agreement. 'Bruce, you'd better throw that thing outside, before it turns all our stomachs.'

As Kyle made instant coffee, Lauren cooked up porridge and a big powdered egg omelette on a two-burner butane stove. Ryan kept snoozing as the others propped on bread crates and ate breakfast.

'UHF pick-up,' James noted, as he crouched over a screen. 'Sounds like someone's in the office.'

The laptop was set to record any voices picked up in the control room. Since the bugs were only producing a crackly backup signal and in Arabic, Tovah shuffled across and replaced the tinny laptop speaker with a set of headphones.

'Two guys bitching about their wives,' Tovah explained. 'Their accents are rough.'

'Meaning what?' Kyle asked.

'Workers, I'd guess,' Tovah replied. 'Waiting for their boss to arrive and give instructions . . . They're bitching about how they were told to be here super early, but there's nobody else there yet.'

'So something's happening today,' James said brightly.

Ryan opened one eye, then sat up when he saw Lauren, Bruce and Kyle looking at him. 'What?' he said, stifling a yawn. 'What I do?'

'Nothing,' James said, smirking. 'As someone who tossed and turned all night, worrying about this shit, I envy your ability to switch off and sleep for ten hours.'

'It's called being a teenager,' Ryan said, giving up on the stifling and going full yawn. 'Besides, what's to worry about? We're just camped out eighty kilometres inside the territory of a dangerous terrorist group who'll torture and chop our heads off if they capture us. Have all the eggs gone?'

Ryan felt pampered as Lauren dished him eggs and Kyle brought coffee. Tovah made him jump by slapping her thighs and yelling, 'We got tha shit, dudes!'

'What you got?' James asked.

'Boss man just arrived. Told the workers to get all the burned control consoles out of the hut, because they have to be cleared out before replacements arrive.'

'When?'

'There's a local electrician coming in to replace the burned-out supply box at 0800. Replacement consoles and the repair team are due in by lunchtime. Then the guy asked when they expected the well to be fixed. Boss guy said it depends on the engineers but hopefully they'll be pumping oil again by tomorrow.'

'Nice,' Bruce said. 'Looks like we timed our arrival just right.'

'Don't want to stick around any longer than we have to,' James noted. 'Be good to have a couple of cameras in the area before it gets too light.'

'We can land a pair of micro-drones on the oil derrick,' Tovah suggested.

'Won't they give the game away if they're spotted?' Ryan asked.

James got up and pulled a boxed micro-drone out of his backpack.

'Three centimetres, weighs less than ten grams, but has an HD camera,' James explained. 'Battery lasts three kilometres in flight, and transmits a picture for up to twelve hours. You just program coordinates, after which it's totally autonomous apart from the landing. In flight, it looks like an insect. Chances of it being spotted in situ are very slim and the plastic is corn starch, so after a couple of days the structure and rotors dissolve and the remaining components look like plastic scrap from a kid's toy or something.'

Ryan picked it out of the box.

'Don't break it,' James smirked. 'That's twenty-seven thousand pounds' worth.'

'Whoa!' Ryan said, thrusting the device back at James.

'Two will give us complete video coverage over the well site,' Tovah said. 'As long as it doesn't rain.'

37. SURRENDER

At 13:05, Ryan lay chest-down on stony ground, sixty metres from the oil derrick. Two bearded men stood outside, using a crowbar to open a crate. When the plywood side panel snapped free, a torrent of Styrofoam packing peanuts subsided to reveal the side of a reconditioned Offshore Marine control console. He looked across at James.

'See the gouge in the side panel?' Ryan said. 'I'd swear I saw that exact machine in Uncle's warehouse five weeks back.'

'Probably did,' James agreed, wiping sweat off his brow as Kam Yuen stepped down from the control cabin.

Kam had grown a wispy beard and walked with a slight limp. He spoke to the guys unpacking, as Gordon Sachs stood around the back talking to the electrician. But while the two engineers were running the repair job, a trio of bulky armed guards never let them out of sight.

'Heavy,' Ryan noted of Sachs. 'Ten kilos at least since the last photos we saw.'

But James was distracted, speaking to Tovah through his in-ear com unit. 'I have both targets in plain sight. Three bodyguards; Ryan and I have clean shots at all of them.'

'Understood,' Tovah said. 'Drone is in position. Lauren and Bruce are in position. Is it a go?'

Ryan looked across as James felt like his chest was being crushed.

'It's go,' James said.

Back at the supermarket, Kyle stood guard while Tovah activated a half-metre-square quadcopter drone, which Lauren had placed on the ground two hundred metres from the well. The rotors spun up and the craft took off for a pre-planned coordinate, thirty metres from the hut. While the direction was pre-programmed, Tovah used a targeting screen with facial recognition capability. It had picked out Sachs, Yuen, the electrician and the three bodyguards.

Tovah used the touchscreen to green-light the three bodyguards' faces, then pressed T on the keyboard to make them active targets. As soon as the *In Range* icon flashed up, Tovah pressed the Q and W keys simultaneously.

Out by the well, James instinctively covered head with hands as the drone skimmed overhead. Its final approach was the last thing the bodyguards ever saw, turning their heads as a pair of drone-mounted machine guns blew them apart.

As Sachs, Yuen and the electrician dived for cover, Lauren and Bruce moved from the opposite side of the derrick towards a line of parked vehicles. Bruce shot the driver of the equipment delivery truck through the head as he stood smoking a cigarette. The two Mercedes that Sachs and Yuen had arrived in had armoured glass, which made them more problematic.

As Lauren lobbed a grenade under the equipment truck, Bruce fatally shot the driver of the first Mercedes as he stood by his car making a call. The second car was an ML-class four-wheel drive people carrier. There was a reserve bodyguard asleep on the back seat, but the driver was at the wheel and got the engine running.

The tyres were reinforced, so Bruce targeted the passenger side window, taking chunks out of the bulletproof glass as the driver hit the gas. Bruce was almost through the glass, when he saw the bodyguard open a port in the side window and take a couple of shots back.

'Shit!' Bruce shouted, starting to run as the Mercedes roared off and the grenade under the equipment truck exploded.

While Lauren and Bruce dealt with vehicles, James and Ryan approached their targets.

'Come with me,' Ryan said. 'We've got bikes to get you out of here.'

James covered the electrician. 'Wrists together,' he shouted, as he pulled out a set of plasticuffs. 'Put these around. We won't hurt you if you don't give us shit.'

'Where's the boy?' Ryan asked, referring to a lad of about thirteen who'd been running back and forth helping the electrician.

'I think he went to the electrician's van to fetch something,' Sachs said, as he glanced warily at the assassin drone hovering fifty metres overhead.

As James pulled the cuffs tightly round the electrician's wrists, Ryan saw the boy dart out from under the hut and charge towards him with a screwdriver, screaming something in Arabic. Ryan tried to kick him down, but the assault rifle and a heavy pack threw his balance and the kid somehow got the screwdriver deep into Ryan's bicep.

Ryan roared in pain, feeling his arm lock up and his neck muscles spasm.

The boy kept running. James took aim and had a clear shot between the lad's shoulders that would have blown his heart out through his ribs. But the electrician was yelling, 'Have mercy for my son,' in Arabic.

James raised his muzzle a few centimetres and sent the boy scrambling for cover with a shot that went high over his head.

'Get back here, boy,' James yelled, in wretched Arabic.

'He's just going to cuff your hands,' Ryan added, as James fired another warning shot.

As the boy stopped running and turned, hands raised in surrender, Tovah's drone swooped in from behind and ripped him in half with a dozen bullets. James swore furiously as the electrician started screaming. James wanted to say something, but what do you say to a man who just watched his son die? All James could do was keep rolling.

'Bikes,' James spluttered, head spinning as he made hand signals for Sachs and Yuen to get moving. 'Ryan, can you take Yuen with you?'

'Haven't got much choice,' Ryan said, as Lauren and Bruce came running in from the side.

'Mercedes got away,' Bruce said. 'Why'd Tovah shoot the boy?'

'How the hell should I know?' James roared furiously. 'Let's get out of here.'

There were four dirt bikes hidden at the roadside. Smoke from the burning truck cut the air as James grabbed his bike and eyeballed Sachs.

'You been on a bike before?' James asked, as Bruce and Lauren kick-started theirs.

Sachs shook his head anxiously.

'You let *me* ride,' James said. 'Sit up straight, put your arms around my waist. Tight, but not so tight that I can't breathe. OK?'

'There's roadblocks,' Sachs protested. 'We're eighty kilometres from the border.'

'You think we're *that* dumb?' James said irritably. 'Just do what you're told. We need to get out of here.'

The drone stood sentry overhead as Lauren and Bruce sped off across country. Ryan and James made more gentle starts, so as not to terrify their greenhorn pillion passengers.

'Tovah,' James said, shielding his view to avoid a final look at the teenager. 'We're heading out. Bruce said one Mercedes got away, so they could have radioed for help. What can you see?'

'Nothing so far,' Tovah said. 'Drone only has two minutes' fuel. I'm about to crash it into the control building.'

James hoped the cuffed electrician would have had sense enough to start walking before the drone crashed. Riding with Sachs' bulk was hell. His weight made the back wheel slam down on every bump. James had calculated that the 5km ride back to the supermarket would average 30kph and take around ten minutes, but even half that speed was making the bike unstable and Ryan was having the same problem with Yuen.

Back at the supermarket, Tovah made final checks on the planes, while Kyle laid out explosive charges, so that Islamic State didn't get hold of high-tech equipment that was too heavy to fly home. As he laid a charge under the makeshift control desk they'd built using crates and a door, he noticed something on one of the local surveillance cameras.

'Shit,' Kyle shouted. 'Tovah, get over here.'

'I'm rechecking the wing pressures,' she said irritably. 'What's the problem?'

'Dust trails,' Kyle said as he zoomed a surveillance image. 'Looks like a pick-up truck with a big gun on the back and a couple of cars.'

Tovah ran so fast that she skidded and almost turned

her ankle. 'How the hell can they know we're here?' she yelled.

'Maybe someone saw the bikes leave,' Kyle suggested. 'Or heard Bruce's shot.'

'Doesn't matter how,' Tovah said, as she picked up her assault rifle, then pulled a radio off her belt to speak to the four riders on their com units. 'We've got incoming,' she warned. 'Get here as fast as you can and don't be surprised if you have to shoot at something when you do.'

38. CLUSTER

Two pick-ups headed towards the mall from the east. A Toyota, closing at speed with six guys bouncing in the back, and a Mitsubishi double cab, with five plus driver inside and a 20mm anti-aircraft cannon welded into the rear compartment. From the west the bulletproof M-Class Mercedes threw up a trail of dust, with a white van right behind.

'Planes are ready to roll,' Tovah told Kyle, as she stood inside the supermarket stuffing things into her backpack. 'I'm gonna hold these dudes off. You run communication, OK?'

'Right,' Kyle said, as Tovah swapped her headset for an in-ear com unit, snatched her assault rifle and dashed through the remains of plateglass windows.

The Mitsubishi crawled tentatively into the parking lot as Tovah took cover behind the rubbled side wall of a florist's shop. The rear cab door flung open and two guys jumped out, keeping low as they headed towards the fuel station. The rest drove deeper into the lot.

Tovah watched through her rifle sight, seeing the confused body language of a team with nobody giving orders. At the same time, the Toyota had circled to the rear of the mall. It stopped by an exit on to the main road and the men in the back started jumping out.

Lauren's voice came over the intercom, the engine of her speeding dirt bike in the background. 'Bruce and I have the mall in sight, over.'

'Circle around and deal with the Toyota,' Tovah said. 'Be aware there are two hostiles near the gas station.'

'Roger that,' Lauren said.

As the Mitsubishi slowed down, Tovah turned the polarising filter on her gun-sight to cut out the reflection coming off the windshield. The instant she had a clear view, she aligned the crosshairs with the driver's nose and took a shot.

The truck jerked forwards as his head exploded. Doors flung open and panicked guys jumped out. IS clearly sent its best troops to forward areas, because these were guys in their fifties, armed with careworn Kalashnikovs, plus a kid of about sixteen.

The teenager was first to die. A shot in the gut and another through his head as he crumpled. Tovah was aware of shots coming from the guys getting out of the Toyota, but her position was well covered and only a freak ricochet could cause a problem. The old guys getting out the other side were trickier, because the pick-up gave them cover.

Tovah dug into her trouser pocket, pulled the pin on an anti-personnel grenade, then bobbed up and made a ground-skimming throw that ended with the grenade bouncing off the underside of the truck. The grenade was filled with hundreds of metal flechettes and screams erupted as the blast lifted the back end of the Mitsubishi, and knocked the men on its opposite side unconscious.

Tovah bobbed up, thinking she might be able to take the vehicle and use the big rear-mounted gun, but the hot metal had also punctured the fuel tank. The rear end was ablaze and she didn't fancy being this close when strands of 20mm ammunition clips heated up.

As Tovah scrambled out the back of the crumbled florist shop, Lauren and Bruce jumped off their bikes and took cover, squatting by the mall's perimeter fence, fifty metres from the Toyota and five middle-aged guys taking sporadic shots at Tovah's position.

Lauren was a good shot, but she felt sick as she crashed down in the dirt beside Bruce. 'You ever killed anyone before?'

Bruce shook his head nervously. 'There's a lot of them and a few of us. Gotta make it count.'

Lauren took a one-knee firing position and looked through her scope. 'I'll work from left.'

'Roger that,' Bruce said. 'Ready?'

'As I'll ever be.'

Lauren felt grim as she looked through her sight. Greying hair, sweaty necks. Someone's husband, someone's granddad. She shot two guys between the shoulder blades, while Bruce did exactly the same. The fifth target was in front of the truck, but seemed to think the bullets were coming from Tovah's direction and actually stepped out of cover and right into Lauren's field of view. It was so easy it seemed unfair.

'Shit, yeah,' Bruce shouted, as he whacked Lauren on the back. But she was shaking and he realised he'd hit the wrong tone. 'You OK?'

'No,' Lauren said, choking back tears. 'No I'm not.'

Bruce realised he needed to take charge. They were less than two hundred metres from the supermarket, so it seemed pointless going back to the bikes. 'Let's roll,' he said, as he rubbed Lauren's back. 'You'll be fine, mate.'

Tovah came enthusiastically over the intercom. 'You kiddies can shoot!' she yelped. 'Kyle, what's the situation with incoming?'

'James and Ryan are almost here,' Kyle said. 'Looks like the Mercedes and the van didn't like what they've seen and are presently keeping their distance.'

'Copy that,' Tovah said as she started running in the open towards the Toyota. 'There's still two hostiles out by the garage.'

'Will they attack after we just wiped their buddies out?' Bruce asked.

By this time, Tovah had jogged to within speaking distance, and could see that Lauren was shaken up. 'Our wings are an eight-metre target and one shot will deflate them,' Tovah said. 'We can't have *anyone* close enough to take pot shots.'

Bruce nodded, but Lauren seemed spaced out. 'Get back inside with Kyle,' Bruce told her soothingly. 'Get your plane running and leave when you get the all-clear.'

'Right,' Lauren said, unable to keep her eyes off the dead bodies.

'You and me drive,' Tovah told Bruce, glancing about warily as she opened the driver's door of the Toyota, and pleased to spot a key in the ignition.

'I've had my eye on them,' Kyle said, over the com. 'They're around the garage. They've definitely not made a run for it.'

'Roger that,' Tovah said, as Bruce jumped into the rear of the pick-up.

The garage was five hundred metres, heading away from the supermarket. The drive was a straight line, interrupted only by a couple of speed humps. Tovah kept super low, peeking over the dashboard as she rammed the accelerator. In the distance, she heard James and Ryan's dirt bikes approaching from the opposite side of the supermarket. Then she jolted in fright as a bullet shot through the cab, shattering both front and rear screens.

'Crap!' Bruce shouted, shielding his face as glass showered the open rear compartment.

Another shot hit the engine block as Tovah threw the pick-up sharp right and stopped close by the garage's buckled roof.

'One up top,' Bruce gasped, bashing his shoulder as his body slammed the pick-up's metal casing.

As Tovah scrambled out, Bruce bobbed up and took

three quick shots. The last one hit a guy crouching in the buckled roof canopy. It was only a shoulder shot, but Tovah scrambled around the side of the bombed-out gas station and shot him through the chest before he'd landed.

'One down,' Tovah yelled.

They circled the canopy, meeting up at the far side. The small garage shop was levelled and offered no hiding place. They were both mystified until Bruce spotted the holes where the underground fuel tanks had blown open.

'Can't be anywhere else,' Bruce whispered, as he pulled a grenade and rolled it into a hole.

'*Laa, laa,*' a small figure shouted as it clambered out of the hole. Not even a teen yet, yelling the Arabic word for *no*.

Tovah lined her pistol up to shoot, but Bruce saw that the figure was unarmed and knocked Tovah's hand, sending the shot ripping through the canopy.

'You already killed one kid today,' Bruce shouted.

'I targeted someone I saw running away,' Tovah yelled furiously. 'Drones don't recognise surrender gestures.'

As Tovah backed up, Bruce yanked out the small body, scrambled a few metres and dived for cover. Fortunately, the buckled canopy absorbed most of the blast, and Bruce's combat helmet took the sting out of a fist-sized chunk of concrete.

With ears ringing and dust subsiding, Bruce thought about the boy trapped beneath him. Why had he taken a dumb risk? What if the boy was about to pull the pin on a grenade?

Bruce flipped into combat mode, grasping the boy's arms. If he was unarmed, Bruce figured there was no harm in kicking him up the arse and sending him on his way. But when he rolled the boy on to his back, there was a rip in his grubby turquoise T-shirt. Beneath the rip, tightly strapped bandages had slipped down, exposing a boob.

'You're a girl,' Bruce blurted.

'Come on,' Tovah shouted to Bruce. Then to Kyle on the com, 'We're clear to fly. Start launching.'

The girl looked tearful and started babbling in Arabic. 'I don't understand,' Bruce said. 'You're no threat to us. You can leave.'

Tovah shook her head. 'She's saying she can't be seen with her ripped shirt. She says if they find out she's a girl, the religious police will torture her, and force her to marry a soldier.'

Bruce gawped. 'How old are you? Who looks after you?'

Tovah looked emotional as she pointed towards the back of the garage. 'She's twelve. Her older brother looks out for her, but I think we just killed him.'

'Bloody hell!' Bruce shouted, as Kyle's voice came back over the com.

'Looks like more vehicles closing in,' Kyle said. 'You need to get back here. Repeat, back here *now*.'

'We can give you a T-shirt,' Tovah said in Arabic, grabbing the girl's hand as Bruce started running towards the supermarket. James was out in the car park, clearing some debris from the fighting as Lauren drove her microlight out of the supermarket, with Sachs' chunky frame squeezed in the back.

'Good to go,' James shouted, giving his sister a double thumbs-up.

As Lauren put her lightweight plane to full throttle and rattled off across the parking lot in one direction, Bruce, Tovah and the Syrian girl sprinted towards the shed. Before Lauren was even off the ground, Ryan rolled out of the supermarket, with Yuen as passenger. His heart thumped as he ran through checks he'd done fifty times before at the hostel. Fuel, navigation, flaps.

'All set,' Ryan said, taking a glance back at his nervous passenger and forward at Lauren leaving the ground, before going full throttle for take-off.

The next two planes were some way off being ready for take-off.

'Who's this?' James asked, surprised to see Tovah with a raggedy Arab accomplice.

'She needs a T-shirt,' Bruce said. 'Tovah's probably closest to her size.'

'No,' Tovah said firmly. 'We'll fly her out. She's not safe here without her brother looking after her.'

'There's no empty seat,' Kyle said.

'Three planes,' Tovah said, pointing across the hall. 'We brought a backup. I had to take some parts off to replace a faulty navigation unit on Ryan's plane, but I can fly eighty clicks in daylight without one.'

The building shook as something hit the front wall.

'That's a twenty-millimetre shell,' Tovah said, glancing

at the screens. 'I'd say they're wary of coming close after we took the first wave out, but it looks like they're gonna be shooting from a distance. James, you fly with Kyle. Bruce, you take the girl.'

'Maybe she'd be more comfortable with you,' Bruce suggested. 'Being female and speaking good Arabic.'

'I'll be last out in case any of you have a problem on take-off,' Tovah said. 'And the faster she's out, the safer she is.'

'It's too hairy out there for my tastes,' James said, casting a wary glance back at the monitors, as two more 20mms shook the building.

As James and Kyle pushed their little plane towards the exit and clambered inside, Tovah spent a few seconds explaining to the girl that Bruce was going to fly her to a safe place and that they would find a good family to look after her.

'What's her name?' Bruce asked, as he realised that nobody had thought to ask.

'Zahra,' the girl said.

Bruce smiled. 'I'll try and be a good pilot,' he said warmly.

Zahra smiled, even though she didn't understand much English. James powered up his engine as Kyle rolled their plane out into sunlight.

'It's cold up high,' Tovah said, as she handed Zahra a sleeping bag they'd been planning to leave behind. Then she helped the girl fix her five-point harness.

Kyle was about to board James' plane when he remembered the detonator in his shirt pocket.

'If you're leaving last,' Kyle explained, as he handed it to Tovah.

As Kyle buckled up behind, James upped the throttle and trundled out on to the tarmac. More 20mm shells were thumping the far side of the supermarket and a vehicle had parked up, shielding behind the two fast-food restaurants at the lot's far end.

'Full throttle,' James announced, deciding that the risk of staying on the ground for an extra minute was greater than the risk of not making final checks that Tovah was sure to have done at least twice already.

Bruce throttled up before James was even off the ground and there was now small ammunition coming towards the planes from behind the garage.

'Tovah, don't hang around,' Bruce warned over the com, as he pulled up the flaps, following James and Kyle into the air.

Tovah was out on the concrete within seconds of Bruce taking off. As she hit the throttle she heard shots coming from all sides and tried not to think about the frailty of her air-filled wing. As she neared take-off speed, she felt something hit the runway in front, then bounce up and smash the front wheel. As an instructor-level pilot, she instinctively raised the flaps slightly, so that the nose lifted and the plane continued its take-off balanced on two rear wheels.

Another half-dozen shots ripped off as she finally got up to speed and since she was flying solo and manual, she put the little plane into the steepest climb that she dared. James and Bruce's craft were visible, their grey wings merging with the colour of clouds high above.

Tovah took one last glance back at the supermarket as she pulled the remote detonator, waited a few more seconds to be certain that the explosion vortex didn't suck her in. Then she pressed a button and blew the whole place to hell.

39. TENTS

Cruising at eight hundred metres, cold air blasting from the east and the autopilot making corrections with the flaps. The world seemed beautiful from up here, but Lauren couldn't get the bodies out of her head. She'd killed a man on her first mission, aged eleven, but that was a him-or-me. This had been like some weird one-sided video game.

All that CHERUB training, versus some grandpas. Lauren felt naive now, jumping at a chance to relive old times when James called her up. Now she wanted to get back to Texas. The little house she shared on the edge of a racetrack. Rat making scrambled eggs in his mechanic's overall. Kissing her neck and saying how much he loved her.

Touchdown was seven hundred metres inside the Turkish border. An unfinished eight-lane highway, leading to a border crossing planned before Syria's civil war. As Lauren flicked off autopilot for landing, the dirty white ground west of the road emerged as a neat grid of refugee tents. As Lauren took the plane down, Sachs looked down into the refugee's world: standpipe queues, trash piles and street football.

Tovah had taken off last, but without the weight of a passenger she'd arrived first, pulling off a delicate landing on undamaged rear wheels. Bruce had touched down a minute before Lauren, though she didn't understand why Zahra was climbing out the back.

'All good?' Tovah yelled, jogging alongside as Lauren locked her ground brake and ripped off her helmet.

'Clear run, no bother,' Lauren said, as she straddled out.

Sachs was a big man, and while gravity had helped him bed in, he tilted the little plane as he tried getting out. Lauren and Tovah tugged from either side, and Sachs burst out laughing as he popped out.

'I was proper wedged,' Sachs beamed, then moaned in pain as his knee gave way to cramp.

'Whoa,' Lauren said, grabbing the big man's arm.

When Sachs' helmet came free, Lauren saw red eyes and tears streaming down his face. Arms matted with thick hair pulled her into a sweaty hug.

'Rescued by a beautiful young lady,' Sachs sobbed. Then roared, 'You little hero!'

'It's OK,' Lauren said, smiling helplessly as Sachs thumped her on the back.

'I thought they'd kill me,' Sachs said. 'Cannae wait to

get a pie, a pint and a round of golf!'

The greater good, Lauren thought to herself. But she still pictured dead bodies as Ryan and Yuen made a bumpy touchdown. Yuen was another happy camper, making his own way out and getting into a triumphant man-hug with Sachs.

Ryan wasn't doing so well. His right arm seemed paralysed and his hand was dark red from blood that had run down inside of his shirt and soaked his cuff. After removing his helmet one-handed, Ryan squatted down and Lauren saw that he was pale and breathless.

'OK, pal?' Lauren asked, as she rushed over.

'Been better,' he confessed.

Ryan had told everyone inside the supermarket that his arm was OK and they'd been too busy to do anything but take his word. Now, Lauren studied a gory mess around his upper arm and realised that the screwdriver he'd been stabbed with had snapped at the handle, leaving the metal shaft sticking out of his bicep. It hadn't caught a vein or artery, but Ryan's pallor suggested that he'd lost a lot of blood.

Lauren yelled at Bruce to find a medical kit, as she pulled a hunting knife holstered to her belt and slit Ryan's shirt open, just above the wound.

'Where's your stab proofing?' Lauren asked.

'I took it off in the night,' Ryan said. 'It's tight, I hate it.'

Bruce had found a first-aid kit and overheard as he closed in. 'Lucky you quit CHERUB,' he noted. 'You'd get at *least* two hundred punishment laps for skimping on protective gear.'

Ryan winced as Lauren pulled the slashed shirt over Ryan's hand, exposing a well-muscled but bloody arm.

'I'm not pulling out the screwdriver in case it spurts,' Lauren said. 'He needs a proper doctor.'

James and Kyle were ten metres from touchdown as Bruce and Lauren carried Ryan towards a waiting minibus.

The refugee camp was separated from the abandoned highway by fifty metres and a wire fence. But the fence had breaks and curious kids who'd spotted the gliders landing were edging closer.

'We have to ship out,' Tovah shouted, as James and Kyle hopped up. 'The last thing we need is a brat with a camera phone. Get your wings deflated and your planes in the back of my truck.'

'You heard the lady,' James shouted, as Kyle opened the valve to start deflating their wing.

Sachs and Yuen helped out, collapsing the carbon fibre strut work of Lauren's plane, then lifting it into the back of an unmarked truck. Kyle and James lifted their plane in last, giving some of the others a noisy shove to make room.

'That's the lot,' James told Tovah, as he glanced back along the road to be certain. 'Not a bad result.'

'I guess it's goodbye,' Tovah said, as Kyle grabbed a swinging handle and pulled down the metal shutter on the back of the truck.

James hugged Tovah and cheekily whispered, 'Free Palestine,' in the Israeli agent's ear.

'Screw you,' Tovah said, smirking. 'Keep safe and give Kerry my love.'

Bruce was attending to Ryan in the back of a waiting minibus. Sachs and Yuen were climbing in through the little bus's side door, but Zahra stood awkwardly in the middle of the tarmac.

'Are you taking her?' James asked Tovah, as she climbed into the driver's side of the unmarked truck.

'What am I gonna do with her?' Tovah asked, as she pointed towards the increasing gathering of kids. 'There's a refugee camp right there.'

James considered this as Tovah started the engine and pulled off. He wasn't an expert on Syrian ethnicity, but knew that most of the refugees camped in northern Turkey were Kurds, and since Zahra and her brother had been with Islamic State, she most definitely wasn't.

'We can't leave her here,' James told Kyle, before dashing across and grabbing Zahra's arm.

The girl looked back, frightened and uncertain. Two strange men with assault rifles and body armour, marching her towards a waiting minibus, as Tovah roared off in the truck. She seemed better when she got inside and sat next to Bruce. Ryan was the only one who spoke good Arabic, but he was sprawled out in the rear, babbling.

'I should have worn the stabby vest,' Ryan said, grinning. 'I'm sorry, James Adams. Mr Mission Controller . . . Sir, yes sir!'

'Gave him a morphine shot for the pain,' Lauren explained, clambering into the driver's seat, as James pulled shut the sliding side door. 'I'll drive, if we're all in?'

'Sure you're a good enough driver?' James teased, as he took the front passenger seat.

'Oh you're witty,' Lauren said, feeling more like herself now that she was among friends and had stuff to do. 'According to the mission plan, there's a private clinic five kilometres from here. Twenty-four hours, with doctors that speak English.'

'Sounds like a plan,' James said, looking behind as Lauren hit the gas pedal. 'Everyone else OK?'

Sachs and Yuen nodded happily. Bruce and Kyle were stripping off weapons and body armour. Zahra didn't look too bad for a kid who was in a strange country, with strange people, including the one who'd shot her only living relative two hours earlier.

James opened the glove box and was pleased to find British diplomatic passports, for everyone except Zahra. Plus a plastic wallet containing a selection of mobile phones and personal effects that they'd abandoned before setting off the day before.

After taking his phone and passport and passing the wallet back to the next row, James dialled the control room on campus. John Jones answered.

'We're all out, one moderate injury and we picked up a stray,' James said. 'We'll take Ryan to the clinic. How's our ride out looking?'

'RAF have a jet on standby in Cyprus which can be with you in ninety minutes,' John said. 'Now Sachs and Yuen are safe, I'll contact MI5. Hopefully Uncle and his associates will be behind bars before he hears about the rescue.'

'Nice,' James said, as Lauren turned the minibus off of the unfinished highway, pulling into a tight gap on a busy local road. 'You might as well get that plane dispatched from Cyprus. I'll stay back here if Ryan needs to stay in hospital, but there's no reason everyone else can't head straight home.'

'Roger that,' John said. 'It's a pity this is an off-the-radar mission you know, James. This could have done your career a lot of good.'

James cracked a wry smile. 'I'll *still* have your job in two years, boss,' he joked. 'Chairman of CHERUB before I turn thirty-five.'

'You can *have* my job,' John grunted. 'Ning's here with me in the control room, she's got a call to patch through.'

There was a bit of fiddling at the other end, before James reached behind and handed his phone to Kam Yuen.

'It's for you, buddy.'

'Hello?' Kam said curiously, then burst into tears when he heard his daughter's voice. 'I'm so happy, baby,' he blubbed. 'I thought I was never going to speak to you again.'

40. BROMANCE

Six weeks later

Zahra pulled a plastic chair up to a desk, bruised and slightly breathless. The twelve-year-old wore muddy boots, combat trousers and an orange CHERUB T-shirt splattered with chicken blood. CHERUB's chairman Ewart Asker sat across the desk, half smiling.

'You did very well on the recruitment tests,' Ewart began. 'Your English is improving, but we'll need to work some more on that, along with your upper body strength and swimming before you'd be able to commence basic training.'

Zahra smiled at the news. 'How far to then?' she asked.

'Basic training lasts one hundred days. If you progress well, I would like to think that you'll be more than capable of joining the trainee group that commences at the beginning of April.'

'OK,' Zahra said. 'I will try. And to work very hard.'

'But I must ask one more thing,' Ewart said. 'Your father died fighting to free Syria from the Assad regime. Your brother died fighting for Islamic State, and was killed by a former CHERUB agent. How does that make you feel?'

Zahra's face was a puzzle, as she struggled to answer in a language she'd been learning for less than two months.

'I like to learn,' Zahra said. 'Learn science and math. Police stop all girls learning my home. Brother make me boy. He stop me from being forced to marry or get raped. He was not a real Islamic fighter. But no jobs. He *only* make money as fighter.'

Ewart nodded and smiled. 'I understand.'

'I like campus very much and not frightened of work hard,' Zahra continued. 'Theo, who showed me around, was very nice. I might make world better if I am live here.'

'I think that's *exactly* what you're going to do,' Ewart said, as he reached across the desk to shake hands. 'Congratulations and welcome to CHERUB.'

*

CHERUB campus was January cold as Ryan Sharma waited outside the mission control building. The entry system was having a hissy fit until James Adams came and let him in.

'Good to see you, buddy,' James said. 'Come on through. How's the arm?'

Dressed in a white CHERUB T-shirt, Ryan waved to a couple of familiar faces in the control room as they set off for James' office.

'It's healed,' Ryan said. 'Two more sessions with the physiotherapist.'

'See this?' James said, as he pointed to the door of one of the small offices along the hallway. The sign read *Kerry Chang, Junior Mission Controller*.

'So you're her boss,' Ryan said, smiling.

'I'm a full mission controller,' James said. 'So I'm senior to her, but I'm not her line manager or anything, thank god.'

'Is she in?'

James shook his head. 'Still in a leg brace. Had to go down to London to see her surgeon today.'

'Ning said you set a date.'

James laughed. 'Ning has a big mouth, it's supposed to be on the QT . . . But yeah, I've got some leave booked for Easter time. So we're getting hitched in Vegas, then we're driving up Route 66 to Chicago for our honeymoon.'

'Nice,' Ryan said. 'Motorbikes!'

'I wish,' James said. 'Kerry does ride, but she's not into bikes like I am.'

'The way you ride, I'm not surprised,' Ryan noted.

James tutted. 'So I found a company that hires out old cars and we're gonna do it in a vintage Ford Mustang. Plus, Lauren's season will have started, so we're going to see a couple of her races along the way.'

By this time they'd entered James' office. Ning sat at

James' desk dealing with some admin and she cracked a big smile and jumped up to hug Ryan.

'What are you doing here?' Ning gasped, surprised. 'I've not seen you since Christmas.'

'You're always busy whenever I want to meet up in town,' Ryan explained. 'But I had to come back to campus today to pick up some new identity papers and consolidated exam certificates for my uni applications.'

'And for this,' James said, pulling an envelope out of his desk drawer. 'It's all on paper because I don't want an electronic trail.'

Ning looked curious as Ryan took the envelope. 'Really appreciate this, James.'

'You'd bloody better,' James said. 'I had to go into follow-up files from the Aramov mission. I could *totally* get my ass kicked off campus for doing this.'

Now Ning was practically bursting. 'What are you two up to?'

James smirked. 'Think Ning can keep a secret? The way I keep quiet about the twenty-four-year-old boyfriend she's got stashed away in Thailand?'

Ning covered her face with embarrassment. 'James,' she squirmed.

'That's still a thing?' Ryan asked.

'Bruce *just* set me up with a gap year in Thailand,' Ning protested. 'That's all it is.'

James shook his head. 'Every time I walk into this office, she's on Facebook Messenger with Bruce.'

'Sod you!' Ning said. 'And you said yourself, Bruce is a really nice guy. Now stop changing the subject and tell me what's in the envelope.'

Ryan opened the envelope and showed Ning a picture of an eighteen-year-old girl.

'Natalka,' Ning gasped.

Ryan had met Natalka on a mission in Kyrgyzstan four years earlier. He'd fallen in love, and wound up with a broken heart when he had to go back to campus.

'There's a bunch of stuff in the file,' James said. 'Natalka was released from reform school when she turned eighteen. I managed to find an address that's about three months old and three possible mobile phone numbers. The latest information is an arrest for petty theft, on January 2nd, but she's not due in court until March.'

'I've never stopped thinking about Natalka,' Ryan confessed to Ning. 'I begged James to help me to find her.'

Ning was aghast. She found it sweet and romantic that Ryan hadn't forgotten about Natalka. And how cool was it that James was prepared to bend the rules to help Ryan find his true love? She couldn't think of any other CHERUB staff member who'd do something like that. But she was also shocked, and that's the side that came out.

'You're both *bloody* bananas,' Ning blurted. 'You're not supposed to contact people you met on missions for all sorts of very good reasons. James, you're the most highly regarded young mission controller on campus. John is retiring in three years and you could easily be his successor as senior mission controller.

'And Ryan, you haven't thought this through, have you? You were only fourteen. How much have you changed as a person since you last saw Natalka? And Russia's a tough country—'

Ryan interrupted. 'I don't care,' he blurted. 'I can handle Russia. My dad was Russian. I speak the language.'

'But what if you arrive and Natalka's got a boyfriend?' Ning continued. 'What if she's got a drug problem? What if she's about to get sent back to prison?'

'I don't give one shit,' Ryan shouted back. 'I've kissed girls on campus, but all I think about when I'm with them is that they're not Natalka. When I was with her, it was like we were one person. I haven't seen her for three years, but I still think about her. Wondering where she is, what she's doing, if she's happy or sad. If she still thinks about me.'

'But what are the odds this will work out?' Ning asked. 'What if you come back with another broken heart?'

Tears welled in Ryan's eyes. 'Maybe she'll break my heart. But even if the odds it'll work out were a million to one, I'd still want to find her and ask.'

Ning saw the intensity in Ryan's face. 'You want me to go to Russia with you?' she asked.

'Nah,' Ryan said. Not wanting to cry in front of James, he rattled the folder and headed for the exit. 'I owe you a big one, James.'

Ning wondered when – or even if – she'd see Ryan again as he walked out, with a manila envelope in one hand, and the other smudging tears out of his eye.

She gave James Adams a look. It was the look his mum gave when he'd gotten in trouble at school, the look Lauren had before she kicked him for doing something dumb, the look on Kerry when she found him in bed shagging the pizza delivery chick . . .

'You risked your whole career because Ryan's crushing on a girl,' Ning said, stifling a smile. 'You look all grown up, but there's still a mischievous twelve-year-old inside your skull.'

James shrugged. 'You'd rather I was some guy in a grey suit, barking orders?'

Ning thought for a couple of seconds, then surprised James with a peck on the cheek. 'Don't ever grow up, James Adams,' she told him. 'The world wouldn't be the same if you did.'

EPILOGUE

All information accurate as of December 2017
The Paedophile Hunting Network (PHN) video of
NIGEL KINNEY was viewed over 160,000 times in its
first three months online. During this period several
people approached PHN with allegations of other sexual
offences committed by Kinney.

Following a police investigation, Kinney was charged
with eight serious sexual offences and found guilty of
charges relating to six of them. After being assaulted by
fellow prisoners, he is currently serving his twelve-year
sentence in an isolation cell at York House prison on
the Isle of Wight.

PHN actions have led to numerous similar paedophile
convictions, though police and government continue
to say that their brand of vigilante justice is dangerous
and of limited use in obtaining real convictions of
sex offenders.

OLIVER LAKSHMI, more commonly known as Oli, was moved to a foster home in North London following the robbery and vandalising of Uncle's print shop. Despite numerous small altercations and some bullying incidents, Oli has now returned to normal schooling. He is doing reasonably well and his social worker reports that he has found a stable and age-appropriate friendship group for the first time in his life.

Police moved in to arrest MARTIN JONES aka UNCLE a few hours after James Adam's glider rescue operation was completed. By this time MI5 had been investigating his operations for over a month. In all, twenty-six people involved in the smuggling of OME equipment were arrested. Two men linked to Uncle were also later charged with the drug-related murder of CHRIS CARLISLE.

Uncle received a life sentence for terrorism and money laundering offences. All of the OME equipment at his Birmingham scrapyard was destroyed, and oil companies around the world have agreed to destroy OME equipment when it is decommissioned, so that it cannot fall into the hands of terrorists.

Due to the secret nature of the rescue operation, the kidnapping and return of GORDON SACHS and KAM YUEN was never publicised, and nobody within Uncle's organisation was charged with offences relating directly to their kidnapping.

The two engineers returned to peaceful retirement,

although they are still viewed as kidnap targets and now carry emergency alarms and have had passive tracking devices inserted in their buttocks.

ZAHRA's first attempt at CHERUB basic training ended on the thirty-second day, following a fall that led to an eye injury. She recommenced training three months later and is now a fully qualified CHERUB agent, awaiting her first mission.

After their return from the summer hostel LEON and DANIEL SHARMA faced no further punishment for their involvement with the Paedophile Hunting Network. Daniel received his black CHERUB T-shirt following a solo mission in early 2017. The twins remain active CHERUB agents, along with their younger brother THEO SHARMA.

Following two short, final missions, FU NING retired from CHERUB as planned in summer 2017. She currently works as a teacher at a Muay Thai dojo in Thailand. She is planning to study at an Australian university and is in a relationship with former CHERUB agent BRUCE NORRIS.

Because he had recently worked as CHERUB staff and commenced the relationship while Ning was still an agent, Bruce has been permanently banned from working on CHERUB campus and from returning to campus at all for three years. He says that falling in love with Ning totally made it worth the ban.

RYAN SHARMA travelled to Russia at the end of January 2017. He was able to locate his lost love NATALKA and used most of the resettlement money he'd been given by CHERUB to pay bribes to local police in order to drop various criminal charges that could have led to her serving a lengthy spell in prison.

Ryan and Natalka then spent the summer of 2017 travelling around Europe. The couple currently live in Cambridge, where Ryan is in his first year studying History. Natalka works as a waitress and is studying for GCSEs part-time at a local college. The couple's relationship has been described by friends as, 'Extremely volatile and unlikely to last.'

LAUREN ADAMS enjoyed a successful first season in saloon car racing, finishing the twelve-race series in third place and being voted 'Rookie of the Year'. Lauren intends to compete in the same series in 2018, and has also been invited to become a test driver for a NASCAR team.

KERRY CHANG underwent three operations to remove and replace her damaged kneecap and was able to fully begin her role as a CHERUB mission controller in June 2017.

The complex nature of Kerry's surgery, along with work commitments, meant that JAMES ADAMS eventually married Kerry at a Las Vegas casino in September 2017. Several friends attended the wedding, including KYLE BLUEMAN, who served as best man.

During Christmas dinner on CHERUB campus, Kerry announced that she and James were 'Surprised but delighted' to be expecting their first child.

READ ON FOR A TASTE OF
ROCK WAR . . .

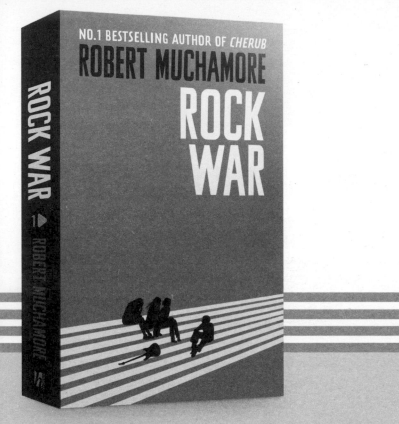

MEET JAY. SUMMER. AND DYLAN.

JAY plays guitar, writes songs for his band and dreams of being a rock star. But seven siblings and a rubbish drummer are standing in his way.

SUMMER has a one-in-a-million voice, but caring for her nan and struggling for money make singing the last thing on her mind.

DYLAN'S got talent, but effort's not his thing ...

These kids are about to enter the biggest battle of their lives. And they've got everything to play for.

Hodder
Children's
Books

Also available
as an ebook

ROCKWAR.COM

Prologue

The stage is a vast altar, glowing under Texas moonlight. Video walls the size of apartment blocks advertise Rage Cola. Close to the stadium's fifty-yard line, a long-legged thirteen-year-old is precariously balanced on her big brother's shoulders. She's way too excited.

'JAY!' she screams, as her body sways. 'JAAAAAAAY I LOVE YOU!'

Nobody hears, because seventy thousand people are at it. It's noise so loud your ears tickle inside. Boys and girls, teens, students. There's a ripple of anticipation as a silhouette comes on stage, but it's a roadie with a cymbal stand. He bows grandly before stepping off.

'JET!' they chant. 'JET . . . JET . . . JET.'

Backstage the sound is muffled, like waves crashing against a sea wall. The only light is a green glow from emergency exit signs.

Jay is holding his queasy stomach. He's slim and easy on the eye. He wears Converse All Stars, ripped jeans and a dash of black eyeliner.

An immense roar comes out of the crowd as the video walls begin a thirty-second countdown film, sponsored by a cellphone maker. As Jay's eyes adjust to the light, he can see a twenty-metre-tall version of himself skateboarding downhill, chased by screaming Korean schoolgirls.

'THIRTEEN,' the crowd scream, as their feet stamp down the seconds. 'TWELVE, ELEVEN . . .'

On screen, the girls knock Jay off his skateboard. As he tumbles a smartphone flies out of his pocket and when the girls see it they lose all interest in Jay and stand in a semicircle admiring the phone instead.

'THREE . . . TWO . . . ONE . . .'

The four members of Jet emerge on stage, punching the air to screams and camera flashes.

Somehow, the cheering crowd always kills Jay's nerves. Thousands of bodies sway in the moonlight. Cheers and shouts blend into a low roar. He places his fingers on the fret board and loves the knowledge that moving one finger will send half a million watts of power out of speaker stacks the size of trucks.

And the crowd goes wild as the biggest band in the world starts to play.

1. Cheesy Crumbs

Camden, North London

There's that weird moment when you first wake up. The uneasy quarter second where a dream ends and you're not sure where you are. All being well, you work out you're in bed and you get to snuggle up and sleep another hour.

But Jay Thomas wasn't in bed. The thirteen-year-old had woken on a plastic chair in a school hall that reeked of burgers and hot dogs. There were chairs set out in rows, but bums in less than a quarter of them. A grumpy dinner lady squirted pink cleaning fluid on a metal serving counter at the side of the room, while a banner hung over the stage up front:

**Camden Schools Contemporary Music
Competition 2014**

Debris pelted the floor the instant Jay moved: puffed wheat snacks, speckled with cheesy orange flavouring. Crumbs fell off his clothes when he stood and another half bag had been crushed up and sprinkled in his spiky brown hair.

Jay played lead guitar in a group named Brontobyte. His three band mates cracked up as he flicked orange dust out of his hair, then bent over to de-crumb a Ramones T-shirt and ripped black jeans.

'You guys are *so* immature.'

But Jay didn't really mind. These guys had been his mates since forever and he'd have joined the fun if one of them had dozed off.

'Sweet dreams?' Brontobyte's chubby-cheeked vocalist, Salman, asked.

Jay yawned and picked orange gunk out of his earhole as he replied. 'I barely slept last night. Kai had his Xbox on until about one, and when I *finally* got to sleep the little knob head climbed up to my bunk and farted in my face.'

Salman took pity, but Tristan and Alfie both laughed.

Tristan was Brontobyte's drummer, and a big lad who fancied himself a bit of a stud. Tristan's younger brother Alfie wouldn't turn twelve for another three months. He was Brontobyte's bass player and the band's most talented musician, but the other three gave him a hard time because his voice was unbroken and there were no signs of puberty kicking in.

'I can't believe Jay gets owned by his younger brother,' Tristan snorted.

'Kai's the hardest kid in my year,' Alfie agreed. 'But Jay's, like, Mr Twig Arms, or something.'

Jay tutted and sounded stressed. 'Can we *please* change the subject?'

Tristan ignored the request. 'How many kids has your mum got now anyway, Jay?' he asked. 'It's about forty-seven, isn't it?'

Salman and Alfie laughed, but stifled their grins when they saw Jay looking upset.

'Tristan, cut it out,' Salman said.

'We all take the piss out of each other,' Tristan said. 'Jay's acting like a baby.'

'No, Tristan, *you* never know when to stop,' Salman said angrily.

Alfie tried to break the tension. 'I'm going for a drink,' he said. 'Anyone else want one?'

'Scotch on the rocks,' Salman said.

Jay sounded more cheerful as he joined the joke. 'Bottle of Bud and some heroin.'

'I'll see what I can do,' Alfie said, before heading off towards a table with jugs of orange squash and platters of cheapo biscuits.

The next act was taking the stage. In front of them three judges sat at school desks. There was a baldy with a mysterious scab on his head, a long-limbed Nigerian in a gele headdress and a man with a wispy grey beard and leather trousers. He sat with his legs astride the back of his chair to show that he was down with the kids.

By the time Alfie came back with four beakers of orange squash and jam rings tucked into his cheeks there were five boys lining up on stage. They were all fifteen or sixteen. Nice-looking lads, four black, one Asian, and all dressed in stripy T-shirts, chinos and slip-on shoes.

Salman was smirking. 'It's like they walked into Gap and bought *everything*.'

Jay snorted. 'Losers.'

'Yo, people!' a big lad in the middle of the line-up yelled. He was trying to act cool, but his eyes betrayed nerves. 'We're contestant seven. We're from George Orwell Academy and we're called Womb 101.'

There were a few claps from members of the audience, followed by a few awkward seconds as a fat-assed music teacher bent over fiddling with the CD player that had their backing track on it.

'You might know this song,' the big lad said. 'The original's by One Direction. It's called "What Makes You Beautiful".'

The four members of Brontobyte all looked at each other and groaned. Alfie summed up the mood.

'Frankly, I'd rather be kicked in the balls.'

As the backing track kicked in, Womb 101 sprang into an athletic dance routine, with four members moving back, and the big guy in the middle stepping up to a microphone. The dancing looked sharp, but everyone in the room really snapped to attention when a powerful lead vocal started.

The voice was higher than you'd expect from a big black guy, but he really nailed the sense of longing for the girl he was singing about. When the rest of Womb

101 joined in for the chorus the sound swamped the backing track, but they were all decent singers and their routine was tight.

As Womb 101 hit their stride, Jay's music teacher Mr Currie approached Brontobyte from behind. He'd only been teaching for a couple of years. Half the girls at Carleton Road School had a thing for his square jaw and gym-pumped bod.

He tapped in time as the singing and finger clicking continued. 'They're really uplifting, aren't they?'

The four boys looked back at their teacher with distaste.

'Boy bands should be machine-gunned,' Alfie said. 'They're singing to a backing track. How's that even music?'

'I bet they win as well,' Tristan said contemptuously. 'I saw their teacher nattering to the judges all through lunch.'

Mr Currie spoke firmly. 'Tristan, if Womb 101 win it will be because they're really talented. Have you any idea how much practice it takes to sing and dance like that?'

Up on stage, Womb 101 were doing the *nana-nana* chorus at the end of 'What Makes You Beautiful'. As the song closed, the lead singer moved to the back of the stage and did a full somersault, climaxing with his arms spread wide and two band mates kneeling on either side.

'Thank you,' the big guy shouted, as the stage lights caught beads of sweat trickling down his forehead.

There weren't enough people in the hall to call it an eruption, but there was loads of clapping and a bunch of parents stood up and cheered.

'Nice footwork, Andre!' a woman shouted.

Alfie and Tristan made retching sounds as Mr Currie walked off.

'Currie's got a point though,' Jay said. 'Boy bands are dreck, but they've all got good voices and they must have rehearsed that dance routine for weeks.'

Tristan shook his head and tutted. 'Jay, you *always* agree with what Mr Currie says. I know half the girls in our class fancy him, but I'm starting to think you do as well.'

Alfie stood up and shouted as Womb 101 jumped off the stage and began walking towards the back of the room to grab drinks. 'You suck!'

Jay backed up as two of Womb 101's backing singers steamed over, knocking empty plastic chairs out of the way. They didn't look hard on stage, prancing around singing about how great some girl's hair was, but the physical reality was two burly sixteen-year-olds from one of London's toughest schools.

The one who stared down Alfie was the Asian guy with a tear-you-in-half torso.

'What you say?' he demanded, as his chest muscles swelled. 'If I see *any* of you boys on my manor, you'd better run!'

The boy slammed his fist into his palm as the other one pointed at Alfie before drawing the finger across his throat and stepping backwards. Alfie looked like he'd filled his BHS briefs and didn't breathe until the big dudes were well clear.

'Are you mental?' Tristan hissed, as he gave Alfie a hard shoulder punch. 'Those guys are from Melon Lane estate. Everyone's psycho up there.'

Mr Currie had missed Alfie shouting *You suck*, but did see Tristan hitting his brother as he got back holding a polystyrene coffee cup.

'Hitting is *not* cool,' Mr Currie said. 'And I'm tired of the negativity from you guys. You're playing after this next lot, so you'd better go backstage and get your gear ready.'

The next group was an all-girl trio. They dressed punk, but managed to murder a Paramore track by making it sound like bad Madonna. Setting up Tristan's drum kit on stage took ages and the woman judge made Jay even more nervous when she looked at her watch and shook her elaborately hatted head.

After wasting another minute faffing around with a broken strap on Alfie's bass guitar the four members of Brontobyte nodded to each other, ready to play. When the boys rehearsed, Salman usually sang and played, but Alfie was a better musician, so for the competition he was on bass and Salman would just do vocals.

'Hi, everyone,' Salman said. 'We're contestant nine, from Carleton Road School. Our group is called Brontobyte and this is a song we wrote ourselves. It's called "Christine".'

A song I wrote, Jay thought, as he took a deep breath and positioned his fingers on the guitar.

They'd been in the school hall since ten that morning. Now it all came down to the next three minutes.

CLASS A

Robert Muchamore

Keith Moore is Europe's biggest cocaine dealer.

The police have been trying to get enough evidence to nail him for more than twenty years.

Four CHERUB agents are joining the hunt. Can a group of kids successfully infiltrate Keith Moore's organisation, when dozens of attempts by undercover police officers have failed?

MAXIMUM SECURITY

Robert Muchamore

Under American law, kids convicted of serious crimes can be sentenced as adults. Two hundred and eighty of these child criminals live in the sunbaked desert prison of Arizona Max.

In one of the most daring CHERUB missions ever, James Adams has to go undercover inside Arizona Max and bust out a fellow inmate!

THE ESCAPE

Robert Muchamore

Hitler's army is advancing towards Paris, and amidst the chaos, two British children are being hunted by German agents. British spy Charles Henderson tries to reach them first, but he can only do it with the help of a twelve-year-old French orphan.

The British secret service is about to discover that kids working undercover will help to win the war.

Book 1 – OUT NOW

Also available as an ebook

www.hendersonsboys.com

Hodder
Children's
Books